JAM...
The Squared Circle

◆ "A vivid, heartrending story of a top athlete struggling to leave the glory road and find his own path . . . Bennett displays profound knowledge of the game's history and play. . . plus the rare ability to create complex characters of both sexes; this is at once a set of penetrating psychological portraits and a sobering look at the pleasures and temptations of big-money athletics."
— *Kirkus Reviews,* pointered review

"An acutely perceptive account of a young man's emotional and intellectual awakening . . . Bennett sketches out the pivotal episodes in Sonny's coming of age, inviting the reader to piece them together rather than assembling them, Chris Crutcher-style, into a single bombshell. His startling ending is sure to leave his audience with plenty to talk about."
— *Publishers Weekly*

"Spellbinding . . . It is difficult to adequately describe the power of this book. It is a masterpiece."   — *Voice of Youth Advocates*

"[Bennett's] story is fictional, but his sobering indictment of Division One college athletics is right out of the daily sports pages. . . . This is a sobering read that should be thrust into the hands of any high school students who are contemplating playing revenue-producing sports at major universities."
— *School Library Journal*

"Wow! What a book, the best I've read in a number of years. Shocking and colorful and wild and angry and occasionally funny and real and honest about life . . . It's mercilessly real."   — *English Journal*

An ALA Best Book for Young Adults
Voted 1995's Finest YA Novel by Voice of Youth Advocates
Voted Best YA Book of 1995 by English Journal

Other Signature Titles

Crusader
Edward Bloor

Dakota Dream
James Bennett

Danger Zone
David Klass

Freak the Mighty
Rodman Philbrick

I Can Hear the Mourning Dove
James Bennett

Slam!
Walter Dean Myers

Somewhere in the Darkness
Walter Dean Myers

THE SQUARED CIRCLE

JAMES BENNETT

SCHOLASTIC ■ SIGNATURE

AN IMPRINT OF SCHOLASTIC INC.

NEW YORK TORONTO LONDON AUCKLAND SYDNEY
MEXICO CITY NEW DELHI HONG KONG BUENOS AIRES

ISBN 0-590-48672-1

Copyright © 1995 by James Bennett.
All rights reserved.
Published by Scholastic Inc.
SCHOLASTIC and associated logos are trademarks and/or
registered trademarks of Scholastic Inc.

12 11 10 9 8 7 6 5 4 3   3 4 5 6/0

Printed in the U.S.A.   01

First Scholastic paperback printing, February 2002

Author's Note

I would like the reader to understand that even though real place names (for the most part) comprise its setting, *The Squared Circle* is exclusively a work of fiction. All characters — as well as events — in it are products of imagination, with no basis in any actual person, living or dead.

The setting for *The Squared Circle* is real because it is designed to function centrally in the story. The southernmost tip of the state of Illinois, traditionally referred to as "Little Egypt," has long been a basketball hotbed, particularly at the high school level.

As an author with southern Illinois roots, I hold Southern Illinois University and its athletic program in high esteem. All coaches, players, fans, administrators, and events in this story are fictitious; no link to SIU history or procedures is intended.

THE SQUARED CIRCLE

=1=

Snell asked the question as if what he expected from Sonny was an admission of guilt: "Did you shoot free throws after practice?"

"What d'you think?"

"How many?"

"What d'you think?"

"You shot a hundred, right?"

"Yeah."

"How many did you make?"

"I just told you. I made a hundred."

"I said how many did you *shoot*, not how many did you make."

Sonny looked up from his book. He had already decided he didn't like Snell. "I told you. I shot a hundred and I made a hundred."

"You're saying you made a hundred in a row?"

"No, Snell, *you're* saying it." Sonny decided to go back to the paragraph he was trying to read.

"You hear this shit?" said Snell to Robert Lee. "He says he made a hundred free throws in a row after the workout."

Robert Lee was leafing through a recent copy of *Penthouse*. Without looking up he said, "That's what I know. Tell me something I don't know."

"You believe him?"

Robert Lee shrugged. "I've seen him do it before. I

don't think he'd leave the gym without his hundred straight free throws."

"I've never seen him do it," said Snell.

Sonny put the book down again. "That's because you're never around after we scrimmage. If you want to see it, you'll have to hang."

"Right. I'm going to hang out afterwards, just so I can watch you shoot free throws."

"Then get off my case."

Sonny and his two pledge brothers were sitting in one of the upstairs study rooms in the fraternity house. They were waiting restlessly for the second lineup of the year. Mounted on the wall were a few fraternity paddles made of blond polished wood. The paddles were half an inch thick and 26 inches long. On each paddle, the names of pledge father and son were burned in charred capital letters: MIKE '97 from DOC '96. TONY '98 from NILES '96.

Robert Lee and Snell were both scholarship basketball players like Sonny, but from what Sonny could tell from the pickup games in Davies, the old gym, Snell was going to be a practice player strictly, while Robert Lee was an overachiever, one of those guys who got by on desire.

The book Sonny was trying to read was one on chimpanzees by Jane Goodall, assigned by his Intro to Anthropology professor. His interest was so marginal that he kept rereading the same paragraph. The obstacles to concentration began with the imminent lineup, but continued with Robert Lee's interruptions to show beaver shots from his magazine. For his part, Snell was amusing himself by setting his own farts on fire with a Bic lighter.

Snell still wasn't finished with his agenda. He turned to

Robert Lee again and said, "Youngblood shoots his hundred free throws a day, and we don't even start real practices for another week. Then he'll have to shoot his free throws after he wins the wind sprints and the suicides."

There was no answer from Robert Lee, so Snell went on, "You know what you are, Youngblood?"

"I give up," said Sonny.

"You're a fuckin' fanatic. You're a basketball junkie. It's like there's nothing else in life but hoops. You're a fucking fanatical basketball junkie."

These remarks pissed Sonny off. He was about to answer, *And you're nothing but a glorified walk-on*, but then suddenly, the door was kicked open. It was Pinky, a chunky sophomore. Across his flushed face was a mad grin. Sonny felt his stomach constrict.

"Guess what, slugs?" asked Pinky. "Guess what it's time for?"

"We know, we know," said Robert Lee with a weary expression.

"You know shit!" roared Pinky. He was full-out drunk. In his right hand he was holding what was left of a gallon of Mad Dog wine; his pudgy index finger was looped through the glass ring at the bottle's neck. "A fucking slug knows jackshit!"

Robert Lee lowered his face and murmured, "Yes sir."

In his left hand, Pinky had a firm grip on his fraternity paddle. "It's time for the goddamn lineup," he declared. He tilted up the jug to drink some wine with a gurgling sound. Finished, he wiped his mouth with the back of his hand and belched loudly. Twice. "I said it's time for the goddamn lineup. Get off your dumb butts and follow me downstairs. Fucking slugs."

Dutifully they followed Pinky, who swayed as he walked. At the last study room before the stairs, they stopped before the open doorway. Wayne Burkhart was in the study room, lying on a couch, reading a book.

"Time for the lineup, Wayne," said Pinky. "You wouldn't want to be late."

"We'll see." Wayne, a senior, was Sonny's pledge father; but having nothing in common, the two of them had little contact with each other.

"Hummin' you!" shouted Pinky at the top of his lungs. He twirled the gallon jug like a lariat, then released it through the open door of the study room. It smashed against the wall behind Wayne's head before he had a chance to duck. The bottle shattered. Red wine streaked down the wall.

"You asshole," said Burkhart.

"HaHA!" Pinky threw back his head and laughed. Sonny wasn't too surprised; he'd seen Pinky *hum* people before.

"Asshole," Burkhart said again. Looking at the shattered glass and moisture on his clothes, he sat up and put the book aside.

"Let's go, slugs!" commanded Pinky. He led them down the stairs.

They went through the parlor and the living room. In the living room, there was a large stone fireplace against one wall. Once, when Stinky was drunk, Sonny saw him take a piss on the gold carpet; there was still a stain, in front of the fireplace.

Lineups were always held in the dining room. Sonny, Robert Lee, and Snell were the last ones. The other pledges were already in place, seated in their chairs.

"Well," said Harris sarcastically. "Glad you children could join us."

"Fucking slugs," muttered Pinky. He belched loudly again.

When the three took their seats, all nine pledges were in place. In a lineup, it was a requirement that you had to sit rigid on your wooden chair, with both feet flat on the floor, and keep your arms folded across your chest. Your chin had to be pulled in tight, and your eyes staring straight ahead at all times.

Harris, the house president, would lead the lineup. He held his fraternity paddle in his right hand and wiggled it back and forth. He was known for his sarcasm, but usually it went over Sonny's head.

Sonny sat stiff and staring. He focused his eyes on a knothole in the tongue-and-groove pine paneling opposite. He could feel his palms begin to sweat; to him, the lineups felt like betrayal. Everyone said that lineups were illegal, but that didn't seem to prevent them.

As soon as the noise died down, Harris started to speak. "I'm glad to see you, Robert Lee. I've got some plans for you."

"Yes sir," said Robert Lee, his eyes straight ahead. "Thank you, sir."

"Don't thank me yet, but you and I have a score to settle. You know what I mean, don't you, Robert Lee?"

"I think so, sir."

"You bet your sweet ass. You get your buns ready." Harris spoke quietly, but his eyes were glittering.

"Yessir."

By now, the room was silent. Harris lit a cigar before he continued, and clenched it between his teeth. "A few of you guys are going to get your ass burned tonight. Robert Lee won't be the only one."

Sonny swallowed hard and sat ultra-still, hoping not to be noticed. But at six feet five inches, it was never easy to be inconspicuous.

"In a few months," Harris went on, "several of you slugs will become active members of this house, although God only knows why. Most of you are too dumb to find your ass with both hands."

"They show me no hair!" shouted Pinky.

As if on cue, the 35 actives in attendance pounded their fraternity paddles on the floor like baseball bats. Then stopped abruptly.

"We can't blame anybody but ourselves," the president continued. "We chose to pledge you losers, and now we're stuck with you. And you thought we had perfect judgment, didn't you, Youngblood?"

It was several seconds before Sonny realized that Harris was speaking to him.

"I said, you thought we had perfect judgment, didn't you, Youngblood?" Harris's voice was hard. He was touching Sonny's forehead with the tip of his paddle.

"Yes, I did," said Sonny. But he could feel how dry his mouth was.

"Yes, you did what?"

"Yes, I did, sir."

"Try to stay with us, Youngblood; the questions may get harder."

Skinner came forward to stand next to Harris. At six feet four and 235 pounds, he was the starting tight end on the football team. He was massive in the arms and upper torso from years in the weight room. He rested his paddle easily on his right shoulder. "I'm gonna have to bust Woodson's ass," he said simply.

"Be my guest."

"Woodson, get your ass up here," ordered Skinner. Woodson got up from his chair to step forward.

"Fucking slugs, keep your eyes on the wall!" shouted Pinky. Paddles pounded on the floor for emphasis. Staring straight at the wall, Sonny still had Woodson and Skinner within his range of vision.

"Assume the position," said Skinner.

"Yes sir." Woodson bent over. His head was even with his knees. His right hand cupped his genitals, while his left hand gripped his left ankle.

Skinner drew the paddle back slowly, then drove it powerfully against Woodson's buttocks. *Crack!* Immediately after the blow landed, there was the exclamation point of paddles pounding on the floor.

With a scarlet face, Woodson stood up to face Skinner. "Thank you, sir, may I please have another?"

"We'll see. First, I want you to tell everybody how many classes you cut last week."

"Eight, sir."

Sonny could barely hear him.

"Louder!" commanded Skinner. "And keep your goddamn eyes on the wall!"

"I cut eight, sir." Woodson answered, in a louder voice. "I cut eight classes."

"Why, you lying bastard," Harris interrupted. "You told me you went to all your classes. Assume the position."

Woodson assumed the position, but Harris stepped back. Skinner administered another board with another loud report.

"Thank you, sir, may I please have another?"

"Hell no, you're not worth it. Go sit down, girlie man."

Woodson resumed his seat at the other end of the row. Sonny's lower back was getting stiff, but he tried to hold his rigid position while staring at the wall. There was no breeze in the room, so he was beginning to sweat. He fought the urge to scratch, for fear that someone would notice him. The hope in a lineup was always that they would overlook you.

For Sonny, the hope ended as soon as Geisel, the house academic chairman, stepped to the front. "Youngblood! Youngblood, get up here."

Sonny got out of his chair and stepped stiffly to the front. He stared at the wall. Harris stood on his left, while Geisel was at his right. Geisel was fat, but strong. He was as sarcastic as Harris, and he didn't attempt to hide his contempt for freshmen on athletic scholarships.

"Youngblood, did you think we were going to forget about you?"

"Not much, sir."

"Louder!" shouted Grimes. "Speak up!"

"I didn't think about it much, sir," said Sonny, louder this time. He felt ridiculous.

"You smart ass," sneered Harris. "You lying bastard. You've been thinking about nothing else since you parked your ass in that chair. Am I right?"

"I guess so."

"You guess so what?"

"I guess so, sir."

"Are you going to make grades this semester?"

"I hope so, sir."

"You hope so, sir," Geisel mocked. "What the hell is that supposed to mean?"

"I just mean I hope so, sir," Sonny repeated. He had to stop to lick his lips. Sonny's marginal academic history wasn't any secret. He searched the room quickly with his eyes, looking for Burkhart. Burkhart was his pledge father, maybe he would stand up for him.

"Keep your goddamn eyes on the wall, slug!" Pinky exploded.

Sonny flinched and stared straight ahead.

Geisel repeated the question, which really didn't sound like a question at all: "You're not gonna make your grades, are you, Youngblood?"

"I hope so, sir."

"Assume the position."

"Yes sir." Sonny bent over. The tile on the floor was alternate red and black squares. He could smell Geisel's beer breath and his body sweat.

The paddle slammed against his butt. The pain, which was shocking, licked its way like shooting flames down his legs. He stood up quickly, his face burning. "Thank you, sir, may I please have another?"

"We'll see."

Sonny felt the ridicule of all the eyes watching him. He had the urge to turn on Geisel and give him a shot in his blubber gut. You couldn't do that here, though, because everything was stacked against you. *Where the hell is Burkhart?* Probably still upstairs reading Plato or some other shit.

Then Pinky, the drunkest of all, stumbled forward swinging his paddle. "I'll tell you something else. Youngblood spends most of his spare time hanging out with niggers."

"Is that a fact?" asked Harris.

"Fucking-A. This stupid slug is a nigger lover. Niggers are his friends, right, Youngblood?"

"Some of them are going to be my teammates, sir. You usually make friends with your teammates, because you play a lot of pickup games with them."

Geisel put his face right next to Sonny's ear. "You asshole, do you know anything at all about house loyalty?"

"I think so, sir."

"Then why the hell aren't your own brothers good

enough for you? What makes you think you need to spend your time with the niggers?"

"A friend is a friend, sir."

"*A friend is a friend,*" sighed Geisel. "Isn't that special? I think I might wet my pants, I really do. Is there something wrong with your own brothers, for Christ sake?"

"No, sir, I like my brothers."

"Then why the hell do you spend your time with the fuckin' niggers?" demanded Pinky. "If they were on fire, I wouldn't piss on 'em to put it out." The actives pounded their paddles to show approval.

Sonny could feel his scalp burning. He said to Geisel, "There's a logical explanation."

"There's a logical explanation WHAT?"

"There's a logical explanation, sir."

"Goddamnit, Youngblood, keep your eyes on the wall!" Harris shouted.

Sonny focused quickly on the knothole. Geisel was giggling. "A logical explanation?" He turned to all the brothers: "Wouldn't y'all just love to hear the *logical explanation?*"

The furious pounding of the paddles signified yes.

"Go ahead, slug," said Harris to Sonny. "We're all just dying to hear your logic. Just be sure you keep your goddamn eyes where they belong."

Sonny swallowed first, and then he said, "I don't get much chance for free time. We have informal workouts every day and study table at night. I would be with the black guys a lot, even if I didn't want to be. That's how it is when you're on scholarship; other people decide how you spend your time."

Harris whistled his scorn before he spoke in reverent tones: "Great god almighty, Youngblood, your logic is so airtight I'm about to suffocate. When basketball season is over, you'll probably be recruited for debate."

Pinky faced the group to slur out his contempt: *"When you're on scholarship??* Y'all hear this shit? Are we supposed to be impressed?"

Sonny had no idea the question was meant for him. Pinky wobbled closer. "I asked you a question, stupid slug. Are we supposed to be impressed because you're a high school all-American? You think you're the first big-time jock this house ever had?"

Sonny swallowed again. "No sir."

"He's a high school all-American from Abydos, so we're supposed to kiss his ass!"

Geisel took over again. "You know what that all means here, Youngblood? You know what the all-American crap means on this campus? In this house? It means jackshit, that's what."

"Yes sir."

Geisel finished it off in his terse, even voice: "What you are here is a slug. What's a slug, Youngblood?"

"A slug is the lowest form of life, sir," answered Sonny.

"Keep that in mind the next time you do your wrap-around dribble. What you are is a goddamn slug."

"Yes sir."

"Assume the position, Youngblood," said Pinky. "I'm gonna board your all-American ass."

For what? wondered Sonny. Puzzled, he turned to look at Pinky.

"You got some reason to be looking at me, slug? I told you to assume the position."

"Yes sir." Sonny assumed the position, but he was tense. He knew how drunk Pinky was.

When the blow came, it lashed across the back of both his thighs. It scalded him clear to his ankles. He stood up immediately, at least eight inches taller than his drunk tormentor, but powerless and humiliated nonetheless. "Thank you, sir, may I please have another?"

"Not now," interrupted Harris. "It's time to settle my score with Robert Lee. Go sit down."

Sonny returned to his seat.

"Robert Lee, front and center!"

Robert Lee jumped to his feet. Sonny used his sleeve to wipe his sweaty face before he got back into the required position in his chair. Feelings of anger and betrayal roiled inside, replacing the humiliation. Part of it came from his knowledge of Robert Lee's imminent ordeal.

"Did you think I was going to forget about it?" Harris asked Robert Lee quietly.

"No sir."

"You bet your ass. Now just so everybody has a little background on this whole thing, I want you to tell the group what we had for supper last night."

"Fried chicken, sir." Robert Lee worked for his weekend meals by serving in the house dining room.

"Did you say fried chicken?"

"Yes sir."

"Now then. In a voice loud enough for everybody to hear, tell us what you served me for supper."

"I'd rather not say, sir."

"You dumb shit, assume the position."

Harris hit him hard, then Skinner did the same.

"Let's try again, okay?" said Harris. "Once more, what did you serve me for dinner?"

"An olive, sir."

"Louder!"

"An olive, sir."

"One olive, slug?"

"Yessir, one."

Skinner came up close in a hurry. "An olive? You douche bag, you served Harris an olive for supper?"

"Yes sir."

"Why the hell did you do that?"

"I thought it might show some hair, sir."

"You thought it might show some hair? Robert Lee, stupid slug, what is an olive?"

"An olive is the lowest form of food, sir."

"Why?"

"Because it's used in the olive race, sir."

Harris asked him, "What is the olive race like, slug?"

"Sir, the pledges — "

"— the WHAT??"

"The slugs, sir."

"That's better. Go ahead."

"The slugs carry the olives in the cheeks of their ass from one block of dry ice to another. The losing team eats the olives, sir."

"And you thought it would show some hair to serve me an olive?"

"I thought it might, sir."

"Buster, you just lost the biggest olive race of your life. Assume the position."

"Yes sir."

Skinner boarded him a hard one, which was followed up immediately by the clatter of paddles pounding the tile. Robert Lee stood up. "Thank you, sir, may I please have another?"

"Keep your shirt on," said Geisel, who had joined those in front. He was holding a one-quart Mason jar, full most of the way with green olives. "Do you know what this is, stupid slug?"

"I think it's a jar of olives, sir."

"Do you know how many olives are in here?"

"No sir."

"Let me tell you then. There are forty-eight. Each one of these olives has spent a little time in the asshole of one of the active members of this house. Are you starting to get the picture?"

"Yessir, I think so, sir."

Then Harris took over. "You just lost the olive race, slug. You get to eat these. All of them." He took the jar from Geisel.

"Open up, slug," ordered Harris.

The room was so quiet. Sonny felt like he was watching an execution; it made his stomach turn. He resisted the urge to wipe the sweat that riveted its way down his face and neck. From the corner of his eye he could see Robert Lee.

When Robert Lee opened his mouth, Harris ordered: "Wider!" He opened wider.

"Now," Harris instructed, inserting the first olive, "swallow only when I tell you to." One by one, he put eight olives into Robert Lee's mouth. Then, and only then, did he say, "Okay, chew 'em up and swallow."

It took Robert Lee a long time to chew up the eight olives and finally swallow. "Now assume the position," said Harris.

As soon as Robert Lee bent over, Harris boarded him.

They repeated the procedure five more times. Each time, Harris pressed the eight-olive quota inside Robert Lee's mouth. Each time slower, Robert Lee chewed them up and swallowed. Then he caught a board. It was agony for Sonny just to watch; even worse than when he himself had been the victim.

Finally all 48 olives were gone; the jar was empty.

Harris spoke to Robert Lee one more time. "Now go and sit down. You think long and hard before you ever serve me an olive for dinner again."

"Yes, sir," said Robert Lee. He returned to his chair.

Before he dismissed them, Harris delivered a short speech on house loyalty, but Sonny didn't pay much attention. The breakup was a weary one without much conversation. Sonny went back upstairs to the study room, passing Burkhart's closed door on the way. From downstairs, he could hear several of the actives talking in loud voices about going out to do some more drinking.

There were three bathrooms on this floor. Sonny found the first one, went inside, and closed the door. It was too bright, but at least it was private. He pulled off his soggy shirt and T-shirt, then rolled them into a ball. He had to stoop down to look at his red face in the mirror. He scrubbed with tepid water from head to belt buckle, then toweled off with special effort to dry his wet hair.

When he was done, he put on his nylon UCLA windbreaker over his bare skin and zipped it up. He put the rolled-up shirts under his arm.

Back in the study room to retrieve his textbook, Sonny found Robert Lee prone on the couch, a wet washrag draped over his face. Sonny felt bad for him. "You okay, Robert Lee?"

Lee lifted a corner of the washrag to speak. "I couldn't be better. I just hope we all get to do it again tomorrow night."

"I'm really sorry, what they did to you. You gonna be okay?"

"Shit. If we scrimmage again tomorrow, I'll be right in your face again."

Sonny laughed. It was amazing, the way you couldn't get him down. Couldn't *keep* him down, anyway.

Robert Lee lifted the corner again. "I suppose you're going to shoot now."

"Most likely," Sonny answered.

"You'll be going over to Davies to see if it's unlocked. One workout a day ain't enough for you."

"Most likely." Then Sonny had a thought. "You want to come with me?"

This time Robert Lee lifted the whole rag. "Are you out of your freakin' mind? You saw what they did to me."

"Yeah, right. Sorry."

Just after Robert Lee got the washrag back in place, Harris came into the room, walking slowly. He was trying to relight what was left of the short cigar. Without looking at Sonny, he tilted back in a wooden chair against the bolster next to Robert Lee's head. Harris made Sonny nervous; everything he did seemed arrogant.

"How we doin', *amigo*?"

Robert Lee answered without lifting a corner. "Who, me? Hell, I'm just great, how about you?"

Harris was Robert Lee's pledge father. He chuckled as he blew his smoke in twin nostril streams. "Any gastrointestinal distress?"

Robert Lee cut loose with a whopper of a belch. "You mean something like that?"

Harris laughed out loud and pretty soon Robert Lee joined him, until the two of them were hysterical like little kids. Robert Lee took the washrag away and rolled on his side. Sonny didn't laugh at all; if there was something funny, it eluded him. *They fucked him over like they did and now it's funny.*

Harris tipped forward in the chair so all four legs were back on the floor. He handed Robert Lee the cigar so he could have a drag. "My son, you make me proud."

"I'm sure."

"The olive gambit was the best I've seen. That was big-time hair."

Robert Lee took a second drag, then passed back the smoke. He exhaled just before belching again. "Next time, don't be so proud, okay? My ass is still burning."

"That's the beauty of it," chuckled Harris. "Big-time hair, Robert Lee."

Sonny didn't get any of this. He stood up to leave.

Harris turned to look at him for the first time, the smile still on his face but all the humor gone out of his eyes. As if he could read Sonny's thoughts he said in a flat voice, "You don't get any of this, do you, Youngblood?"

Sonny's voice was tense, but his answer honest: "No, I don't."

"No you don't what?"

"No, I don't, sir."

"What *do* you get, Youngblood? Other than a double team or a pick-and-roll, just what the hell do you get?"

Sonny hated the contempt. He knew he had to leave, he was on the verge of telling Harris to go fuck himself. Instead he said, "I have to go now."

"You have to go what?"

"I have to go, sir." He headed out the door without looking back. Over his shoulder he said, "See you, Robert Lee."

He headed for the quad by way of Thompson Woods. It was a still and warm October night. In the mist, the pole lamps looked like London streetlights in old Jack the Ripper movies. The soggy fallen leaves beneath his feet crowned the blacktop with a slick layer of thatch.

He tried to stop thinking about the lineup. Burkhart didn't come down at all. Was there something meaningful that a pledge father was for? Something that he was supposed to do? Whatever it was that bonded Harris and Robert Lee was beyond Sonny's understanding. *You don't get any of this, do you, Youngblood?*

He knew he would get what he needed at Davies, where he found a side door unlocked. The old gym was obsolete since the opening of the new arena, but you could never obsolete a ten-foot rim affixed to a rectangle. He shot layups and jump shots for nearly an hour, stripping eventually naked to the waist. Left-handed, right-handed, left-handed, right-handed, the old, ragged nets plopped on short shots and snapped on long ones. Sonny cozied into this warm and private freedom like a bird in its nest. Custodial workers came and went without taking notice of him; they were used to this.

It was nearly midnight by the time he sat beneath the basket where he began pulling on his shirt. Sonny felt in no hurry to leave. He spun the pebbled texture of the ball across his fingers where it soothed like the touch of a lover. The fraternity was mostly for the purpose of satisfying his uncle Seth anyway; he said out loud, as if speaking directly to Harris, "You don't get any of this, do you?"

2

There was a coffee shop in the east wing of the clinic, and it was there that he ran into his cousin Erika, an SIU art professor. When she asked him to join her he agreed, but not with much enthusiasm; even though she was family, and he knew her well enough to call her by her nickname, Sissy, there were years and space between them.

While Sonny was easing his long limbs under the small table, she said, "I forgot how tall you are. You look as if you could drop the ball right in the basket without jumping up."

"No, I have to jump for that." It must have been a funny remark somehow, because Sissy laughed. Sonny assumed the conversation wouldn't be about basketball, but Sissy said, "I keep reading all about you in the papers."

"I always heard you weren't into sports," said Sonny.

"I'm not enthused about the excesses of major college athletics," she replied, "but how could I be indifferent to the heroics of Sonny Youngblood?"

"Let's don't say 'heroics.'"

"Are we modest, Cousin? When I was in the hospital, I read the column in the *Post-Dispatch*, which characterized you as the white Michael Jordan."

Sonny felt a little foolish. He looked down, with no reply.

"Sorry I embarrassed you," Sissy said. Then she asked him why he was at the clinic.

"I'm here for drug testing. I'm waiting for the results to be signed by the lab."

"Drug testing?"

"It's just routine. I never touched a drug in my life. But if you're on a varsity team, you have to have a specimen analyzed every week. When you get the results, you have to take them back to the athletic director's office."

"But why are you being tested now, Sonny? Isn't this the football season?"

She sure does ask lots of questions, he thought. "It doesn't matter if your sport's in season or not," he answered. "You still have to be tested on a regular schedule."

"How comforting to know that the integrity of our games is monitored with such vigilance."

"I guess," said Sonny. He decided to ask her a question. "So why are you here?"

"I'm having some blood work done. I had surgery last month."

"Are you okay?"

"I'm doing well, thank you. I have to take it easy for a while, and my teaching load is reduced to half-time this semester."

Sonny had only a few memories where Sissy was concerned, but she seemed thinner. She had a cotton ball taped to her arm over a bruised vein.

"How is your mother?" Sissy asked.

His mother's condition was never a comfortable subject. "I haven't seen her this month. She's the same."

"I saw her last month. I paid her a visit just before I had the surgery."

"You did?" Sonny was surprised. As far as he knew, his mother never had visitors other than himself and

Aunt Jane. Once in a blue moon, Uncle Seth. "Did she know you?"

Sissy shrugged, and then she smiled. It was a nice smile. "Yes and no. She didn't speak, but I brushed her hair and braided it. Her hair is so long and fine. She seemed to enjoy the procedure, so I choose to think that some part of her knew who I was."

Sonny noticed the gray streaking Sissy's own hair, which was thick and black. Some of her fingernails were long, but some were broken. At the cuticles there were traces of residue like steel-blue paint. He decided his professor cousin was too sophisticated; it seemed like pressure trying to keep up his end of the conversation. When she asked him what classes he was taking, it only felt like filler.

"Composition, Nutrition, P.E., Earth Science. And Introduction to Anthropology."

"Is everything going well? I know people who play sports have large demands on their time."

"Yeah, everything's fine." He could have added *except Composition and Anthropology*, but he didn't. His Coke was finished and he felt certain that the test results would be finished by now, so he stood up. "I better be goin'."

Sissy was smiling at him. "Have a nice day," she said. Her teeth were nice and straight. He wondered if she was teasing him somehow, but he didn't know her well enough to tell.

The car itself wasn't much to look at — an '88 pale yellow Toyota with significant body rust — but Uncle Seth assured him it was a good runner. If it would run, Sonny was happy to have it.

Uncle Seth always seemed to have lots of free time, but plenty of money. He had quite a few irons in the fire. One of the irons was used cars. He owned at least one used-car dealership that Sonny knew of, besides which he'd always been ready to buy and sell from his own backyard. It seemed like there were always half a dozen beaters of various descriptions parked between the house and the barn. They came and went like weather fronts.

Sonny sat at the breakfast table in the huge kitchen, Seth on his left and Aunt Jane making perfect fried eggs with no burnt edges, and Bob Evans sausage patties, thinly sliced. While Sonny wolfed down breakfast, Seth read the newspaper by concentrating on the business section and the classifieds. He lit up one cigarette after another. Every once in a while, he made a note on a napkin about cars or real estate or public auctions. He needed a shave. He wore a sleeveless undershirt with coffee stains; his big belly hung over the top of his khaki trousers.

Through the kitchen window, Sonny could see the Toyota sitting near the back of the large gravel parking lot. Right next to a Buick station wagon with a sprung door on the passenger side. Beyond, through the gray mist, he could see the rest of Uncle Seth's property, from the tenant farmer's drafty-looking house on top of the hill, to the acres of timber with the marshes in back. Sonny knew he would have to leave soon or else he'd be late for the press conference, but he didn't want it to look like he was just grabbing the car and running.

He thanked Uncle Seth for the car.

"Don't give it a second thought," his uncle replied. "How you s'posed to get around the campus without a car?"

Sonny tried to think of the vehicle as a necessity. While he was making the effort, Uncle Seth added, "I should've got you one sooner. You been in school more 'n two months and no wheels. I should've got you one sooner."

Uncle Seth had bad teeth and bad breath. He was a slob, there was no getting around it, although Sonny felt guilty thinking that way because it was Seth who'd helped Sonny and his mother back on their feet again when his dad took off. Let them move in for awhile, found them the apartment, even got his mother a job at the phone company.

Aunt Jane turned away from the skillet to make her contribution: "Besides, if you have your own car, maybe you'll come to visit more often."

"Maybe so," said Sonny.

"We're goin' to the press conference," said Uncle Seth. "Think we'd miss that? I better get myself cleaned up."

Sonny drove fast on the way back to Carbondale to give his car a test run, but any speed over 75 and it started to shimmy and shake. It didn't matter; it seemed to be a good runner, just like Seth claimed.

For the press conference, the players were required to wear their maroon and white warm-ups, the new ones with the angular, bionic saluki dog extended across the zippered chest. By the time Sonny slipped his on and got to the arena, he was late, but just barely. Uncle Seth and the cronies had already arrived.

It seemed like Minicams were perched on a hundred shoulders. Student assistants and S.I.D. staff kept trekking back and forth from Lingle, the office complex, bringing the coffee and donuts, publicity material, and stacks of printed handouts. It was the biggest media event for SIU basketball that anyone could remember. So big in fact that none of the conference rooms was spacious enough to accommodate the throng of reporters and photographers. Everything would be held in the arena, including the press conference. The entire event was open to the general public, who filled nearly half of the lower-level seats on both sides.

For the interviewing, a long table was set up beneath the north goal. There were eight microphones spaced along it. Facing the table, the semicircular rows of folding chairs for reporters reached almost to the center line. In addition to the media people who traditionally covered SIU athletics, there were scores of reporters who represented a wider publicity range. Even the *Tribune*, *Sports Illustrated*, and ESPN were there.

Before the formal stuff started, Sonny made a try at small talk with Uncle Seth and his friends. Seth wanted to introduce him to Hufnagel.

"We've met before," said Hufnagel to Uncle Seth. He told Sonny, "I saw you in the Mount Vernon game when you were a junior. You scored forty-seven points. I think you made nine threes in a row."

"Right," said Sonny, shaking Hufnagel's hand. He tried to remember exactly who Hufnagel was, or what it was that he did, but Uncle Seth had introduced him to so many guys, all the way back to ninth grade. Sonny was pretty sure about one thing, though: He'd never made nine treys in a row, at least not in a game.

"Look at this," said Uncle Seth, waving his hand at the congregation of media visitors. "This is recognition. This is respect."

"I never saw anything like it," said the man named Grant.

"Nobody has," Hufnagel observed. "Your team is going to put us on the map, Sonny. We haven't had any real recognition since the NIT team of '67."

Grant, an insurance man who'd followed Sonny's high school career like a homing device, was one of the biggest honchos in the SIU booster club. He said, "Maybe this year we won't be suckin' hind tit to the Big Ten and the Big Eight."

"There's a thought," said Uncle Seth. "You're going to be playing Michigan in the Big Apple NIT, Sonny. Do me a favor, huh? Don't just *beat* the sonsofbitches, bury 'em."

"You do that, and you're on the map right away," said Hufnagel. "I mean, beating Michigan on national TV."

Hearing this kind of talk was no source of comfort, especially since he hadn't even played a single college game yet. "We'll have to see," said Sonny, "I know Michigan's really good." He thought to himself, *We're supposed to make these men feel important.*

For the press conference, Sonny sat near the end of the head table, Luther on one side and Robert Lee on the other. It wasn't possible to be far away from the microphones, but Sonny made sure he was no closer than he had to be. Robert Lee nodded his head at the huge gathering and said, "This is intense, man." But he was clearly enjoying it. Luther, who had a grin a mile wide, leaned back in his chair and locked both hands at the back of his neck. "Ain't it a rush?" he chuckled.

To begin with, Coach Gentry made a brief statement about how hard the players had been working in practice. He talked briefly about the schedule. Coach Gentry was only in his second year as SIU head coach, but he was a sophisticated, polished man, at ease even in this much limelight. His three-piece suit was stylish, and not a hair was out of place. When Sonny looked at him, he couldn't help but think of Brother Rice, his old ninth-grade coach, that other time he was a freshman.

Rice was a crude, blunt slob who let it all hang out, while Gentry was like a corporate executive. Even in practices he was detached and low-key, like a CEO handing out duties to his vice presidents.

Coach Gentry drank some water and leaned over from the lectern while the sports information director whispered in his ear. He nodded his head several times before he straightened up to tell the reporters, "Jesse informs me that the only home games with tickets remaining are three conference games in late February and early March."

The first question was one about pressure. A reporter asked, "Some publications are ranking you as high as ninth or tenth in their preseason reports. What kind of pressure does this put on you and your players?"

"None on the coaching staff, and we hope none on the players," the coach answered. "We want to be the best team we can be, but we don't talk about polls or media expectations. We can't stop players from watching television or reading newspapers, but any pressure they feel will be self-generated; none of it will come from me or my assistants."

"Is it fair to say you expect to win the Missouri Valley Conference without much difficulty?" It seemed like a loaded question and it came from a reporter Sonny didn't recognize; he wondered if the guy came from Chicago.

Coach Gentry's crisp answer was, "It's fair to say we expect to play hard in every game and do our best to win."

Someone asked the coach if he knew who his starting lineup would be, but he answered, "It's premature for that kind of speculation. We're just evaluating at this point, trying to determine our strengths and weaknesses."

A few of the reporters chuckled in a smug kind of way, and the group as a whole seemed somewhat restless. One of them stood up and asked, "What kind of a contribution should we expect from Luther and Sonny?"

Coach Gentry adjusted his necktie before he said, "Let's start with the obvious. Luther has the advantage of two years' experience at the junior college level, while Sonny is a true freshman. They aren't at the same point in their development. They're both excellent players, as you know."

"Are you saying they might not start?"

Gentry took off his glasses. "Luther and Sonny are both outstanding talents, players any program in the country would be delighted to have. But everyone needs to remember that we were seventeen and eleven last year, and most of our veteran players are returning. Let's not forget that Otis Reed is one of the best point guards in the league, and Royer is one of the best centers in the league."

"But your returning players are going to be much better with Luther and Sonny on the floor at the same time."

Gentry got a big laugh when he said, "Is there a question in there somewhere?"

Sonny could hear Luther whistling with his tongue along the roof of his mouth; this was all like a party to him. The first question directed at a player went to Royer, a six-foot-ten senior center. He was asked how he liked having Luther and Sonny on the team.

"Who wouldn't like it? I'll probably go through the whole season without being doubled down."

"No jealousy on the team?"

"None that I know of."

The questioning rotated to Luther Cobb and he was asked how many games he expected the team to win. Luther said, "Might as well win 'em all."

"Every game?"

"Ain't no reason to be losin' any of 'em."

It didn't take the reporters long to warm to Luther's absence of caution. A writer from the *Post-Dispatch* wanted to know, "You're predicting an undefeated season? Are we talking national championship here?"

Luther's grin was ear-to-ear, his straight white teeth gleaming in high profile against his ebony skin. "All I'm sayin' is, ain't no reason to be losin' any games."

The writer from the *Sporting News* asked Luther, "Do you think you have the potential to play in the NBA?"

Luther Cobb's facial expression was an unlikely blend of humor, contempt, and astonishment, as if the reporter had asked him if he could touch the rim. "*Potential?* I can take those guys down in the summer leagues right now. *Potential.*"

Everyone was laughing by now, including Sonny. It would suit him fine if Luther's brashness preoccupied the reporters altogether. But he didn't expect it; he knew he wouldn't be overlooked in this setting, and he wasn't. The next question was for him.

"Sonny, you scored over three thousand points in high school, one of only five players to do that in IHSA history. Do you have any goals for yourself this season?"

All these eyes suddenly on him and Sonny couldn't think of a thing. Ballpoints poised everywhere he looked. "I'm not sure what you mean," he said quietly.

"Personal goals. Scoring, rebounding, that sort of thing. Have you set any?"

It seemed like a long time he had to think. Finally he

said the only thing that came to his mind: "I just want to play."

A reporter near the back shouted, "Louder, please? Could you speak into the mike?"

Sonny leaned forward to pull the mike closer. "I just want to play," he said again, this time loud enough for everyone to hear. It was the reporters' turn to be astonished, and their guffaws revealed just how much.

A woman reporter, one of the few present, asked Sonny, "Is this something you enjoy, Sonny?"

It was a curious question for sure. Sonny said, "You mean press conferences?"

"I mean press conferences."

Sonny wasn't sure, but he thought she might have been from the *Chicago Tribune*. "No, I don't. I just want to play."

So she turned to Luther. "Luther, you seem to enjoy what we're doing here. How would you evaluate Sonny Youngblood as a player?"

Luther sat up straight and didn't flinch. He took back the mike. "Sonny's the best white boy I've ever seen. He can *play*."

This remark brought down the house, but it also brought Coach Gentry back to his feet. Luther's brashness was the kind of color to gratify the media, but clearly not the press conference mode the coach preferred. For the next 30 minutes he restored equilibrium by answering questions about injuries, offensive and defensive strategies, and the strengths of other teams in the conference.

It was much less formal after the press conference. With the warm-ups on, and then off, the players posed for picture after picture. Still pictures, action pictures, group pictures, and posed pictures. The videocams wanted action footage of dunks, shot-blocking, and three-pointers.

But the more time passed, the more they wanted Sonny and Luther. Luther was basking in the singular attention, but Sonny felt sorry for the team's veterans, the guys who played last year, especially C.J. Moore, a stylish six-foot-five swingman who was a big-time talent. Media folks had none of these concerns; they wanted Sonny and Luther together, spinning basketballs on their fingertips, dunking each other's lobs, until the two had in fact worked up game-condition sweat. The cheering coming from the assembled spectators seemed gamelike as well.

A final dunk-off between Sonny and Luther, requested by ESPN's Chris Berman and cleared with Coach Gentry, was set up for any technician with a videocam on his shoulder.

Luther went first. He came in from the side, along the baseline, and hammered home a two-handed reverse slam. He even hung briefly on the rim before he jackknifed himself up and away. In his wake, the backboard was shaking like a leaf. The crowd erupted like a conference championship had just been claimed.

It was competition now, so when Sonny's turn came he passed quickly into the zone that left everything behind. No more regrets for last year's players, no camera lights, no residual tension from the ordeal of the head table with microphones. No nothing.

He stood on the spot where his heels covered the free throw line. If he looked straight at the rim, ignoring the net, the circle met the square. Sonny never did have a way with words, but something about it was perfect. If he looked straight at and through the rim, it formed a kind of flattened disc framed just exactly right by the square on the backboard behind it. Not too big, not too small, the outer edges of the circle made just the barest contact with the four edges of the square. It was all within, but just.

In place at the free throw line, six feet five inches and 206 pounds. Where his long, sinewy arms hung at his sides, each large hand palmed a bright orange basketball casually. The crowd of onlookers, quiet as a church and without access to the inner chamber where Sonny was locked in his vision, might have been looking for sure at one of God Almighty's lightbulb afterthoughts: *Hot damn! Before I call it a day, I think I'll just sit me down and design the perfect basketball player!*

But if Sonny looked to others like a pilgrim standing reverently before a shrine, he didn't linger long for meditation: The floorboards squeaked as he vaulted himself suddenly forward. He launched like a missile, two quick strides and a flight at the iron. He dunked both balls in a blink, first the right and then the left, in a succession so rapid it looked like an optical trick. It took a moment to absorb, but then the crowd's astonished approval erupted like a volcano.

It was the mystery of *Checkpoint* that made it a source of apprehension. For his own information, Sonny wanted to know if Coach Gentry was going to be present, but Gardner told him no.

"What about Coach Price?"

"Coach Price won't be here either. This is strictly routine, Sonny. It's not like you're in any kind of trouble." While he was offering this reassurance, Gardner was directing people to be seated by gesturing at the chairs around the table. As compliance officer, Gardner was a member of the athletic staff, but not a coach.

Sonny assumed his basic duties were to monitor all the rules and regulations published by the NCAA in order to guard against possible violations.

"Shouldn't I be at practice?"

"Would you relax, Youngblood? Coach Gentry knows where you are, you're covered."

The setting was a conference room on second-floor Lingle. Maria, one of the basketball secretaries, was bringing ice water and coffee in thermal pots. Quackenbush and Burns were from NCAA headquarters in Kansas. With their short haircuts and their crisp suits and shiny briefcases, Sonny thought they looked like FBI agents or Mormon missionaries. They were polite, though, when they asked Sonny if he wanted these proceedings taped.

Sonny said, "I don't know." He looked at Gardner, who squinted his face, then shook his head back and forth.

"I guess not," said Sonny.

"We'll be taking notes," Quackenbush told him, "but it's your right to have all you say on tape if you request it."

"I guess not," Sonny repeated.

"Fine. *Checkpoint* doesn't presume any wrongdoing. It's strictly routine, just as your compliance officer is telling you." He meant Gardner.

Quackenbush went on, "We've been conducting exactly the same interview procedure with incoming freshmen all over the country. We were targeting football players during the summer, but now we're concentrating on basketball players. The object, of course, is to help maintain the integrity of NCAA athletics. I'd like you to have this pamphlet, which explains the history of the program, its goals, and its development. Maybe in your free time you can read it over. We advise that you do." He pushed the pamphlet across the table.

Sonny picked it up indifferently. It was a simple trifold in red and black. The word *Checkpoint* was printed in large letters on the front. He put it down; maybe there was no reason to be nervous, not with Gardner right there to oversee everything.

The format they followed had Quackenbush asking most of the questions, while Burns took most of the notes. Right away, they wanted to know about academics. A composite score of 20 on the ACT and a high school record where C's prevailed, wasn't exactly a "strong academic history." They wanted to know how his classwork was going.

"Okay, I guess."

"Have you received midterm grades yet?"

"Yeah, we got them."

"And how's your progress? Are you doing well?"

Sonny thought of his English Comp and the Intro to Anthropology. These questions seemed personal and embarrassing. But when he looked at Gardner, he was smiling comfortably. "Go ahead, Sonny, you can answer their questions."

"Can I have some water?"

"Sure."

After he drank half a glass, Sonny said, "I need to pull up my grades in a couple of courses."

"Not flunking anything, are we?"

"No." But he wasn't positive.

"Have you declared a major yet?"

Sonny shook his head. "I don't have a major. Just general studies."

"Fine," said Quackenbush. It seemed to be a word he liked. The questions turned to recruiting. Burns asked him if any coaches or institutions ever offered him any illegal inducements.

Sonny wasn't precisely sure what the question encompassed. "I doubt it," he said.

"Did anybody buy you anything or offer to buy you anything? Think before you answer."

"No, I don't think so."

"You're not sure?"

"Yes, I'm sure." Sonny glanced sidelong again at Gardner, who was amusing himself by twisting rubber bands.

"Did any coach or institution promise you anything if you signed a letter of intent?"

It seemed like the same question. Sonny thought for a few moments. "Most of them told me I could start if I came to their school."

"We don't mean that," said Quackenbush. "Were you ever promised cash, or a vehicle, or special living privileges? That kind of thing."

"No."

"Sonny, do you have adequate spending money?"

"I guess so. I don't buy much. Just drugstore stuff, maybe a few meals."

"Girls? Dates?"

"Not very often. Probably more if I had the time."

"But you have enough spending money to meet your needs."

"I'd say so."

"And where does it come from?"

"Mostly from my uncle Seth. I have a savings account, but it isn't much. I didn't earn a lot of money during the summers because I was in so many camps."

"You're talking about basketball camps."

"Yeah. The Nike camp, the Prairie State Games. You know."

"Yes," said Quackenbush. "We do know. How much money does your uncle give you?"

Sonny felt like his privacy was being invaded, and why were they trying to make him feel guilty? It was annoying, but apparently not to Gardner, who seemed utterly placid. Sonny decided not to mention the Toyota. He told them, "It varies. Sometimes he gives me a hundred."

"This is a generous uncle," observed Quackenbush.

"I guess he is. Is there something wrong with it?"

"Probably not."

"I've lived with him and my aunt since my sophomore year." He needed some more water.

Quackenbush poured himself a cup of coffee before he continued. "Sonny, when did you decide you were going to enroll at SIU?"

"I signed my letter of intent last November."

"That's what we have on record. What I mean is, when did you make up your mind?"

He had to think before he could answer. "By the time I was a junior, I was pretty much decided."

"Pretty much?"

"I was decided. My mind was made up."

"Fine. Did you make official visits to UCLA and the University of Illinois last fall?"

Gardner interrupted for the first time: "It doesn't seem in very good faith to ask him what you already know."

"Okay," nodded Quackenbush, "fair enough. When you made those campus visits, Sonny, did you tell those coaches that you had already made up your mind to go to SIU?"

"Not exactly. I told them I was leaning, but they wanted me to come for the visits anyway."

"Why UCLA?" asked Burns.

Sonny provided the only answer he knew, "I always liked the Bruins on TV, and I wanted to visit the campus."

Burns looked up quickly from his notes. "You wanted a free trip to California."

Sonny blinked. The way everything seemed to have a double meaning added to his tension. "I wouldn't exactly put it that way."

"How would you put it, then?"

"I already told you how I put it."

It was Gardner's turn to make another interruption: "Let's be fair here. Sonny was entitled to five official visits, but he only made three. Lots of prospects sandbag their way on a much bigger scale than that. Let's be fair."

Burns seemed impatient. "Why the U of I?" he wanted to know.

"When I was a sophomore, that's where I wanted to go," Sonny told him.

"Why?"

"I wanted to play in the Big Ten. It seemed big-time, almost like the NBA."

"Did University of Illinois coaches make you any offers of cash or other gifts?"

"No," answered Sonny. "I thought I already told you nobody offered me anything illegal."

Quackenbush said, "You wanted to play in the Big Ten, and then you chose to come to SIU. What changed your mind?"

It was the easiest question yet. Sonny told them, "My uncle Seth is an SIU alum. It was important to him for me to play here."

"So you chose SIU to please your uncle?"

"It's not quite that simple. My mother's in the state

hospital in Anna. My aunt pointed out how I wouldn't be able to visit her if I went away from home too far."

"Family loyalty then, primarily?"

"That was a big part of it, but I like Coach Gentry and the players, too. It meant a lot to me when I found out Luther Cobb was coming here."

"You wanted to play with Luther Cobb?"

"Sure. Who wouldn't?"

Then Quackenbush asked, "Is it fair to say that you wanted to go to the U of I, but your uncle exerted enough influence to change your mind? Is that a fair statement?"

They are twisting this, Sonny thought to himself. *And why do they care so much about Uncle Seth?*

Gardner complained, with unconcealed impatience: "Would you expect a high school sophomore to have his mind made up about college plans? Especially one who's getting pressure from college recruiters day and night on the phone?"

Sonny appreciated the supportive intervention, but Quackenbush simply said, "Fine. Is it fair to say you accepted free campus visits to the U of I and UCLA after you had your mind made up to attend SIU? Is that fair?"

It seemed so argumentative that Sonny felt defensive. He looked at Gardner, who simply smirked and gave it a wave of his hand. Which Sonny interpreted to mean, *It's all just a matter of routine, so go along*.

But Sonny had his own impatience by this time. He said to Burns and Quackenbush, "It's a basically accurate statement, but I don't know if it's fair or not."

When the interview was over, Sonny went straight to practice, an hour late.

After supper, he called his uncle to tell him about the *Checkpoint* interview. Uncle Seth told him not to worry.

"It's strictly routine, just going through the motions."

"Easy for you to say, you weren't there. You know about this?" Sonny asked him.

"A little. I may be an old fart, but I get around some."

"I didn't even know this was comin'," said Sonny.

"Don't worry about it," Seth repeated. "You need any money?"

"Not really."

"Maybe you should. Spend a little money, have a little fun."

"Right." But when he hung up the phone, Sonny felt relieved.

Another walk in the rain, through Thompson Woods, heading for study table. This was cold rain, falling steady through bare branches. The occasional lamps, if they weren't burned out, lighted the path, but it was an especially dark night.

Sonny wore his Cardinals baseball cap, but it didn't prevent some of the rain from splattering his face. He thought how strange it seemed, the way things could turn ironic. *Checkpoint* was being somebody. So were press conferences, phone calls from reporters, microphones in your face, and the hot light of the Minicam. Sonny was *somebody*. When he was a senior at Abydos, they ran his picture in *Street and Smith*. He didn't care about it; he only cared about the game itself, and even that was a kind of vacuum of its own, the way he played it in his private zone of intensity that blotted out the cheering crowds and the backslappers. Maybe most of life itself. *Was basketball fun?*

A tutor helped him with gerunds and participles but what little interest he had was brief. It was between 9:30 and 10:00 when he ran into Warner at the Pizza Hut on the lower level of the student center. Warner was a sportswriter for the Carbondale paper, the *Southern Illinoisan*, whom Sonny had known for a long time.

"Would you like to tell me about *Checkpoint*?" Warner asked him.

Sonny had to smile. "How come you know so much?"

"It's a reporter's job to sniff these things out. But if I knew so much, as you put it, I wouldn't need to be asking you any questions." He was smiling.

It was a long line they were in, and they found themselves near the end of it. People stared at Sonny, but he was used to it. Warner was a tall, gaunt man with a perpetual twinkle in his eyes. He'd been covering Sonny's games since his sophomore year.

"So where's your pencil?" Sonny asked.

"I don't need a pencil for porch talk. It's too late to be on duty anyway. I tried to raid the refrigerator but there wasn't anything in it except for health food like carrots and celery."

"They say it's just routine," Sonny stated.

"*Checkpoint*? Yeah, that's all it is."

"You might think different if you were there. I wonder who else they're going to interview."

"You mean here at SIU?"

"Yeah."

"Nobody," said Warner. "Only you. They only screen the top fifty freshmen in the country. If you're looking for recruiting violations, that's the most likely place to find them."

"But what about Luther? He was a junior college all-American."

"He was, but that's just it. Luther's a junior college transfer, not a freshman. If he went through *Checkpoint*, he probably went through it two years ago."

"Well, did he?" asked Sonny.

"I don't know," Warner answered. "Maybe not. The NCAA doesn't usually take too much interest in guys who go to junior college. Look at it this way, Sonny, it's an honor to be chosen."

"Let's believe that." But he wondered why this information had to come from a newspaper reporter. Why not from the basketball staff, or the athletic director's office, or the compliance officer?

It was their turn to order. "Buy you a slice of pizza?" offered Warner.

"Sure. Why not?"

Warner was smiling again, but this time in an indulgent way. "Why not is because it would probably be a violation. If I buy you something to eat, that's a gift. I'm not an SIU alum, but anybody who spends as much time as I do on this campus would be seen by the NCAA as a representative of SIU athletic interests. *Ergo*, I would be providing you with an illegal gift."

"Okay, okay. Gardner goes over all this stuff, but it's too complicated."

"Complicated it is. It's a game you have to play like you're walking through a minefield."

Sonny looked him in the eye, which meant he had to look down. "It's not the game I care about," he said. "The only game I care about is the one played on the court."

"I believe that," admitted Warner.

When they found a table and started eating, Warner said, "I don't want to alarm you, Sonny, but I'm going to put a bug in your ear. *Checkpoint* may be simply routine, but what's coming is not."

"What's that supposed to mean?"

"It means an NCAA investigation. Does the basketball staff discuss this stuff with you people?"

"No, we never talk about anything like that, just the rules. Today was the first time I ever answered questions from the NCAA."

Warner finished chewing, swallowed, and drank some of his Coke before he continued. "I probably shouldn't mention any of this, but it seems like *somebody* should. There's going to be an investigation, and I mean full-scale."

"You mean of our program?"

"That's exactly what I mean. The NCAA is going to conduct a full investigation, which won't be routine at all."

"How do you know?"

Warner shrugged and smiled. "I got hold of some information. Trust me on this."

"I trust you. When will they have this investigation?"

"There's no way to tell. The NCAA is overloaded, and they're incredibly slow even when they're not."

Sonny could feel a knot forming in his stomach. *I haven't even played a game yet.* "Are they going to have it this year?"

"They'd probably like to, if they can get their act together, but who knows? Time will tell."

Sonny didn't say anything for a while. He ate his pizza instead, and tried to remember details of his recruiting trips or specific conversations with coaches. He remembered when Uncle Seth finally set up a separate phone line with an answering machine.

Warner said, "I really wasn't sure if I should mention this to you or not. I wouldn't want to do anything to upset you. You're a good kid, Sonny; I've always liked you."

And what good does it do to be a good kid? "It's okay, Warner, I'm glad you told me."

"I hope so."

"I'm not afraid of an investigation," Sonny said. "I've never done anything wrong."

"I'm sure you haven't." Then Warner changed the subject: "Are you ready for the Big Apple?"

He was talking about the NIT in New York City. "That's not for another week," Sonny replied. "I'll be ready when the time comes."

Sissy's office was in ancient Allyn Hall on the perimeter of the old campus quad. Although he'd passed it many times on the way to informal workouts at Davies, he'd never been inside the building. If there was a comfortable way to talk to her, Sonny didn't know what it might be, so he started with an irrelevant question. "Do you think Uncle Seth will be pissed when he finds out I quit the fraternity?"

"I have no idea, Sonny. Are you in a fraternity?"

"I was, until last week. I dropped out."

"I'd like to see that as a problem, but in my mind a person who separates himself from the Greek system should be commended for an act of intelligence."

Sonny absorbed her remark a moment or two before he continued, "I'm going to tell him I just don't have the time, which is the truth. Not with classes and practice."

"Did you enjoy the fraternity?"

"No."

"Then that should be reason enough for quitting, shouldn't it?"

"Probably. I just don't want to hurt his feelings, I guess."

"Why is it so important what he thinks?" Sissy asked him. "Why are you so concerned about Seth's approval?"

Sonny looked at her. He felt like saying, *He's your*

father, for Christ sake. Instead, he told her, "Where would I be now if it wasn't for Uncle Seth and Aunt Jane? They took me in when my mother went to the puzzle house."

"I know, Sonny. I'm glad for that."

"He supported my whole basketball career through high school. He took care of recruiters, summer camps, and just about everything else. It was like I had my own agent."

Sissy answered, "I'm pleased to hear it. I hope he did it for the right reasons."

"What's that supposed to mean?"

It was somehow her cue to activate some impatient body language. She sat up straighter in her chair. "Let's just say your uncle Seth hasn't exactly made a habit of working at things that don't benefit him personally. Have you never heard of doing the right thing for the wrong reason?"

"He's your father, isn't he?"

"Yes, indeed. Sonny, your uncle and I have a long and checkered history, which you and I don't need to explore at this time. If he supported you, I'm happy to know it. In any case, belonging to a fraternity, or not, has to be your decision."

Of course she was right. He looked out the window where the sycamore limbs, large and bare of leaves, mottled with missing bark, reached their bony branches right up near the glass. It was a clear sky, but the sun in it was the pale November kind.

"Why did you come to see me?" Sissy asked him. "You're not here to talk about fraternities."

"That's true." He was still staring out the window at the branches. "I've got a big problem. I dropped a course."

"What course?"

"Anthropology. Intro to."

"Why did you drop it?"

"I think I was flunking."

"Then maybe dropping it was the right thing to do."

He looked into her eyes. "I've only got eleven hours now; I'm afraid I'm not going to be eligible."

"You're talking about basketball now. Are you saying that you have to be carrying more than eleven hours to be eligible for basketball?"

"That's what I'm saying."

"And you didn't know this when you dropped Anthropology?"

Sonny shook his head. "I probably should have. Robert Lee told me last night. He's one of the other players on the team. I thought eligibility was based on the courses you're registered for."

"And apparently it's not?"

"It gets worse. I might not even be eligible second semester. I might not have what they call *satisfactory academic progress*. Not with just eleven hours."

"Have you talked to your academic advisor?"

"He's on the A.D.'s staff. He'll be pissed big-time."

"Will he know?"

"All our academic stuff goes through the athletic director's office." At this point there seemed more than he could tell her. Or would know how to tell her. There was eligibility, but there was also trust in the athletic administration. Sometimes it felt like your treatment wasn't open. There was the possibility of the NCAA examining everybody's transcript. When the basketball office found out, what if they tried to hide it? *Then where will I be?* Finally he said to her, "Sometimes it's like you can't even take a piss without the right person's permission. Or that's how it seems. Excuse my language."

For the first time, Sissy laughed. "Sonny, forgive me for being blunt with you, but I have no patience at all with varsity athletic programs in college. There are universities where some of the best high school students are denied admission, yet basketball and football players can be admitted with ACT scores of fifteen."

"I know all about that. What am I supposed to do?"

"I'm sorry," she said. "It's a corrupt sort of business, but you're not its creator. Why are you telling me all of this?"

Sonny decided he might just as well say it. "I just thought that since you're a professor, there might be something you could do."

"Do? I don't know of anyone who could reinstate you in a class once you've dropped it."

Sonny was shaking his head. Since he was this far, though, he might as well go for the rest. "That's not it. I only need one hour. I thought there might be something you could do."

At first, she didn't say a word. Slowly, and with some discomfort evident, she wheeled her desk chair close to him, using her feet to propel herself. She clamped his left hand, top and bottom. "Cousin, Cousin. Are you asking me to commit academic fraud for a jock?"

"No, nothing phony." He tried to imagine how preposterous this request must sound, and how vague. "You have to understand, I'm not good at expressing myself. I just thought there might be something; I'm not sure what."

She let go his hand. When she stood up, she did so slowly. "Come with me. I'll buy you a Coke at the student center."

This part was a surprise. "I'll go with you, but I can't accept the Coke."

"Why is that?"

"It's probably a gift. It's probably a violation."

"From your own cousin?" Then she began laughing and laughing, for what seemed like the longest time.

Sonny finally interrupted, "What's so funny?"

"You don't see the humor in this?" she asked him. "I would say it's downright comical."

"All I said was, it might be against NCAA rules."

"Come with me, Cuz."

They sat in the student center McDonald's, but Sonny paid for the two soft drinks. "Let me see your hands," Sissy said.

"What?"

"Put your hands on the table; I want to look at them."

The long, strong fingers he spread covered nearly half of the Formica top on the tiny table. "Why am I doing this?" he asked Sissy.

"You're probably strong as an ox, aren't you?" she asked. When she said "Okay," Sonny put his hands back in his lap. She wanted to know if he'd ever done any carpentry.

"Some, at Uncle Seth's. I always got A's in shop. So what's the point of these questions, anyway?"

"The point is, I may actually have something, unlikely as it seems."

"Have what?" Sonny asked eagerly.

Sissy was rubbing her closed eyes. He noted the long fingers with the irregular nails. Other than the gray in her hair, and the well-defined crow's-feet at the corners of her eyes, she didn't really look her age.

"Have what?" he asked again.

"Do you know anything about art?" she asked.

Even if he needed a favor, Sonny wasn't prepared to lie. "Not actually. I always took shop instead of art."

"I need some help with a restoration project," she said. "I have to get some fresco panels taken down and transported from Pyramid State Park. I'm working on a grant from the National Endowment."

Words like *fresco panels* and *national endowment* didn't mean much to Sonny. "And you could give me credit for helping you?"

"I could give you an hour of independent study. The panels have to be transported safely by second semester. I have a seminar that's going to work on restoring them. It will be hard work getting them here, worth an hour's credit at least."

"Don't forget, I only need one hour."

"I'm not forgetting. I had an art major picked out for this, but he dropped out of school."

"So let me do it," said Sonny.

Sissy searched his eyes for several moments before she answered. "You're so young, aren't you?"

"I'll be nineteen at the end of next month. You know how old I am."

"How's your mother?"

"She's the same, I suppose." *Why is she changing the subject with a question like this?* "I see her about once a month, but I don't think she recognizes me. She's been catatonic. This is off the subject, isn't it?"

"Maybe and maybe not." Sissy was smiling, but it wasn't teasing. It seemed like a patient and fond smile. "Actually, it might work out nicely. You're strong and you have some experience with tools and materials."

Where she was headed seemed promising, so Sonny

didn't say anything. Sissy added, "It would take us clear through December, I imagine, which is well past the end of the semester."

"I don't think that would be a problem. I'd have the team, but no classes; there should be enough free time." In spite of himself, he was starting to breathe a sigh of relief. He waited a moment before he added, "It seems perfect to me, Sissy. You'd have your project ready to go and I'd be eligible. I know you're eligible if you're carrying twelve hours."

"It's perfectly *political*, that's for sure," she replied. "I have no interest in basketball, and you have no interest in art. What could be better?"

It wasn't the first time in his life he'd observed her sarcasm, which could just about blow you away. "It just seems to me like we'd be helping each other out," he said quietly.

"And it seems to me we'd be using each other. Would it bother you at all to earn credit if you have no real interest in the subject matter?"

"No," he said without hesitation. "That's what I do every day. What would bother me is going ineligible. Basketball is my whole life."

She reached upon the table to touch his hand, which was wrapped around his Coke. She gave a long sigh. "Cousin, Cousin. I'm going to need a little time to think about this. There are art majors who could help once the semester is over, but I can't wait that long to get started. Besides that, I have the go-ahead from my doctor to start working on the project. Give me a day or two to see if I can lock my conscience up in the closet."

"Okay," said Sonny. He chose to see this as extremely hopeful.

She searched his eyes again. "It might be nice to get acquainted, huh?"

"Yeah, that would be nice."

"No promises," she reminded him. She was taking a small spiral notebook and a ballpoint from her large canvas bag. "I'll need your phone number," she said.

3

It was Robert Lee's opinion that there were better ways to spend Thanksgiving Day than sitting on a charter flight, but Sonny knew they were headed for New York City and the Big Apple NIT. "No, there aren't," was his terse reply.

Luther announced with contempt that the Salukis were ranked 21st in the country in *USA Today*'s preseason poll. It seemed like a pretty high honor to Sonny, but Luther threw the paper aside. "Shit, man, say twenty teams better than us? No way."

On the trip, Sonny would be rooming with Robert Lee. Snell was left at home because only 12 could make the traveling squad. When they reached their midtown Manhattan hotel, Robert Lee flopped himself on one of the two queen-size beds and wallowed in the luxurious spread. "I could get used to this, man."

Sonny laughed, but his interest in their accomodations was minimal; standing at the threshold of his collegiate career, he was too much on edge. His interest in the sights and sounds of Manhattan was only slightly higher. This was just a town for playing basketball, like Mounds, Illinois, or Cobden.

Madison Square Garden, however, was a different matter, an awe-inspiring shrine permanent on the pilgrimage of basketball holies. "Jesus Christ," said Robert Lee. "I thought our arena was big."

"The Assembly Hall at the U of I is as big as this," said Sonny. But that fact didn't mitigate the reverence he felt. He spent so much time gawking worshipfully at the height and breadth of this basketball mecca that Workman, one of Gentry's assistants, told him, "Time to get in your game head, Sonny. This is just another gym."

"Right."

"Baskets here are ten feet, free throw line is fifteen. This is the same as the playground."

"Right." Sonny began pouring in three-point arcers. The photographers and the Minicams seemed to grow out of the floor like crops.

A free copy of *The New York Times* was perched on each table in the hotel dining room. Tournament coverage in the sports section included pictures of Sonny and Luther, as well as high profile players from some of the other teams. When they were finished eating, Sonny folded the page to take home for Aunt Jane's scrapbook.

The game against Miami was an easy 95–77 win, but the crowd was small. Even though the Salukis had some substantial preseason recognition, Miami had none at all, and neither team was likely to spark a great deal of interest in this east-coast setting.

Nervous during the first half, Sonny relaxed later on and nailed a few threes. He finished with 19 points, but late in the game, a Miami jumping jack named Jerome Williams blocked his shot. It was a breakaway, which Sonny nonchalanted in a finger roll, but Williams swooped from the side to swat it off the court.

Luther Cobb was a monster on the boards. At six feet seven inches and 235 pounds, he pounded out a performance to match his image. After the game, he and

Coach Gentry were the postgame interview for ESPN. Coach Gentry observed that "It was gratifying for an opening game. The rough spots were to be expected."

When asked about the large margin of victory, Luther told the interviewer, "Ain't no big thing."

The 88-channel capability of the cable TV in their room held a powerful fascination for Robert Lee, who manhandled the remote like a video game. "Check this out," he said to Sonny, when he located the late-night triple-X movie channel.

"Who cares?" The restless Sonny Youngblood prowled the room and brushed his teeth three times.

"I know what it is," said Robert Lee. "You're all unglued because you got your shot blocked."

"Nobody ever blocks my shot."

"You scored nineteen points, am I right? You know what your problem is, Sonny? You're just not used to screwing up. You're too good."

"Nobody blocks my fucking shot! The next time I think finger roll, I'll just dunk it. If I'da dunked it, that never could've happened."

"Right," said Robert Lee, who had just located a Cuban channel. "Can we kiss it off now?"

"There has to be another notch in the switch," Sonny muttered. "There will be."

"I said, can we kiss it off?"

The following night, for the Michigan game, the crowd was large, although less than capacity. Rated number three in the country, the Wolverines were heavily favored. During warm-ups, Sonny felt his tension increase when he looked in the direction of Michigan's senior all-American, Alonzo Lipes. "How good is Lipes?" he asked Luther.

"I played against him in a summer league two years ago," Luther replied. "Lipes can play."

When the teams were at the bench for last-minute instructions, Sonny had to go to the locker-room toilet to throw up. A security man was staring at him until Sonny told him to get out. Scarlet-faced, hanging on the porcelain, heaving up phlegm when it was all that was left in his tract, Sonny missed the starting lineup introductions.

He was shaky in the early minutes, but it was a disastrous night for Michigan. The Salukis buried them 102–65, in a game that wasn't even close at halftime. Michigan tried zoning for a while, but zoning a team that counted Sonny Youngblood among its members was a futile proposition. His accuracy from outside the arc was uncanny, while C.J. Moore on the other wing was a deadly perimeter shooter as well.

When Michigan went to the man-to-man, it merely revealed the Saluki balance. Luther's power moves underneath demanded double-teaming, which left the six-ten Royer free for a string of uncontested short jumpers in the paint.

For his part, Sonny was on fire. He led all scorers with a 40-point game. In addition to his breathtaking demonstration of three-point shooting, he ripped home a pair of reverse slams off the half-court trap. Even Robert Lee got enough playing time to root around for 11 points and shake the ball loose several times with his physical, nose-to-nose defense.

With six minutes remaining, and the lead mounted to 40 points, Sonny caught the substitutes lined up at the scorers' bench from the corner of his eye. He stole an errant pass and bolted for the Michigan basket. *Just this one more before Coach takes me out.*

The frustrated Alonzo Lipes flew at him while Sonny soared at the iron, the ball cocked in both hands behind his head. He powered home his monster dunk an instant before Lipes's left hand delivered a glancing blow against the back of his head.

He made his free throw pure to complete the three-point play. As soon as Sonny came out of the game, he went straight to the locker room for more vomiting. It was a different security guard this time. Sonny had the shakes and some uncomfortable palpitations as well. Drained of color and energy, he lay on one of the benches with a wet towel over his face.

A minute before the game was over, Workman came in and said they wanted him for an ESPN interview.

"Forget it," he told Workman, without lifting the towel.

"You okay, Sonny?"

"I'm fine. No interview though."

There was a big party in the hotel ballroom with refreshments, reporters, and photographers. Most of the reporters learned soon enough that Sonny wasn't a good interview, so it wasn't surprising when they tended to gather around Luther and Coach Gentry. One reporter, however, a man from *Newsday*, asked Sonny what he thought about New York City.

"Not much," he replied. He was drinking a large glass of punch and gobbling French pastries on his still-queasy stomach.

"You don't like the Big Apple?"

"I didn't say that. I just don't think about it much."

As poised as Coach Gentry was in the press conference environment, he never seemed comfortable when his players hobnobbed with the media. This time was no exception. At 11:45, he told Price to herd them to their rooms. Even before Sonny and Robert Lee got inside the room, the phone was ringing.

It was Uncle Seth, drunk and in the company of several cronies. He told Sonny, "We've been sitting here counting the rings. We got up to one hundred and sixty before you answered."

"Hi, Uncle Seth."

Seth and the other revelers took turns on the receiver, proclaiming the glory of this moment in loud, slurred syllables. Sonny held the receiver three feet from his head so Robert Lee could hear as well.

To win the finals the next night, they had to beat St. John's. Not regarded as a great team, St. John's had upset favored Louisville to reach this title game. Since St. John's was a New York City team, the Redmen would enjoy a huge homecourt advantage. Before the game even started, the noise level from the 16,000 partisans was like a tidal wave, and it was hostile. Sonny could feel his stomach churning, but it wasn't enough to give him nausea.

The intimidation generated by the roaring crowd didn't endure past the 14-minute mark, when the score was 15–14. At halftime, the SIU lead was swollen to 47–25. By the time the blowout was over, 94–63, the crowd had thinned out considerably; Madison Square Garden was as quiet as a practice gym.

Reporters swarmed the locker room, but Coach Gentry moved everyone quickly in order to meet the midnight flight from La Guardia. Because he was chosen the Most Valuable Player for the tournament, Sonny did have to stick around for a center-court ceremony and a brief interview with cable hookups. One writer described his style of play as that of a "dervish." Another labeled him the "Tasmanian Devil of the hardwood," whatever that meant. But at 18 years and 11 months, Sonny Youngblood was averaging 32 points a game against high-level competition, and bringing home the MVP plaque from the Big Apple NIT.

Lights out on the plane, but it seemed to Sonny that he was the only one having trouble sleeping. He twisted his long limbs this way and that in search of a comfortable space. His stomach was still queasy from game-generated tension and gorging on available snacks. His racing mind permitted only intermittent dozing, in and out.

In the disorientation of this racing mind, he found himself out of time and place. The vivid images in his brain were not of the NIT, but somehow of the freshman team back in Abydos. He wasn't on a plane at all; he was back on the bus to Tamms, in the ninth grade. It was a long and winding ride in the dark, especially after the driver, who was new, got lost and ended up in Thebes. They had to use secondary roads cutting through the Shawnee National Forest. There were patches of frozen snow along the shoulder and every once in a while Sonny caught a glimpse of the naked trees along the bluffs.

Most of the other guys didn't seem as tense as he was, but then he was the only one with no previous game experience. Butch Cross played a battery-operated video game, while Julio was listening to a tape on his Walkman. Sonny had a seat to himself, but across the aisle was One Gram, who kept a steady stream of small talk going. With his attention primarily out the window, Sonny didn't hear much of what he said, so he just grunted yes or no every so often.

Brother Rice, who was hulked up in the front seat, wouldn't tolerate a lot of noise on the bus. At the moment, he had Dick Lynch in the "seat of honor," the one right behind the driver. He was talking to Lynch in a conversational tone, while pointing to diagrams on index cards. Sonny couldn't hear what he was saying, but he had Lynch's undivided attention.

When it was his turn, Sonny felt proud because Brother Rice didn't put you in the seat of honor unless he thought you were a significant player. Nerves took over in a hurry, though, and his heart began to thump in his chest. Rice leaned close to tell him, "If we get ahead of this team, I want to use the diamond press in the second half. I want you on this wing." He showed Sonny the index card with the diamond press configuration. He pointed to the X on the right wing.

Rice's labored breathing smelled like cigarettes; there were droplets of perspiration formed on his forehead.

"Okay," said Sonny.

"What did we say about the press in practice?" Brother Rice asked him.

Sonny licked his dry lips. "We have to put pressure on the ball all the time," he said.

"Some of the time?"

"No, all the time."

"And you remember what I said about fouls." Rice's voice was like gravel.

"I remember."

"Okay, tell me. What did I say about fouls?"

Sonny had to lick his lips again. "It's okay to foul because you have to find out what the refs will let you get away with."

"Exactly. A press that doesn't intimidate in every way possible is not worth a shit." Then he clapped Sonny on the knee and said, "Good concentration, Youngblood; just be sure your head is in the game."

During warm-ups, Sonny was careful to shoot only conventional layups, soft off the glass. No finger rolls. Dick Lynch tried a semidunk which was a big failure; all he did was more or less pin the ball dead on the front of the rim. Then he had a sheepish grin when some of the guys hooted him. Sonny didn't say a word. He thought he could outjump Lynch anyway.

The gym was about half full of spectators, which Sonny thought must be a good crowd for a freshman game. He said so to Julio.

"It is a good crowd," said Julio. "But that's what you get when Abydos plays."

"Really?"

"Damn right. You'll see."

When the game started, Sonny was on the bench, about three down from Rice himself. Rice's "head in the game rule" meant that even though your ass was on the bench, your mind better be on the court. You weren't supposed to do any gabbing or goofing off, you needed to concentrate 100 percent on the game, especially on the guy playing your position.

Sonny rooted for Abydos to get a big lead, so he would get to play. It wasn't necessary, though; when the game was only four minutes old, it was only a matter of *how* big the lead would be, and how soon.

The Abydos defensive pressure produced lots of turnovers, which led to easy baskets. On offense, Julio was like lightning at the point guard position, dropping off pinpoint passes for easy baskets, by his teammates, mostly Lynch and One Gram. Abydos had a lead of 24–9 at the quarter; by halftime, the score was 44–24. Watching his team execute and dominate, Sonny felt his adrenaline flow like a river. *It almost takes your breath away*, he thought. *I've got to be a part of this.*

Halfway through the third quarter, Sonny got in. It didn't help his nerves any when Rice started squalling at him to play tougher defense. "Get in his face, Young-blood, what the hell do you think you're gonna do from back there?? You're not playing pocket pool, you're *trapping!*"

Embarrassed and shaky, Sonny took deep breaths. The only sliver of consolation was knowing Rice wouldn't get on your case unless he decided you were worth it. The next time an Egyptian player got trapped on his side, Sonny went straight at the guy and raked the ball loose with both hands. But he also bodied him out-of-bounds and got whistled for a foul. Sonny quickly looked at Rice, but there was no reason to be shook; the coach was grinning the crooked grin and giving him the thumbs-up.

One Gram, who was seated next to the coach, shouted encouragement: "In his face, Sonny, in his face!"

While they were lined up to shoot the free throws, Sonny watched as the Egyptian coach, Barnes, walked over to Rice. Barnes wanted to know why Rice was putting on the press with a 30-point lead.

"Kiss my ass," was all Rice said to him, without even looking in his direction.

On offense, Sonny turned down several jump-shot opportunities. It felt safer just to make quick passes; it got him into the flow of the game and over feeling stressed. Twice in the fourth quarter he anticipated the path of the pass that the trapped Egyptian player would have to make. Both times he stepped up easily to intercept, and with two quick strides and a single dribble, made the soft layup. Both times it all happened so fast there was no time to think, like it was instinct, like it was *inner.*

*　　*　　*

What was *not* inner was the air turbulence over Cleveland. Sonny sat up straight in his seat, along with several of the other players. There was some low-level murmuring and grumbling. He was surprised to find Coach Workman sitting beside him, but maybe he shouldn't have been; of Gentry's three assistants, it was Workman whose emotional bond with players was most secure. "You okay, Youngblood?"

"Yeah, why not? Is this okay?"

"It's just a pocket of turbulence, nothing unusual. Have you done much flying?"

"No. Only when I made a visit to UCLA. That, and the flight back."

"You want something?"

"Have you got something?"

"Just these. They help sometimes."

Sonny looked at the two tiny white pills. "What is this, Dramamine?"

"Something like that. You were talking in your sleep. Are you havin' bad dreams?"

"Not exactly," he laughed. "I was back in the ninth grade playing against Egyptian."

"You played for Brother Rice, didn't you?" Workman asked him.

Sonny was surprised. He downed the pills and rubbed his eyes before he said, "You know about him?"

"Oh yeah. I never met him, but I sure *heard* about him. He's got a reputation, or at least he had one when he was still coaching."

"He's in a nursing home now."

"He was one corncob sonofabitch, from everything I ever heard."

"Yeah," said Sonny. "I guess maybe. I'm never sure. I

never would have been a player without him, though."

More turbulence made the aircraft drop again, but Workman just smiled. "So why don't you tell me about Rice?"

"That would be a long story."

"Okay, come up with a short version."

Sonny had to think for a moment. He knew Coach Workman was trying to calm him. "I always remember the Anna–Jonesboro game," he said. "I was a starter by then, scoring lots of points, etcetera. My uncle Seth was already introducing me to businessmen and other people who were supposed to be important. The high school coaches were always at our games, even college coaches. Uncle Seth said they were primarily there to watch me, to see if I would be a starter in my sophomore year."

"So what about the Anna–Jonesboro game?"

"It wasn't the game itself, we probably blew 'em out." But the rest, Sonny remembered crystal clear. After the game, in the milling around near the scorers' bench, Barb told him what a great game he played, and so did Andrea. Uncle Seth introduced Sonny to an insurance man, but Sonny was watching from the corner of his eye where he saw Rice talking to McAllister, the head coach at the high school.

By the time he peeled off his jersey in the locker room, most of the other guys were already showering. That was when Rice walked in and said, "Youngblood, I need to talk to you for a minute; come into the office."

"Right now?"

"Right now. Follow me."

As soon as they were both inside the basketball office, Rice closed the door. Sonny sat on a folding chair whose cold metal shivered his warm flesh. Rice parked in the swivel chair and groaned it like everything; he lit up a Marlboro Light.

"Youngblood, we need to talk. I'm going to give you some advice, which you may or may not decide to take. Players don't usually choose to listen to advice, because they think they know it all."

"I can listen to advice," said Sonny. His voice broke a little; the shortness of breath was from the tension created by going one-on-one with Brother Rice.

"You're not tired, are you?"

"No," said Sonny. "I'm not tired."

"Good. Bad things happen to players who are tired. Mistakes, lapses in concentration. Even a player with very little talent can be in shape. You, of course, have lots of talent."

Sonny flushed a little. It was very matter-of-fact the way the coach said it, like he was counting his change or talking about the weather, but it was a high compliment. Rice searched for the ashtray that was hiding somewhere on the desk beneath piles of folders, mail, circulars, and sports literature. Even the telephone was mostly buried under paper.

Rice took a deep drag before he exhaled upward toward the steampipe ceiling. He continued, "Right now, it's talent that's getting you by. At this level it's enough. At the next level, it won't be."

Sonny wasn't sure where the coach was headed, but he did know one thing: when you talked to Rice, your job was to listen.

"You don't know yet what it means to play hard. You can coast and win because of your natural ability. I can't see you playing with the sophomores next year, and neither can McAllister. You'll be on the varsity. From freshman basketball to the high school varsity is a big jump.

What's going to happen when you're challenged?"

The compliments were nice, but Sonny couldn't help feeling wounded. He thought of the countless hours he practiced on his own, any time of year, any place, any kind of weather. "You don't think I try hard?"

"I think you play as hard as you know how. The time will come when you'll need to know how to play harder. Youngblood, I've seen thousands of players and coached hundreds. There's lots of talented players out there, but the thing that separates them, what makes the great players, is mental toughness. These are the guys with the switch inside; there's always another notch on the switch, so they can always turn it up one more level. They have the inner voice that keeps telling them 'I can play harder than this' each time down the floor."

Smoke streamed from Rice's nostrils while he paused to crush out his cigarette. Sonny tried to think of this as something other than a put-down; he knew his coach wouldn't waste this kind of time and energy on an average player.

"You see what I'm saying, Youngblood?"

"Sort of, I guess."

Rice tipped back in the straining chair. He locked his fat fingers on the enormous belly. "You ever watch *Nova*, Youngblood?"

"No, my mother does."

"They're running a series on sharks. You should see the sharks in a feeding frenzy, turning the water red." He was smiling his crooked smile. "Ferocious and single-minded, but somehow in control. Here's what I want to say to you: Some players *will not lose.* The tougher it gets, the more they turn up the switch. If you can learn something about mental toughness, you can be a great player."

Rice closed his eyes. *A great player?* Sonny asked himself. *Is that what he said?* He studied Coach Rice, with the usual confusion. Could such a lard-ass as him ever really play the game? He was a sonofabitch but he was also a brilliant coach, the primary reason Sonny and his teammates whipsawed their way through every opponent. After the long silence Sonny asked, "Is it okay if I take my shower now, Coach?"

Rice opened his eyes and leaned forward in the chair. "Just one more thing. Let me see your hands."

Puzzled, Sonny held out his hands. "Here, hold up your left one flat," Rice instructed. When he did, Rice pressed his own large, fat hand against Sonny's palm, fingers spread. Sonny's fingers were longer.

The coach told him, "Your hands are big and strong, Youngblood; you must have a twelve-inch span here. One of these days, you're going to grow into them."

Once their hands were separated, Rice continued, "I wouldn't be surprised if you grow to be six five or six six. If you do, you could play just about anywhere on the floor. Posting up, facing the basket, hell, your ball-handling is good enough you might even work as a big point guard."

Then the coach took his usual long pause to get his breathing reestablished. "Now look at your hands again. There's *two* of them, not one. At this point, you're too right-handed. You need to do everything you can to develop the left. Practice with your right arm tied or in your belt. Hell, you can even put it in your pocket if you don't get distracted and start to play with yourself."

Sonny laughed. He was still looking at his hands held out in front, with his fingers spread. Feeling foolish, he put them down.

"Left hand, Youngblood, think left. Left hand, left

hand, left hand. The more ambidextrous you are, the more versatile you become."

"Thanks a lot, Coach." Sonny wasn't sure why he said it, but it seemed as appropriate as anything else.

Brother Rice looked him in the eye. "Maybe I underestimate you, Youngblood. Maybe you do know how to take advice. Now go get a shower; you're stinking up the place."

Workman was laughing. "He must have been a piece of work."

"I'd say so," Sonny agreed. He noticed the roughness had gone out of the ride. "It looks like the turbulence is behind us," he suggested to Workman.

"Looks like," Workman agreed. "Maybe Brother Rice was one of those evil geniuses. You run across people like that from time to time, and you can find them in any field, not just sports."

"Maybe. Whatever." Sonny was very drowsy at this point. It must have been the pills kicking in. He fell sound asleep like a baby for the rest of the flight.

The bleary-eyed players deplaned at 2:30 A.M. Central Standard Time at the Carbondale Airport. Even at that hour, and in freezing rain, more than a thousand fans waited to greet them. Monday morning's *USA Today* would show that most polls now ranked the Salukis number four in the nation.

Sissy's house was in the high timber, about a mile above the artsy village of Makanda on the western edge of Giant City State Park. A narrow blacktop serpentined the incline to get there, but needed plenty of downshifting. Her property was at the road's end, where the blacktop turned to rutted gravel for a couple of hundred yards. The cluster of old pines and cedars provided major shade even in late November, with the oak and sycamore branches stripped clean.

Sonny asked her, "What do you do when there's snow and ice?"

"It can get very tricky," Sissy admitted. "Sometimes this road is the last to be plowed, and that's when we're lucky. You didn't tell me you have a car."

"Uncle Seth gave it to me."

"Mmm. Before we get any equipment loaded, I wonder if you could help me move some studio materials?"

Sonny shrugged. "Sure."

Her property was a farm once upon a time, but looking at the steep, wooded terrain, Sonny couldn't see where there was much suitable space for growing crops. The house was a tired-looking two story with faded yellow paint. The barn, which looked solid enough, was closer to the house than the dilapidated tractor shed. Outside the shed was an old, gray Ford tractor, and behind it, an uneven pile of barn siding that must have come from a torn-down building. There were only three of them, the bags of clay that Sissy wanted him to carry from the Bronco to the barn, but they were the 80 pounders. It took Sonny three trips.

Most of the lower barn, which she used for a studio, had evidence of recent remodeling. "But there's a lot more that needs to be done," she told him, "to make it an adequate studio. It needs a skylight for one thing — how about it, Carpenter?"

Sonny laughed. "I think that would be a little over my head." There were three large worktables that looked like shop benches, galvanized garbage cans with tight lids, a roomy sink area, and an assortment of sculptor's tools, which Sonny knew nothing about. The heat came from a Franklin wood stove. She asked him if he would store the clay in the floor-level cabinets.

"I do appreciate this, Cousin. Since it's not in the syllabus, we'll call it extra credit."

Remembering about her surgery, he said, "You're probably not supposed to do any heavy lifting."

For the most part, this was going to be an equipment run. With a load of tools familiar and unfamiliar, Sonny drove the Bronco down toward Makanda slowly while Sissy made notes on a clipboard.

The village was so tiny, a church on a slope and a small stretch of quaint storefronts, that you could take it all in at a glance even without a high-ground advantage. An abandoned, ramshackle building with peace-sign graffiti spray painted on its weathered siding slouched next to the defunct railroad tracks. And on the right, where Sonny pulled the Bronco to a pause, a basketball court: incongruous and central, a young slab of concrete, maybe 20 by 20. An erect basketball goal with fan-shaped metal backboard and orange rim in good condition.

"Why are we stopping?" Sissy looked up from her notes.

"Why is this here?"

"I have no idea."

"But who plays here? It looks like nobody even *lives* here."

"There are a few people who live here, although no basketball players that I know of. Maybe it's a shrine," she said sarcastically. "Maybe the gospel according to Little Egypt dictates that even Makanda must have its own fieldhouse."

"Very funny." The storefront where they got out sold wood carvings by local artisans. In the back was a huge shop with modern power tools for woodworking. A black man with no legs was sitting in a swivel chair and sweeping sawdust from beneath a band saw. Sissy was starting the introductions when the man said, "Shit. You're Sonny Youngblood."

Sissy said, "Oh Lord." On her face she wore the pained expression that begs for patience. "Sonny, this is Willie Joe."

Willie Joe's rolled-up overalls covered his stumps, above or below the knees, Sonny couldn't tell. "Sonny Youngblood, give me five. Man, did you kick some ass in the NIT!" Sonny gave him five.

"Willie Joe," demanded Sissy, "if I showed you a picture of Paul Klee, would you recognize him as quickly?"

"Depends who he played for, Baby! Ha!"

Sonny laughed.

"Drumroll, Baby!"

Sissy simply shook her head before she said, "It must be a sickness I'll never comprehend. The way boys will be boys."

"You need to be careful of this one, Sonny; she's a man-eater."

"She's my cousin," said Sonny.

"Oh, sorry." Willie was using a wire coat hanger to scratch his left stump.

"It's okay, the two of us are more or less just getting acquainted anyway."

Sissy asked Sonny, "Don't you find it peculiar the way he apologizes to you but not to me?"

Willie Joe began asking questions about Luther Cobb and the Arkansas game, but Sissy said, "We need to get started, Willie Joe. Where are the crates?"

The packing crates, some of them as large as pallets, were stacked behind the building. As soon as Sonny loaded three into the Bronco, there wasn't any more room. Sissy said, "It's kind of Willie Joe to let me use his work space, but it's also inconvenient. I'll be a much happier camper when my own studio is finished."

Then they were on their way, driving in silence, while Sissy put on her glasses and wrote more notes. They were clear north of Carbondale before she put away the clipboard and broke the silence: "It was a train."

"You mean how he lost his legs."

"It happened more than thirty years ago, when he was only eighteen. He was drunk and it was a dare."

"That's really sad," said Sonny.

"Yes, it is. On a happier topic, the newspapers are full of your glory this week. According to the experts, the professional league looms for you in the near future."

Talk of the NBA was always embarrassing. "I'm just getting used to college basketball."

"*Au contraire, Liebchen,* your modesty aside, the *Post-Dispatch* writer says you won't need to stay at SIU any longer than your sophomore year."

"That's bullshit. It only makes me nervous to hear talk like that."

"Then we'll change the subject. How much do you know about frescoes?"

"Probably zip." It seemed like honesty was still the best policy.

"Frescoes are wall paintings. The one we're going to try and rescue is mural-sized; it covers an entire wall. It was really painted on wet plaster, which is an old technique. The pigment of the paint actually penetrates the plaster."

"Why can't it just stay where it is?"

"Because it's in an old lodge building that's no longer in use. It's going to be torn down to make room for parking. The lodge was built by WPA workers during the Depression, and presumably it was a WPA worker who painted the mural. But whoever he was, his identity isn't known."

If he asked her what the WPA was, it would probably make him seem stupid. He said, "The mural has to be transported in sections; that's what the packing crates are for."

"Yes. Next semester, the seminar group will try and restore it. In addition to its age, it has water damage from flooding."

"Where will it go when it's restored?"

"That isn't finalized yet. The new art building has a wing on it that may have an Egyptian emphasis; if the restoration is successful, it might end up there."

The fallen timber on the ridges near the entrance to Pyramid State Park was evidence of recent bulldozer activity. The hills were scraped back along the uneven gravel road that led the way along the marshy string of lakes. There was a bottom-level strip of measly corn stubble. The lodge itself, built of limestone and native timber, was dark, and smaller than Sonny expected.

No sooner did Sissy turn on the lights than she started bitching: "Goddamnit, the heat's out again." She flung down the folded dropcloth she was carrying.

Sonny set both toolboxes down. It was cold for sure.

"I have to talk to Smith about this," she announced. She left in a hurry.

Sonny looked around at the clutter of dropcloths, tools, and lumber. There was an appliance dolly and some five-gallon cans of solutions that were unfamiliar. No furniture other than a large worktable and some metal folding chairs. He had no idea who Smith was or where Sissy might go to find him, but he could see that the room's only heat would come from a large gas space heater.

He tried to light the pilot with the propane torch but the flame wouldn't hold. There were box wrenches in one of the toolboxes, so Sonny took off the thermocouple; he cleaned it with some thin wire and by blowing through it. When he reconnected, the burner came on full blaze and shortly after that, the fan kicked on.

Still waiting for Sissy, he checked out the mural. Cracked and fading, it covered a 30-foot wall from floor to ceiling. It seemed to tell a story. In addition to the river that reached clear across, there were recurrent scenes of the same man and woman in Egyptian costume, a coffin, and a shallow boat. To Sonny it looked clumsy, the way the junior class used to paint the storefront windows in downtown Abydos at homecoming. A small refrigerator concealed one of the scenes at the end.

When Sissy returned, she was still agitated. "I couldn't find him," she declared. Then she put her hands out, as if testing for rain. "There's heat. What happened?"

"I fixed the furnace. It was just a dirty thermocouple."

"A dirty what? Never mind. Sonny Youngblood, you're already an asset to the project."

"I told you I got A's in shop."

"So you did. Have you been examining the fresco?"

"Yeah, but what does it mean?"

"It tells the story of Isis and Osiris," she answered. "Part of it, at any rate."

"Who are they?"

"They were Egyptian deities. Gods. After Osiris was betrayed and dismembered, Isis wandered the world to rescue and restore him."

"That's weird," said Sonny.

Sissy turned to him. "Is it? Is it more difficult to comprehend than the parting of a sea or a god who sends plagues of locusts?"

Now she was talking about the Bible, but it was the sarcastic kind of question. Sonny didn't answer. She went on, "The myth has other parts. If you want to find out more, we have a very good library on campus. It's called Morris."

Sonny didn't appreciate the patronizing, especially right after he'd fixed the furnace. He'd been to Morris Library plenty of times. "What's next?" he asked tersely.

"We need more crates. I want each panel to have its own crate so we can keep it packed for storage until it's time to work on it."

"Let's try and get them all today," said Sonny. "I've got practice tomorrow."

It took two additional trips because the Bronco could only accommodate three or four crates at a time, depending on their size. On the last trip, they bought a pizza at LaRoma's on the way through Carbondale. "This is going to be cold by the time we eat it," said Sissy.

"Who cares?" Sonny flipped the rearview mirror down to the night mode.

Sissy sliced out the pizza while Sonny unloaded. The room was so warm by this time they had to turn back the thermostat. Holding open the refrigerator door, Sissy told him, "All that's in here is wild berry wine cooler. Will that be okay?"

Sonny's experience with alcoholic beverages was almost nil. "I guess it has to be."

On a spread-out canvas dropcloth, eating the pizza and drinking the wine cooler, she asked him: "Do you suppose boozing it up will get you kicked off the team?"

Sonny took a long swallow of the fruity, effervescent

drink. "Who's going to know? Will it get you kicked off the faculty?"

Sissy laughed. "I have tenure. Much as some people might like to kick me off, they won't have an easy time doing it."

Sonny ate a second and a third slice rapidly. Because the mural seemed amateurish to him he asked her, "How good is this painting anyway?"

"In an art contest, it wouldn't get far; it probably wouldn't even make the finals. It's the unusual combination of elements associated with it that makes it worth preserving."

"Oh."

"In the first place, it's a true, or *buon*, fresco, which is remarkable in and of itself. In the second place, it may have been painted with two- or three-inch brushes instead of conventional artists' materials. I'm talking about the kind of brush used for painting woodwork or the siding on a house."

Even without knowledge of art, Sonny could see how difficult it would be to make a painting with a house brush. "So who was the guy who painted it?"

"Probably one of the workers who helped construct this building. He might have done it after work or in his spare time. He had to have at least one co-worker, someone who could lay on the wet plaster ahead of him."

"He might have painted it while he was drunk," laughed Sonny.

"Or at least fatigued," Sissy said. "It's also very unusual for its choice of subject matter. Most of the artwork done by WPA painters had a social or political theme such as workers' rights. This one deals with Egyptian mythology." She went to the refrigerator to get them each another bottle.

"You know what I used to wonder?" asked Sonny. "Whenever we went to play in towns like Karnak, or Dongola, or Cairo, I used to wonder, why all the Egyptian names? How did we ever get to be *Little Egypt?*"

Sissy clucked her tongue. "Goodness me, Cousin, were you speculating on namesakes when your mind needed to be on the game? I can only hope your coach never found out."

"My head was always in the game. I wondered about it on the bus."

"How reassuring. Still, it shows us that reflection is part of your makeup."

"You really think I'm stupid, don't you?"

"Of course not. The most common theory is that the tip of the state, located between two major rivers, reminded early residents of the Nile delta. Major flooding every spring produced a bottomland effect of fertile cropland. The same river that destroyed was also a preserver."

The more she talked about it, the more remote her words seemed to become. Sonny didn't mind, though; he felt full and mellow, leaning against one of the support posts and peeling his second Bartles & Jaymes label.

Sissy closed the empty pizza box. "You really should take some interest in ancient cultures, Sonny. That's where the game of basketball has its origins."

"You keep telling me you don't know much about basketball."

"I don't. But I do know something about ancient cultures. A game similar to modern basketball goes back thousands of years, at least as far as ancient Mayan civilization."

"I think you're mistaken. Basketball goes back a hundred years to Springfield, Massachusetts."

Sissy ignored the attempt at humor. "The Mayans played the game in an outdoor amphitheatre. The baskets were rings set high in stone walls. They were positioned vertically, though. A player would have to pitch the ball through the ring from the side."

"In basketball you don't pitch the ball, you shoot it."

"Whatever." Sissy was lying on her back, using her hands to prop her head. Sonny could see that she didn't shave her underarms, which might have seemed gross except he was mellowed out by the wine cooler. He felt peaceful inside all of a sudden, like bolts were loosened.

Everything with Sissy seemed to go so deep, but he could remember talks something like this with Barbara Bonds, the only girl he ever went steady with. *Improving his mind* talks. He peeled labels with her, too, usually at Goldie's Cafe, the labels on the large bottles of orange Gatorade.

In his mellowed condition, instead of the low-lit room with the crude but valuable mural and his prone, sleepy professor cousin, Sonny seemed to be looking at the downtown gazebo where they often stopped when he walked Barb home. The gazebo, which was in the center of the Abydos town square, had wooden benches built into its perimeter. Barb was asking him about the algebra again.

"I don't want to think about it," Sonny declared. "I must have a mental block or something."

"I could help you if you want. We could study it together." It was March, but the sun was so warm she took off her coat. With her arms raised, Sonny couldn't resist a long stare at her major profile of tit, thrusting forward like an artillery shell. He wondered if the actual details of her body matched the ones that characterized his fantasies and his sticky dreams.

She found a clean spot on the weathered wooden bench to sit down, but he was still standing. "I don't want to study algebra," he reminded her.

"I don't mean now, I mean some night after supper. You could come over." She was smiling at him with her teeth so white and straight. He wondered if anything was ever hard for her. At home, or at school, or making friends. One Gram said that all girls liked to masturbate; for the briefest moment, Sonny tried to imagine Barbara doing it. It didn't fit.

He looked at the woodrot along the eaves of the gazebo, the flaking paint, and the broken bottle litter. "This was probably a nice place at one time," he said.

"It used to be real nice. My parents brought me here for concerts in the summertime when I was little. You're changing the subject, though."

It wasn't easy with her. "That's what happens when people talk."

"I'm just asking if you'd like to study together."

It was so frustrating because he would do almost anything to be with her, but if they had to study math, he would freeze up and seem so stupid. Restlessly, he prowled the perimeter of the gazebo. It was a round structure, but the benches made straight lines that formed an eventual octagon. "I'll think about it. I'm real dumb when it comes to math. Maybe I didn't inherit any math brains from my parents."

"You never talk about your father," said Barbara.

"He left."

"I know, but what was he like?"

"He was big."

"Was he really big or did it just seem like it because you were small?"

"No, he was big."

After a moment Barbara said, "Would you stand still, Sonny? Your mother is tall, maybe you'll be real tall when you stop growing. That would be good for basketball, wouldn't it?"

He didn't want to talk about *growing up*, either. Not when she was such a finished woman and he felt like such a boy. He said, "I don't remember that much about him."

"You must remember something though."

Sonny looked her in the eye. "He was big and he liked sports. He was a salesman some of the time."

"What did he sell?"

"I can't remember. Different things, I guess. He must not have been very good at it, though, because we were always poor. He was gone a lot. Eventually, he was gone so much of the time it was like he didn't even live with us anymore. That's when Uncle Seth and Aunt Jane took us in."

"I'm sorry, Sonny, I really am."

"I try not to think about him because he screwed us over; he's gone now and he's not coming back."

"I'm really sorry," she repeated. "I don't mean to pry about things that are private."

Sonny felt two dollars in his pocket. "You don't have to be sorry, you didn't do anything wrong. I'll buy you a Pepsi at Goldie's."

At Goldie's, there were flies. The elderly waitress who stalked them with her flyswatter wore a hairnet and dangled a cigarette from her lips. Goldie's special of the day, chicken fried steak, was written in chalk on a blackboard behind the counter.

Back on the sidewalk with the Pepsis in hand, they walked north. Sonny was nervous as always about keeping up his end of the conversation; he thought about offering to carry her coat for her, but that seemed too geeky.

As they approached St. Mary's Church, they could hear organ music. Some of the windows, the ones that weren't stained glass, were open, clearing the way for *fortissimo* strains of "O For a Thousand Tongues." Sonny wanted to keep right on walking, but Barb wanted to stop at the church steps because she thought the music was so beautiful.

Sonny felt his stomach tighten up; he knew it was his mother playing the music. To make it worse, she was supposed to be at work. "Maybe we should just keep on going."

"Let's wait just a minute. It's kind of neat, don't you think?"

"What's neat?"

"Just the weather and the music. Don't you like to stop and smell the roses every once in a while?"

Sonny shrugged. "If you like church music."

"It must be Protestant music," she said.

"It's Baptist music," said Sonny glumly.

"Do you and your mother go to church?"

"We used to." He longed for a way to change the subject.

Unexpectedly, Father Breen did it for him when he came out through the wooden doors of the church. Sonny remembered the time he came to visit at their apartment. The priest greeted the two of them: "How about if an old man passes a few minutes with the two of you? I think these ancient bones can still make it down here." He groaned himself into a seated position on one of the stone steps. He asked Barb for help to remember her last name.

"Bonds," she told him.

"Bonds, that's it." said the priest. "Barbara Bonds, B.B., that's very nice. Do you remember your catechism, Barbara Bonds?"

Smiling, she said, "I hope so."

Father Breen smiled, but all that did was show his rotten teeth. "If I asked you a few basic questions right now, you could answer them successfully?"

"Maybe, but we were just listening to the music."

"Just to humor an old priest, hmmm? You were always so exceptional in CCD class."

Barbara didn't say anything and Sonny felt sorry for her because Father Breen was going to put her on the spot. You couldn't miss the booze on his breath, either.

"Why are we put here on earth, Barbara Bonds?"

"We are here on earth to learn to know God, to love and serve Him, and one day to live with Him forever."

"Excellent. Why do we say God is truthful?"

"We say that God is truthful because He always speaks the truth. He can't be mistaken or tell lies."

"Excellent again. And why do we say that God is faithful?"

"Our Father is faithful because He always does what He has promised."

This quizzing made Sonny edgy. He looked at the stone facade of the church, which was old and gray. There were weeds sprouting up through the cracks of the sloped stone steps. His mother was now playing "And He Walks with Me."

"Are you as solid on the Blessed Virgin as you seem to be on God the Father?" asked the priest.

"I'm not sure." Now she sounded annoyed and looked away.

"Let's find out. One of the prayers to the Holy Mother perhaps?"

"I'd rather not, Father." She was looking him straight in the eye. Sonny was impressed by her swift answers, but even more so the way it seemed like she was standing up to him.

"So be it, then." agreed the father. He gave Barbara a chummy clap on the shoulder. "If we did it all over again, you would still stand at the head of the class."

Then he said to Sonny, "Your mother plays a spirited repertoire of sacred music, young man."

Sonny looked down. "She likes to play the organ," he murmured.

Father Breen said, "Not only likes it, but excels at it, I would say."

"It's your mother who's playing the organ, Sonny?" asked Barbara.

While she belongs at work, Sonny thought. *Why did this priest have to butt in anyway?*

"If only we could get her to come to Mass," said the priest, "and bring her son with her."

Sonny avoided his eyes. "She tries sometimes, but she usually can't get her hair right." It sounded stupid, but it was true.

Father Breen was lurching to his feet. It took a while, and a while longer before he looked steady. "Maybe the son will lead the mother, then. Speak to him about the spring retreat, Barbara Bonds. Remember what the church teaches about ministry to scattered Christians."

"I remember." But no enthusiasm in her voice.

Father Breen was gone then, heading slowly south on the sidewalk, watching his steps carefully.

"Oh, I'm so glad he's gone!" said Barbara, when the priest reached the corner. "He can be so irritating some imes."

Sonny was glad, too. He hoped she was ready to go now.

"I think he's getting senile, too."

Sonny didn't know the word but he wouldn't ask its meaning because that would make him seem stupid. It must be something to do with his drinking. "Are you ready to go now?"

"Sonny, you didn't tell me it was your mother playing. Let's go inside and listen for a while."

"Why would that be any better than listening out here?"

"I've never met her. Please."

The bind was, if he argued her out of it, he would probably make her mad, especially since she was already pissed at Father Breen. Reluctantly, he followed her inside the church.

It was his first time ever inside a Catholic church. It seemed like a large cavern away from the world; maybe that was part of the attraction for his mother. There was dark wood, low lighting, and the strong, rich smell of furniture wax. There were small statues in hollows in the side walls, and a large statue of the Virgin Mary near the altar. The huge organ was way behind the altar, so they could only see the top of his mother's head bobbing.

In the center aisle, just before finding a seat in the last pew, Barbara lowered herself to touch one knee against the floor. When she stood up to take a seat, Sonny followed nervously.

There were many small candles burning on the altar, casting up most of the light in that end of the sanctuary. If Sonny's mother knew Sonny and Barbara were there, she gave no indication; she went right on playing. In a very low voice Barb asked him what hymn it was, but Sonny didn't know.

This was very tense. What were you supposed to do in a Catholic church in the middle of the afternoon, sitting next to your girlfriend? And your mother playing hymns on the pipe organ when she was supposed to be at work at the phone company? He asked her what the statues were in the wall hollows.

"Those are the Stations of the Cross." Her answer came between clenched teeth because she was clamping two hairpins in her mouth. She was reshaping the mass of hair at the back of her head with a small, silver elastic band.

"Oh." His mother was playing something Sonny had never heard. She must have all the stops pulled, he thought, the way the notes came tumbling out of the dark, vaulted ceiling like an avalanche.

"What's she playing now?" Barb asked in a louder voice.

"I don't know."

"You can tell it's something classical," she said. "It's nothing like a church hymn. She has a lot of talent, doesn't she?"

"I guess she does, but I don't know much about music."

After another ten minutes, it was plain that his mother intended to keep on playing. "She won't be stopping for quite a while, will she?" Barb asked.

"I doubt it. Maybe when it's too dark to see the notes."

"Maybe we should go then."

"Sure," said Sonny, relieved.

"I can meet her some other time."

"Sure." On the way out of the church, Barbara stopped long enough to do the knee-touching thing again, but Sonny didn't feel like asking her about it. On the walk she asked him, "Why did Father Breen bring up the spring retreat? Do you want to go?"

"I don't want to go. My mother wants me to go."

"Why?"

"So she won't feel guilty about playing your church's organ. You should see her on Sunday mornings, when she thinks she's going to Mass. Then her hair isn't right, or her makeup. She ends up not going."

"That's too bad, Sonny."

Sonny shook his head. He was feeling impatient. "She doesn't even want to go. What she wants to do is play the organ when there's nobody in the church. The truth is, I think there's something the matter with her mind. She thinks if she goes to Mass, it would give her more of a right to play the organ. But she can't get her act together, so she thinks I can do it for her if I go to a retreat. You know what I'm sayin'?"

"I understand what you're saying."

"Yeah." He didn't say anything about her drinking or the nerve pills. He'd already told her more than he was used to telling.

They were silent for a couple of blocks and then he said, "What's a scattered Christian?" He didn't really care, but it would be better than a long, embarrassing silence.

"That's you," she giggled.

"How is it me?"

"You're not a Catholic, so you're lost. If you're lost, I'm supposed to help you get found. I'm supposed to convert you."

"I don't care about that."

"Don't worry, I would never nag another person about religion. I believe religion is a personal thing; each person has to make up their own mind."

When they got to her house, they stood inside her screened porch. The shadow from the large spruce trees was dense. He kissed her once but then he said, "I'm not going on a religious retreat just to make her happy."

"I don't think you should," she replied. "A person shouldn't do a thing like that just to please someone else."

4

Sonny spent the night in Sissy's guest bedroom. At breakfast, he told her he was having spells where he lost his concentration.

"Spells? Didn't you just score a thousand points in that New York tournament?"

"If you mean the NIT, it wasn't anything like a thousand points. I'm not talking about basketball, anyway. I mean other times and places. It's like getting lost in thought."

"Lost in thought about what?"

"Usually memories. Certain things make me think about other things. Mostly it seems to be about Brother Rice, my ninth-grade coach, or Barbara Bonds. She's an old girlfriend."

Sonny was finishing a bowl of Cheerios while Sissy poured him a tall glass of orange juice. She was wearing an old flowered housecoat with a zipper front and walking around barefoot. "It sounds like normal reverie activity," she told him. "Are they bad memories?"

"Not necessarily. It's just different. It's not something I usually do. The memories seem . . ." *How to say this?* "They seem important."

Sissy poured herself a cup of coffee and sat down across the table. "You're worried because you're having important memories."

"Not exactly worried." Now it seemed so silly he was sorry he brought it up. "I just feel like I'm spacing out."

"Do me a favor, Sonny."

"What favor?"

"Go to class."

"I have to go to a meeting at Lingle first."

"Fine. Go to the meeting, then go to class."

When he got to the meeting, he discovered it was going to be a heart-to-heart with Gardner, the compliance officer, and Price, one of Gentry's assistants.

Gardner started right in talking about his course load. "The thing is, Sonny, you did it without clearance. You didn't get approval for this."

"It seemed like the right thing to do at the time, that's all. I think I'm capable of dropping and adding a course on my own."

"Sure," Gardner agreed. "But you have to understand the unique position you're in as a scholarship athlete. Especially one with a profile as high as yours." Sonny squirmed in his chair while the basketball secretary put some coffee and ice water on the table.

Coach Price said, "The system is carefully set up to help you through the rough spots. When you're a basketball player, you don't have as much time for schoolwork as other students. It means you're going to need an academic support system."

"Look," Sonny repeated himself. "All I did was drop a course and add one. I'm carrying twelve hours."

After sighing, Gardner put his glasses on slowly. He was looking in an open folder on the table. "Art history?"

"Yes," said Sonny.

"Art history isn't a preferred option for a varsity athlete," Gardner declared. "Never has been."

"This isn't exactly the same as art history," Sonny tried to explain. "That's just its name. Besides, it's only one hour of independent study."

"I can read the note here," said Gardner quickly. He was trying to hide his impatience. "One hour of independent art history. With Erika Neil."

"Oh god," Price moaned. "When did you sign up for this?"

This overreaction was puzzling to Sonny. "Last month, but the credit's retroactive. Everything's okay, believe me."

"Sonny, we're trying to run a *program* here." said Gardner. "Do you have any idea who Erika Neil is?"

"Of course."

"She'll bust your balls, man," said Price. "She is the number one ball-buster on this faculty."

Gardner said, "There's not a more anti-jock professor here than Erika Neil. When she was on the faculty senate, she made it her personal agenda to try and strip us down."

Then Sonny informed them, "Erika Neil is my cousin."

This information left Price and Gardner speechless. When they looked at each other, they seemed to lift their eyebrows simultaneously. Gardner turned back to Sonny. "Your what?"

"Erika Neil is my cousin."

"What does that mean, your cousin? What kind of cousin we talkin' here?" It was Price again.

"I mean she's my cousin. My uncle Seth is her father and my aunt Jane is her mother." How could he make it any clearer?

"She must be forty years old, how can she be your cousin?" But Gardner was giving Price the sign to back off. He poured himself a glass of water before he said to Sonny, "I hope you can forgive the unkind remarks about a relative. That was out of line."

"Right," echoed Price, who was adjusting his necktie knot.

Price and Gardner both knew Uncle Seth, of course, from booster club activities, but it was apparent they had no idea Sissy was his blood kin. It gave Sonny some pleasure to see them caught up short. It might have been Price's presence; the assistant Sonny liked was Workman, who was a *player*. Workman would stay after practice and go one-on-one with you until he dropped. But Price was some sort of middle-aged PR grad assistant. Sonny didn't know for sure what he was supposed to be.

"Is Coach Gentry coming to this meeting?" asked Sonny.

"No, he's not," answered Gardner. "He has many duties, but academic compliance isn't one of them."

Price added, "This isn't high school, where the head coach does the laundry and brings the extra socks."

"It's a big, big program," Gardner said. "That's what we're trying to impress on you here. It's so big that we can't make it work without communication and cooperation. You understand what I'm saying?"

"I can see your point."

"Everyone needs to do their job, and everyone else needs to cooperate fully so they *can* do their job. That's why we always need to work through existing channels."

"Are you telling me I can never drop a course on my own?"

"We're simply asking you to cooperate with the program for everyone's benefit." Gardner paused. He took off his glasses, inserted them in the brown case, then put the case in the inside pocket of his sport coat. He sipped some coffee and closed the folder. "This is not something we like to talk to players about, Sonny, but we have had some preliminary investigative overtures from the NCAA."

Sonny wondered what he meant by *preliminary investigative overtures* but he didn't ask. He remembered his earlier conversation with Warner, his sportswriter friend.

"We don't believe it's anything very serious," Gardner continued. "Or anything to be alarmed about, but it does put us in a position where we have to be especially careful."

"We need to know everything that's going on," said Price.

"That's it, exactly." Gardner agreed. "We need to know because we need to be in control. Can you see where we're coming from?"

"Of course I can see, do you think I'm stupid? If you want to break it down, I had an academic problem and I took care of it."

"We'll all hope so. In the meantime, can we count on your cooperation?"

Sonny's impatience was uncharacteristic. "Why are you treating me like a hard case? I'm preregistered for second semester, you know what I'm taking."

"Okay then. We'd like to apologize again for our remarks about your cousin."

SIU's first home game was against Arkansas, rated ninth in the nation, in the early part of December. Not even the snowstorm that began in late afternoon could daunt the huge crowd that converged on the arena and overflowed it, yelping and bawling for blood.

Otis Reed, the point guard, went down with a severe ankle sprain late in the first half, which meant more playing time for Robert Lee. It also meant a closer game; the Salukis won the ragged, physical contest by a score of 82–72. Arkansas used a confusing mix of gimmick defenses, in and out of the box and one, the triangle and two, but Sonny's frustration, whenever it occurred, was never a match for his intensity. He finished with 29 points to share game-scoring honors with Luther. He also had six steals to lead all players in that department.

Among the horde of postgame backslappers and well-wishers, Uncle Seth and three of his friends were front and center. Aunt Jane, who was also there, seemed to get lost in the congestion.

Two easy wins, one over Chicago State and another over Evansville, both at the arena in front of standing-room-only crowds, followed finals week. The Saluki record was thus pushed to 6–0, and when LSU lost a road game at Illinois, Sonny's team found itself ranked third in the nation in the major polls.

The D that Sonny got in Composition was offset by two B's, one in a P.E. class and another in Nutrition. He got a C in Earth Science. Combined with the A turned in by Sissy, his GPA would be above 2.5. He was tempted to photocopy the printout of his grades so he could have a spare to take to his old fraternity and throw in Geisel's face.

On the road to Memphis for the Tiger Invitational, Otis Reed's ankle was still tender. "I could probably play him, but I'd rather see him get another day's rest," Coach Gentry explained to Sonny. "I'd like to try you at the point, at least some of the time."

"Yeah, okay." said Sonny. It was unusual for Gentry

to talk game strategy with individual players. The trip by bus was also unusual, but this was a short distance.

"We'll walk through it as much as we can during the shoot-around."

"Okay."

Warner, who was doing a series of articles on what he called the psychological profile of successful players, was accompanying the team on the bus.

"You just have to throw the switch," Sonny told him. "You have to play with intensity all the time."

"Yes," confirmed Warner, "there's intensity, but then there's what you do."

"He's always popped," said Luther Cobb, from his seat across the aisle.

"What do you mean by that?" asked Warner.

"I mean he's popped on ludes and reds. He's all wired up from the pharmacy."

"Right," said Sonny. Luther laughed out loud.

"But seriously, folks," Warner chuckled.

"I don't know what it is," shrugged Sonny. "It's just a game head. It's just my zone."

It turned out Sonny's zone was just as effective at point guard. He scored 33 points in an easy 94–68 win over Jacksonville. With his long arms, he could snap passes effectively over a 1-2-2 or a 1-3-1 to locate the seams. Against the man-to-man, his explosiveness allowed him the penetration needed to lay the ball off to teammates for easy baskets. When the defense backed off, he simply rose up to shoot the three-pointer. Because the game was such a breather, Otis and his ankle got another day of complete rest.

After the game, Sonny had to sit at the press conference table with Coach Gentry. In response to a question about Sonny's performance at the point, Gentry said, "It might be his best position. But to be perfectly honest, other than posting him up down low, I'm not sure there's any position that wouldn't suit him."

When a reporter asked Sonny if he had any scoring goals, Sonny said no.

The question provoked Gentry to remind the press, by way of a short discourse, of the defensive aspect of the game. "All you people think about is points. Scoring and offense. Don't forget, fifty percent of the game is played on the defensive end. You can't appreciate Sonny's real value to this team unless you appreciate his defense." Hearing his praises sung so publicly was embarrassing to Sonny, but at least Coach Gentry was back in control of the mike. The reporters scribbled furiously.

Memphis State, the host team, was aroused for the championship game. Their arena was full of noisy fans, their players primed, but even so it wasn't close past the eight-minute mark. With Otis Reed back at the point guard spot, and Sonny back on the wing opposite C.J. Moore, the astonishing Salukis were back to full-bore. The final score was 116–84. C.J. had 29 points and Sonny 27, but it was Luther's dominant strength inside that stuffed the Tigers. He horsed the boards for 22 rebounds, blocked eight shots, and scored right at his 21-point average.

On the ride back, Luther wanted to know if Louisville or Georgetown got beat. Warner, sitting next to Coach Gentry, asked, "What difference does it make?"

"Come again?" said Gentry.

"Who wins or who loses. Let's be honest: This team on the bus is number one in the nation, period."

"You can say that if you want," said the coach.

"I do say that."

"Just don't let my players hear you say it."

But Sonny heard it and so did Robert Lee. And especially so did Hooker, the senior, and former walk-on, who had never before played on a ranked team. Hooker's grin seemed to stretch from one ear to the other as he strapped on his Walkman and closed his eyes.

The fresco project was painstaking and tedious, but Sonny's work turned out to be skillful. "You amaze me," was the way Sissy put it.

"Maybe if you didn't always underestimate me, I wouldn't amaze you."

"*Touché. Olé.*"

In addition to its age, the fresco's exposure to uneven heat and humidity had contributed to its unstable condition. Sissy identified where panels might be separated, based on the mural's content and condition. Her dividing lines improved the likelihood of the mural's eventual restoration, but they delineated panels of uneven size and shape. The strength and touch it took to remove them were characteristics Sonny possessed. With his height and leverage, he could even pry out panels next to the eight-foot ceiling while standing flat on the floor.

Sometimes, though, he told Sissy to slow down.

"Don't be silly. I'm fully recovered."

"Let's hope."

"I am five feet nine and one-hundred fifty pounds of focus," Sissy declared. She locked her arms in the pose of a bodybuilder. "I am woman. Hear me roar."

Sonny laughed out loud at the comical image of his middle-aged cousin in the bodybuilder's mode, wearing her Donald Duck T-shirt beneath her Oshkosh overalls.

It was ten P.M. by the time they were on the road back to Makanda. A few snow flurries sprayed the air, but nothing to affect driving conditions.

"Do you mind if I sleep in the guestroom?" Sonny asked.

"Please do. You must be exhausted."

"The dorm's closed and I don't feel like driving to Abydos."

"You don't need to ask permission, Sonny. You're welcome to use the bedroom anytime you like."

When they got to the house, he didn't do any unloading. He went upstairs to the guestroom. There were two books on the nightstand. One was a large hardcover of art restoration, with pages of illustrations and photographs. The corner was turned down on the first page of the fresco chapter. The other book was a paperback about the Isis and Osiris legend. The two books gave him a good feeling because they were gifts from Sissy; they had nothing to do with required reading.

The good feelings did not prevail on another day, later in the week. When he got to her house, Sissy was on the phone. He couldn't distinguish her words, but her tone was one of distinct irritation. She was on a long time, so Sonny made some toast.

Sissy was wearing a blue twill work shirt and Levi's blue jeans. Her annoyance was evident in the aggressive manner she burned her toast and gobbled it down. While Sonny maneuvered the Bronco down the uneven hillside, he thanked her for the two books.

"You're welcome." But her distraction was obvious in her flat voice.

All the way through Carbondale and two-thirds of the way to Murphysboro without conversation. Silence.

Then Sonny told her about the grilling he got from Gardner and Price over dropping Anthropology without permission. It was his attempt to make conversation, but it turned out to be a mistake.

"Please." she said. "What would you expect?"

"It wouldn't hurt if they treated us a little more like human beings," was his answer.

"And why should they do that? Just to pretend there's something humanizing about big-time college athletics?"

"I wouldn't know about that. Coach Gentry has a way of keeping himself out of the picture, more or less."

"Why would you expect him to do anything else? Do you expect him to care for you? He's an overpaid, overprotected broker of a large corporate enterprise."

"This is college competition, Sissy, not the NBA."

"Oh, can you grow up? You're a professional jock who doesn't get a paycheck. You are useful, like a copy machine. You line the pockets of CEOs and media executives. You're a spare part in a professional entertainment industry whose only link to the university is pretend."

Now he was mad. "I can't understand why you're so pissed. And why do you always assume that I'm stupid?"

"Did I say anything about stupid? I wouldn't waste my time on a stupid person. You're just underdeveloped; too much of your brain is in storage."

"I just love basketball; it's as simple as that."

But Sissy wouldn't let up. "You don't just *love basketball*, you're driven. People who are driven are frightened. Tell me what you're afraid of."

"I'm not afraid of anything. Maybe I'm afraid of you."

"Why?"

"I don't know why."

"Are you afraid of yourself? Are you afraid of finding out who you are?"

Sonny was even more pissed. "Would you get off my case? Why is it such a big deal to you what I think?"

"Turn here."

She meant the mini-mall on Murphysboro's edge, which they were approaching. Sonny swerved sharply into the mostly empty parking lot. Sissy got out of the car and went inside.

Times like this, thought Sonny to himself, his cousin could be a real load. Too much of this and he might come to understand why Uncle Seth kept his distance from her. He remembered the Christmas dinner they had years ago when Aunt Jane fixed the huge spread. Sissy was there, which was very unusual. It was around the time of Desert Storm, because Uncle Seth and the two farm neighbors, Oscar and Sydney, kept saying they'd give anything to get Saddam Hussein in the sights of their deer rifles. Sissy called them adolescents with immature gun fantasies. She asked them if they had any plans to grow up.

That got Uncle Seth so pissed that when he got beers from the refrigerator he slammed the door so hard he almost toppled it over. He called Sissy a commie feminist who was disrespectful of the American Way all the way back to the sixties. It was a very tense situation; Sonny's mother started to cry while she picked at her balled-up handkerchief like a bird.

When Sissy returned from the convenience store, she had two four-packs of Seagram's wine coolers and a pack of Marlboro Lights. She lit one up.

"When did you start smoking those?"

"Sometime in the sixties. The harder question would be when did I give them up?"

After they were through town and heading north on Highway 127, she said, "The phone call I got this morning was from the National Endowment office. They may be cutting the grant."

"The grant for the fresco?"

"The grant for the fresco. It may not be renewed."

He was still feeling hurt but he managed to say, "That would be too bad."

"Wouldn't it though? Let's be thankful it won't ever happen to football stadium construction or ESPN triple-headers on Monday nights."

Sonny could see what she was getting at, but it didn't seem like he deserved this contempt. "Would you give me a break?"

Sissy took a drag before turning her head to look out the passenger-side window. "I was just about to say I shouldn't be taking this unhappy development out on you."

It was an apology, more or less, but the day at the worksite was strained. While Sonny tried to make adjustments to the furnace's temperamental pilot light, Sissy lamented how far behind the project was.

"And if they cut your funding it will be worse."

"Of course it will be worse."

Sonny didn't look at her. He was reaming the thermocouple again with some fine wire from the toolbox. "So what's the solution?"

Sissy shrugged. "The seminar will just have to do more transporting and less restoring." She was putting the wine coolers into the fridge. "Are you going to be able to fix that or should I go get Smith?"

"I can fix it."

They worked steadily, but without much conversation other than Sissy's occasional tactical ruminations, when she was essentially talking to herself. Just before dark, a large panel, which included the detail of Osiris's coffin washed ashore, broke a corner when Sonny pried it loose. When it was down, none of the cartons was quite big enough to suit it, and there wasn't enough spare lumber to build a new one. Sissy's frustration seemed to peak; she threw a screwdriver across the room.

She went to the refrigerator while Sonny put on his coat to go outside. Without speaking. He couldn't begin to know the words that might lift her out of her funk, but even if he did, he needed to be away from her. Around back, the shelter that housed the Dumpster was ramshackle, but it still had plenty of good two-by-fours. Sonny had the crowbar. It took an hour, but he pried loose a dozen good ones, by which time his hands were frozen numb while the sweat ran down his face.

He took them inside where he stacked them. Sissy had two bottles of Seagram's down and was working on a third. She was using one of the empty bottles for an ashtray. After his last trip in, when the scope of his labors was evident, she said, "You *are* resourceful, Sonny. I *do* underestimate you."

Somehow, he felt better. Maybe it was being tired. "It's okay," he said, "you're havin' a bad day." He was taking off his coat. Sissy was sitting on the floor now, facing the other direction. From behind, Sonny could see her shoulders heaving; she was crying. Self-consciously, he watched her, paralyzed. He wouldn't know how to comfort her, and besides, anything he might try would probably make things worse.

His inertia lasted longer than her distress. Finished crying, she wiped her eyes and said, "Come have a drink, Hero. You deserve a break for putting up with such a bitch."

"I was going to cut these."

"You can cut them later. If you don't slow down, I'll have to give you two or three credits instead of one."

Sonny put down the Skil saw and went to the fridge. He unscrewed the top from one of the bottles, then sat on the floor beside her. Her eyes were red, but that was all. There was no mascara to run.

"Sonny, you're cut."

He looked down at his right hand, which was dripping blood to the floor.

"Does it hurt?"

He shook his head. "I didn't even know it was there. But my fingers were numb."

"Sit still." She went to the bathroom and returned with the first-aid kit. Sonny was staring at his index finger, but the blood ran so freely he couldn't actually locate the cut. Sissy blew her nose on a Kleenex before she sat down.

"Let me see." She took his hand. First, she dabbed at the blood with a cotton ball, enough to show that the cut was at the second knuckle. The she took the finger into her mouth. It surprised him. He could feel her teeth and tongue working the cut; it seemed awkward, but it didn't hurt. Her left hand folded down the other three fingers. The curious part was how long she kept doing it, much longer than it would take to get the blood off.

When Sissy finally took the finger out, it was clean as a whistle and the short, deep cut was visible. "You're not supposed to suck on a cut," he told her.

"I know, because of the germs."

There were bloodstains between Sissy's front teeth. She put antiseptic on the cut; it stung, but not badly and not for long. Then a Band-Aid. Sonny flexed his hand to see if there was any stiffness.

"I hope this won't ruin your jump shot."

He smiled. "No, but there's blood on your teeth."

She tongued her front teeth as if to remove traces of misapplied lipstick. "You haven't touched your drink."

"It's too cold," said Sonny. "We need something hot."

"A good idea. Let's hop in the Bronco and go get some coffee."

5

The Butler game was an uneventful blowout that the Salukis won by more than 40 points. The usually rabid crowd was mostly subdued. It might have been a boring night altogether, except for a single remarkable moment Sonny experienced just after he and his fellow starters were pulled from the game to make way for the subs.

He got a towel from the trainer, wrapped it loosely around his neck, and then with no warning whatsoever, he felt like he was walking on air. There was no gravity.

It scared him. Without touching the floor, he walked cautiously to the locker room to take a piss and get a drink of water. He heard the muffled roar of the crowd; somebody must have dunked.

Feeling weightless and shaky, he sat on a bench in search of equilibrium. This was eerie, like he was leaving his own body to float on the air. After he took a few deep breaths, though, he felt fine. A little overfatigued and with a touch of drowsiness, but okay. He walked back to the bench with his feet firmly on the floor. He dismissed the incident from his mind. It was nothing.

For his birthday, Uncle Seth bought him a new car. It was a Mazda RX-7 with silver pinstripes on its steel blue paint. Sonny said it was too much, but Seth dismissed it with a wave of his hand. "Nah. It's not really a new car anyway, it's just a *newer* one." He held the keys dangling for Sonny in the den festive with friends, the night after the easy win over Butler.

Sonny felt a twinge that he couldn't quite identify. "It's not my birthday yet."

Seth was well along toward getting sloshed. "What are you nitpicking for? You deserve it. Call it a combination present, Christmas and birthday." It was an approach long familiar to Sonny, whose birthday fell on December 28.

"I can't believe how expensive it must've been."

"Bullshit. You know how these things come and go. It's always on the wholesale index." He winked at Sonny before he said, "What's on your vacation schedule?"

"We've got a lot of time off because we played in the NIT and the Memphis Invitational."

"I know your game schedule, I'm talking about your practice schedule."

Sonny shrugged. "We've got a few practices, but we've got several days off, too."

"Keep the twenty-eighth free, will you? I'm lining up a bash and there's a couple of guys I'd like you to meet. Georgetown's going to be on ESPN that night."

"Yeah, sure, Uncle Seth." Sonny had a soft drink and met a few people, but then he was tired. He left the party early to go to bed.

Even with a shiny new car, Sonny was sometimes bored and often restless with vacation's absence of routines and familiars. Especially on the days with no practice. He spent most of one day, after a heavy snowfall, plowing Uncle Seth's lane and parking area. He spent another day in Makanda, helping Sissy.

On the 24th, he rode with his aunt Jane to the state hospital in Anna, to visit his mother. Every time he saw her she seemed paler and thinner, but that probably wasn't possible. Her hair was long, but it hung without shape like a mop made of sewing thread. Sonny asked her if she still had her favorite hairbrush, but she gave no indication she even heard the question. Her hands were clasped so tightly around a large mass of Kleenex it was as if all the blood was squeezed out; it was hard to tell which was whiter, the mangled tissues or the bloodless fingers.

But this configuration of hands and tissues did spark a memory. It recalled swiftly for Sonny the day the priest first came to visit them in their old apartment. It was a Saturday morning, he could remember that clearly, because he'd gone to bed after his paper route. When he got dressed and walked into the living room, he couldn't be sure which came first, the smell of muffins baking, or the sight of the priest seated on their couch. He'd been so surprised there was no time to alter his course.

"Norman, I'd like you to meet Father Breen. He's a priest at St. Mary's Church." His mother added, "It's a Catholic church."

Father Breen stood up, then came close to offer his hand. He was an old man, a little tacky around the edges, with blotchy skin and razor nicks. His eyes looked filmy. Sonny thought he smelled liquor on the old priest's breath, but that wouldn't be likely, not early on a Saturday morning.

As soon as the priest returned to his seat he said, "Your mother's been telling me about the loss of your father. That would be a terrible thing indeed."

Sonny wondered why a priest would be in their apartment, but then he remembered how Uncle Seth and Aunt Jane were Catholics. It must be that they were the contacts. Sonny finally said, "I don't know if we lost him, but he went away someplace."

"If there's bitterness in your heart," counseled the priest, "try and let it go. If you cherish it, it can destroy you."

Sonny wondered what that was supposed to mean. Maybe he could go now. If his mother wanted to talk to a priest, why did it need to involve him?

Father Breen turned back to his mother. "Is there any likelihood that your husband will return home, Mrs. Youngblood?"

Instead of answering his question, she simply straightened up in her chair until she achieved a supremely erect posture. She was wearing her white ruffled blouse with the long sleeves and was crushing half a dozen Kleenex into a tight ball in her lap. Her hair was perfect. Her eyes were not focused on the priest anymore, but somewhere off to the side. Sonny knew there wouldn't be an answer to the priest's question.

Father Breen must have known it, too. "Do you do lots of baking, Mrs. Youngblood?"

"I used to," she replied. "Now that I'm working I don't seem to find the time. I'm afraid we don't know much about the Catholic church. We've always been Baptists."

"Would you like to come to Mass sometime? Just to visit?"

"It's difficult to say. We're trying to start over, you see. There are better times coming, I feel certain."

"We'd be happy to have you. I'd like to leave you this pamphlet that has our schedule of Masses and other parish activities."

After Sonny's mother looked at the pamphlet briefly, she clutched it tight among her tissues. She asked, "Does your church have an organ?"

"We do indeed. A lovely old pipe organ."

"How many manuals does it have?"

"It's a double manual pipe organ."

"Oh, my!" exclaimed Sonny's mother. She straightened herself in the chair again. "A double manual pipe organ!"

Sonny began to squirm. The priest asked, "Do you like to play, Mrs. Youngblood?"

"Oh, I do so love to play the organ, I might as well confess it. Do you think I could have permission to play it sometime? When it's not inconvenient?"

A puzzled look passed briefly across Father Breen's face before he took out his soiled handkerchief and blew his nose twice, with a loud honk. "There ought to be some way we could arrange for a thing like that."

"It would be so kind of you. My brother Seth has the family pump organ; he says he may bring it here to our apartment sometime." She still wasn't looking directly at him.

Father Breen changed the subject. He locked his fingers around the knee of his crossed leg and said to Sonny, "We have lots of activities for young people, Norman. As a matter of fact, in November we're having our spiritual life retreat. We always welcome guests."

His mother was silent. What did she expect from him? Sonny turned to her and said, "Mother, maybe the muffins are done."

"They must be," she said quietly. "Please bring some. Father Breen, would you care for a blueberry muffin?"

"Straight from the oven? It would be hard to resist a thing like that."

With a small measure of relief, Sonny went to the kitchen where he took the tins from the oven, then brought his mother and the priest a half dozen of the muffins on a large plate. Back in the kitchen, he gobbled down three of his own, laying on the butter in thick squares. He wouldn't have to spend any more time with the stranger-priest; it was simple enough to leave, by way of the balcony and the fire escape, straight from the kitchen.

Even before he reached the bottom step, Sonny could hear the basketball spanking on the concrete at the far end of the alley. The boy's name was Warren something, but everyone at school called him One Gram. Sonny stood at a distance and watched self-consciously while One Gram shot baskets on the goal bolted to the garage. The backboard was a transparent rectangle; it was made of thick plastic, but looked like the real thing.

As uncomfortable as he felt just standing and watching, Sonny didn't want to return home where he would have to deal with the priest. Eventually, One Gram asked him if he wanted to shoot some hoop. Sonny was grateful for the invitation, even if it did seem mostly obligatory. Sonny shot some baskets for the better part of thirty minutes, mostly running one-handers, but his skills were nowhere near those of One Gram; the only sport Sonny had ever played was football, and that only on the playground.

One Gram informed him that in Abydos, basketball was king.

"It is?" Sonny asked.

"You're damn right. The high school team usually makes it to the state tournament and the ninth-grade team usually goes to the Final Four. What's the name of that town where you used to live?"

"Busiris," Sonny answered.

"I never heard of it," declared his new friend.

"It's real small; it doesn't even have its own high school."

"Basketball is king here," One Gram repeated. "You'll see." Then they went one-on-one for awhile, but Sonny was overmatched. He didn't care; he felt accepted.

Before he left, One Gram told him, "Come over any time you like; we'll shoot some more hoops."

"Sure," said Sonny. "That would be great."

Immediately following the priest's visit, and the entrée established to the pipe organ, his mother escalated into a hyper period (the first official diagnosis they ever got on her was manic-depressive). She was suddenly a participant in Sonny's life, even in the early-morning hours. When he sat on the edge of his bed at 4:45 A.M., rubbing the sleep from his eyes, he could see the hall light creeping under his bedroom door, and he could hear his mother's singing voice:

And He walks with me
And He talks with me
And He tells me I am His own

When Sonny got to the kitchen, he found a blaze of lights bouncing from countertops and appliances. His mother's hair was cut off; what was left was like a boy's, but the cut looked so amateur he wondered if she had done the job herself. She was in motion around the stove, poking at bacon strips that were popping in the skillet. "Biscuits in the oven, Sonny Boy," she sang gaily. "Homemade, right from scratch."

It was more than Sonny could comprehend. He always ate his breakfast by himself. Without speaking, he headed back down the hall toward the bathroom, but he could hear her singing hymns again.

He brushed his teeth and combed his hair, but his head was full of questions. Why was she up? Where was her hair? Was she taking the nerve pills? Was she taking too many? And what about the booze?

In the glare of the kitchen his mother set the feast in front of him, framed by a perfect knife-and-fork table setting on a yellow place mat. Orange juice, scrambled eggs, toast, and bacon. He started eating while his mother put the skillet to soak in the sink.

Waiting for her tea to steep, she sat beside him and folded her hands on the tabletop. "I'll tell you what," she said. "Things are going to be different from now on around here. Everything is going to be much better."

Since Sonny's mouth was full, he didn't need to talk. But in his confusion he was sure he didn't know a good sign from a bad one.

She repeated herself: "A whole lot better, I can promise you that."

He waited a moment. "Mother, where is your hair?"

"I got it cut. Do you like it?"

"I'll probably have to get used to it, it just doesn't look like you."

"This is called a pixie cut. When I was a girl, it was a very popular hairstyle. Do you like it?"

How could he smell liquor on her breath when there wasn't any in the house that he knew of? "It'll take a while to get used to it because it's so different," he said again.

Getting her tea, she said, "I know it looks somewhat rough cut, but in 1960, this was very stylish, believe me."

"I believe you, but where's your hair now?"

"It's on the cutting-room floor, I suppose, except by now it's probably all swept up." She sat down again, with her full cup. "Why do you insist on knowing where my old hair is?"

"I just thought you'd never want to part with it. What if you have second thoughts? You can sell hair, too, people buy it and make wigs out of it."

"That all seems like such vanity."

"We read a story about it in English class."

"You probably read 'The Gift of the Magi.' I've read that story, too. Too much attachment to things like glossy hair is worldly. It may even be sinful because it's so vain."

"Whatever," said Sonny, deciding he liked breakfast better by himself, minus the confusion. You couldn't press his mother on a subject anyway.

She asked, "How's the breakfast?"

"It's real delicious," he said.

"I'm so glad. You have no idea the distress I feel thinking of you out there alone in the dark and cold, delivering newspapers."

"It's not so bad. If I get it out of the way, it leaves me free for basketball practice after school."

"Basketball is such a nicer game than football, isn't it? It's just the thought of delivering newspapers to people who aren't up yet. While the world is still sleeping — it seems so out of joint with the universe."

It was one of her mysterious trains of thought. He was about finished with his toast and it was nearly five-thirty, so he would have to be leaving soon.

"If you do it," she added, "I'll feel so much better knowing you're doing it on a full stomach."

"I always eat breakfast before my route. I have cinnamon toast."

"That's not a *real* breakfast, Norman. This is what you need, something nutritious and protein-rich."

Protein-rich? Did this come from a TV commercial? "Does this mean you're going to fix breakfast every morning?"

"Indeed it does. Haven't I already told you that things are going to get much better around here?"

"I guess you did say that. I have to go now. Thanks for the breakfast."

"I love you, Norman."

That was then. It seemed long ago and yet it seemed recent. Sitting with her now, in this hospital lounge, watching Aunt Jane give her Christmas gifts she couldn't comprehend, Sonny had to wonder if the time would ever come when she would rejoin the human race. His mother turned her head to look in his direction, but her sunken eyes, which focused on his chest, seemed to stare right through him and out his back.

Aunt Jane had a Christmas basket of fruits and nuts and jellies, while Sonny had a blue sweater. His mother didn't seem to acknowledge the gifts, but a bubbly nurse's aide made a big fuss and talked baby talk.

Aunt Jane said, "The snow is so deep, your parking lot looks like Pike's Peak." Sonny told his mother how well the team was doing.

They stayed about 40 minutes. When they were leaving, the aide told them, "I'm sure she'll enjoy her presents."

"Right," said Sonny. *If she even knows she's got them.*

"Sonny, you drive. I hate winter driving."

"Okay." When they were east of town, Aunt Jane said, "I had dinner with Sissy last week in Carbondale. She told me how the two of you have been working together on the mural restoration."

"And?"

"I think it's wonderful."

"You do?"

"Oh, yes. Not just the art project, but the fact that the two of you are getting an opportunity to spend time together."

It made sense that his aunt would appreciate the development. "Let's take the interstate. It's out of the way, but it'll be clearer."

"Fine. You're so young, Sonny, you have no idea how much family pain there is when a parent shuns his own child."

"I don't?"

"I'm sorry. I shouldn't have put it that way."

"It's okay, Aunt Jane." But he felt a little hurt.

"What I should have said is that children have their own lives because they make their own choices. Seth expected Erika to get married to the right man, bear children, then become a good wife and mother. I guess I expected the same things, but I've never been disappointed in her. She's a very successful person."

Sonny wondered if his own father ever had any expectations for *him*. He wondered how anyone could be disappointed in a woman who was a Ph.D. and a professor in a university. He tried to imagine Sissy in the wife and mother role, but he couldn't.

"Not that Sissy has ever worked very hard to mend the fences either, but she's tried harder than Seth has. She's very headstrong, but she's so capable."

It was the first time Sonny saw clearly how caught in the middle his aunt Jane's life must be. He said to his aunt, "You have to get to know her," but it sounded so simple-minded.

"Yes, you do. She can be so aggressive, the way she won't ever back down, but there's a lot of love in her, too. It just doesn't come out with a lot of sentiment."

After a long pause Sonny said, "You know what, Aunt Jane? She's so intelligent, she's scary."

She laughed. "It's true, isn't it? I don't know where the IQ comes from, but I know she didn't get it from her parents."

Then Sonny laughed. "Because of her intelligence, you're tempted to put her on a pedestal, like a god or something."

"Like a goddess you mean. I can't tell you how many times she's lectured me on the fact that the first gods were women."

"Yeah, me too. Did you tell Uncle Seth?"

"Did I tell him what?"

"About your dinner conversation. About Sissy and me working together."

"No, indeed, and I don't intend to. Not unless you want some new stress in your life."

"No thanks."

A warm front pushed through the day after Christmas, bringing rain and slush. Sonny drove out to the high school to see if it was open, but it was locked. Among the many memories that passed through his mind in the parking lot, foremost seemed to be the regional championship against Collinsville when he was a junior, a game in which he scored 41 points.

In a state of mind uncharacteristically aimless and restless, he took the Mazda onto wet secondary roads to "see what she could do" on hills and curves. He fiddled with the range of digital dashboard goodies to establish all their functions. He fishtailed around some agricultural curves, then righted his vehicle smartly. *Bored and stupid*, he thought to himself.

His desultory path made its way eventually to the

town square, where he parked the car. The falling drizzle slushed and dirtied the snow around the aging gazebo bandshell, but it was such a memory place it put a lump in his throat. For the briefest moment he thought about calling Barbara; she was no doubt on vacation, too. But that was stupid, that was the past.

Why was it, he wondered, that his developing habit of hypnotic reminiscing, his "lapses in concentration" as he was wont to call them, seemed mostly to target her, and that freshman year? *Was it important? Did it have anything to do with Sissy? But how could it? I walked on air in the Butler game.*

He decided to find out if the old junior high was open. It was only three blocks, though, so he wouldn't take the car; he could walk easily enough. He found the building unlocked because the janitors were waxing some of the floors.

He shot baskets in the gym for about an hour, by himself. In due time, he found it to be an unsatisfactory set of conditions: The lighting was poor and there was no one else to play with. *Why should those things make any difference? Am I losing it?* When he took a seat on the first row of bleachers, well-worn and highly polished planks bolted permanently into their concrete base, when he looked at the chain-link barrier fastened along the high-up windows like a cage, he saw instead that first ninth-grade practice, more than four years ago. It was Brother Rice all over again.

Vividly, he recalled how he had intended, and succeeded, to be first one in the gym. Rice, wearing shiny pleated pants and a gray sweatshirt, was sitting on the first row of bleachers. He was writing on a clipboard, but Sonny went over anyway.

With no expression on his face, Rice looked up from his notes. His gray eyes traveled Sonny's frame from head to toe for the briefest moment, then he tipped his head toward the other end of the gym. "Start running."

"Laps?"

"Yeah, laps. Start running."

To begin with, his feet pounded an echo around the empty gym, but in no time at all he was joined by more and more players. Eventually, the number was 30. Only 12 would make the final cut. Of the 30, more than half were bringing experience from the seventh- and eighth-grade teams. Only a handful were like himself, out for an Abydos team for the first time.

Rice seemed preoccupied with his clipboard, but Sonny ran hard laps all the same, in case the coach ever looked up. Julio Bates was doing a little clowning as he ran, swivel-hipping like a girl; some of the guys were giggling, but it made Sonny nervous. From everything he'd ever heard, you couldn't clown around where Rice was concerned.

When he blew the whistle, the coach told them to stop the laps and take a seat on the first two rows of bleachers. Sonny sat next to One Gram. As soon as Rice stood up to speak, it got silent as a church. When he started talking, he only needed a quiet voice: "It's obvious already that some of you are lazy. If you cut corners with me, I'll cut you off this team so fast you won't even see it coming. You'll be spending your afternoons down at Goldie's playing video games." Then he picked up the clipboard again to write something brief.

So he was watching, thought Sonny. *He must have been watching from the corner of his eye.* Sonny was breathing harder than he should have been; part of it was nerves.

No one talked while Brother Rice was writing. It was the first time Sonny had ever taken a long look at him.

He was over six feet and more than 300 pounds. He was bald, except for some slicked-down hair above his ears. He had to be in his sixties, at least. His glasses had wire rims, and his long, sharp nose didn't seem to fit with the rest of his fleshy face.

After Rice put down the clipboard, he got a basketball from the ball rack. He stood in front of them again. "There are a few things each and every one of you had better understand right away. If you can't get yourself straight on these few things, then don't bother showing up tomorrow; we'll just wash your ass out of here right now."

He paused for a moment, spinning the ball in his fat hands. No one made a sound.

"The first thing you have to understand is that as basketball players, none of you is worth a shit. Absolutely not worth a shit. Make certain you understand this simple premise. *Do* you?"

No one uttered a sound, especially not Sonny.

"I said, do you?"

"Yeah," muttered the boys meekly.

"Then say it."

Still, no one spoke.

"All of you. Say, 'As basketball players, we are not worth a shit.'"

Keeping their eyes lowered and using quiet voices, they all repeated the sentence.

"That's the first thing," said Rice. "I've seen most of you play, on last year's team, or in P.E., or even on the playground in some cases. You might think you're hot stuff, but you're not. You're not worth a shit. If you bust your ass in practice every day, which I will make certain that you do, if you listen and learn something about concentration, you might be worth a shit by the end of the season. But right now, you are not worth a shit. Say it again."

They said it again. "I am not worth a shit," said Sonny.

"You start with humility and there's a chance you might learn something." He spun the ball some more.

"Second. We're not here to have fun. We're not here for a good time. We are here for one purpose and only one, and that is to win. We are here to win every game. If fun is what you want, go join the Boy Scouts or diddle your girlfriend."

It was Rice's pattern to make frequent pauses so that things could sink in. Sonny couldn't take his eyes off the seams of the rotating basketball.

"In the past four years," the coach continued, "the Abydos freshmen have won ninety-two games and lost eight. The eight losses disgust me; I resent them. In the past four years, we have won two state championships. I find it annoying that we didn't win all four years. What are we here for?"

"We're here to win," the boys responded.

"Don't mumble, say it loud."

"We're here to win!" Sonny could feel his own surge of adrenaline, even though he feared he wouldn't make the cut.

"Make certain you understand that. I'm not interested in a lot of horseshit about sportsmanship, or doing your best. Leave sportsmanship for the girls; if the cheerleaders want to deal with it, that's their business. Your business is finding what it takes to win, and nothing else. Is that perfectly clear?"

"Yes." They spoke as one.

"Third. The rules I give you, you will follow to the *letter*. The first time you break a rule, you will take ten additional laps at every practice. The second time you break a rule, don't bother coming back. Your ass will be off the team, and I will expect never to see your dumb face around this gym again. Is that perfectly clear?"

More silence, for more sinking in.

"The first rule is this: When I'm talking, you are listening. You won't be clowning or making noises or staring around the gym. Look at this ball. Are you looking at it?"

Sonny stared at the seams that patterned the leather grain, rotating slowly in the fat hands. He wondered if there was anything else Rice could do with a basketball; there was no way to imagine him dribbling or shooting.

"If you look at the ball at all times, you won't be distracted. Look at the ball, keep your mouth shut, and listen carefully. It's the first and simplest way to learn something about concentration. When I tell you to do something, I expect to tell you once and only once.

"The second rule is this: You will never miss a practice, not for even one minute. At three-forty I expect to see you running laps. That means three-forty, not three-forty-one." After a long pause, Rice said, "Those are the rules, the only rules, and you will follow them to the letter. Are there any questions?"

Sonny couldn't imagine the nerve it would take to speak up with a question, but after a moment or two of silence, Dick Lynch held up his hand and Rice nodded to him. "Does it matter what we wear to practice?" Lynch asked.

Rice shook his head. "It doesn't make any difference. What you're wearing right now is fine. As long as your dick's not hanging out, I don't care about your appearance."

Some of the guys laughed, but Sonny only smiled. It was nervous laughter anyway. There weren't any more questions so Rice said, "We're going to work on defense today. Fifty percent of the game of basketball is defense, but players don't want to work very hard at it. They'd rather be down at the offensive end, sucking up all the glory they can. You don't play for me, though, if you don't play defense. Take five laps, hard ones, then stand under the south basket and I'll tell you what comes next."

Sprinting his laps as hard as he could, Sonny came in near the front. Lynch was first, so he got to lead the first drill. It was running in place in your defensive crouch, going right or left according to which direction Lynch pointed the ball. Left, right, forward, back, in place. Over and over until Sonny's legs shook heavily and he was so winded a sharp pain scorched in his chest.

Rice then ordered them to pair off and get a ball from the rack. One Gram, Sonny's partner, held the ball. Some of the guys bounced their ball on the floor until they got a good look at Rice's face.

"Now listen up. If it's your turn for offense, dribble the ball against your partner and try to advance it toward the north end. Half of you can go the other way, so we've got some room. Okay, let's see if you've got anything at all. Go ahead."

The fifteen pairs went at it. Guarding Warren felt familiar from the times of one-on-one in his driveway, but Sonny felt shaky indeed. After fifteen seconds, Rice blew the whistle. He bellowed at the guys playing defense. "Look at you, for God's sake! You're slouching like you're in line for movie tickets! Some of you are even crossing your feet! Get your feet apart and get balanced. Get squared up to your man and turn it up a notch. Now move it."

Another quick whistle after another fifteen seconds. "Don't look at his head and don't look at his feet. Those are the things he can fake with. Look straight at the pit of his stomach, and I want to see some concentration. Do it again!"

Sonny guarded Warren with Rice's guidelines firmly in mind. From a balanced crouch, he concentrated hard on One Gram's stomach. He moved his feet quickly right or left, straining to keep himself balanced. He couldn't help but notice, when he moved up close one time to try and poke the ball away, that he and his friend were now the same height. Warren was more muscular, but they were both six feet one.

This time nearly thirty seconds passed before the whistle sounded. "I'd like to know the purpose of the three feet of daylight between you and your man. Is your arm four feet long? Do you honestly think you can put any pressure on the ball from back there? Think again, girls. When you play defense for me, I don't want to see any daylight. I want you in his face and in his shirt." On the coach's harsh face was an expression of long-suffering; he shook his head wearily. "Let's try it again," he said.

Sonny got right up on Warren's chest and slapped at the ball, but it was harder to keep his man from going around him. With his feet moving furiously, he fought to keep his balance. About 20 seconds' worth before the next whistle cut them off. "You guys aren't even close; you don't have a clue. You play defense with your feet, not your hands, not by reaching and grabbing. I told you you don't know anything about defense; maybe by now you're starting to believe me. We better say it again, girls. Tell me how good you are."

"I'm not worth a shit," they said, only this time angry and frustrated. Sonny wanted another chance, but Rice told them, "You guys are hopeless. Let's see if your partner is any better."

One Gram handed the ball to Sonny. "Okay, go ahead," ordered the coach.

When practice was over, they took five hard laps before heading to the locker room. Sonny could even remember how Julio had scampered down the row of lockers, snapping jockstraps as he went.

But a custodian was disturbing this reverie by tapping Sonny on the shoulder. "We're going to be working on this floor, Sonny. I guess you'll have to leave."

Startled, Sonny turned to look. The custodian's name was Gus, it said so on his shirt. "What?"

"I'm afraid you'll have to leave now." He spoke so politely.

Sonny stood up. "No problem," he said. Of course the custodian named Gus would be polite. He was speaking not to a shaky ninth-grader in fear of Brother Rice's wrath, but to Sonny Youngblood, SIU all-American, the MVP of the Big Apple NIT, and star of the third-ranked team in the nation.

"Sorry," Gus repeated.

"No problem," Sonny repeated. "I was just thinking of Brother Rice."

"He's in a nursing home now."

"That's what I heard. It's not surprising if you think about his lifestyle. Maybe the surprising thing is, he's still alive at all. I have some place I have to go now anyway. See you later."

The place Sonny had to go was the Abydos Community Library, and with a surprising sense of purpose. The quiet library was dark wood and low lighting. His only real memories of the place were associated with Barb, doing homework together.

Using an encyclopedia of mythology and a book called *The Golden Bough*, Sonny needed the better part of three hours to write a report on Isis and Osiris. The focus he needed to find was all the more difficult because there seemed to be two distinct tales: the one where Isis recovered the coffin of Osiris and brought him home, and the other where he was dismembered, so she had to locate his body parts and reassemble them. Then there was the nasty problem of simply writing it all out, because writing was never easy for him.

At 4:00 the library closed, but he was nearly finished anyway. Outside it was dusk, but the drizzle had stopped and the temperature hovered near 40 degrees. He stopped at Goldie's to see if anyone might be hanging out. Besides some guys from the implement plant who wanted to slap his back and talk about Saluki basketball, Julio Bates and Andrea were in a corner booth.

First they wanted to see his new car, but he talked them out of it. "You can see it before I leave," he said.

"Oh, just another RX-7," joked Andrea.

"You know how it is with my uncle, the cars are always coming and going."

"I wish I knew."

Julio and Andrea were both enrolled at Shawnee Community College in Ullin. Andrea said, "Barb's in Europe right now on a choir tour."

"You see her often?"

"Hardly ever. She's written me a couple of letters."

Sonny asked Julio about basketball at Shawnee.

"It's okay. I've been playin' sixth man, but there's a guy who's goin' ineligible. I might get to start this semester."

"That's good, Julio."

Julio laughed, then he shrugged. "Well it ain't the *Salukis, amigo*. I've been watchin' you guys on the tube." He stopped long enough to shake his head and make a whistling sound through his teeth. "What can I say?"

Andrea made a groaning sound. "Are we going to talk about basketball now?"

"Chill out," Julio told her. "We're talkin' about *numero uno* here."

"Not in the polls." Sonny smiled at him.

"Yeah, don't tell me. I've seen with my own eyes."

"We *are* going to talk about basketball."

"You want to come to a game?" Sonny asked Julio.

"Sure, but there's no tickets. There's *never* any tickets."

"I get comp tickets for every game. I can get you *free* tickets."

"Are you serious?"

"Would I kid about a thing like this? Just pick your date."

"He picks me," said Andrea.

"Not that kind of date, a date on the schedule."

"Can you get two tickets?" asked Julio.

"Not a problem," Sonny assured him. "I can get up to six tickets."

Julio laughed, then reached across the table to give Sonny a high five. They knocked over a Coke. Andrea started blotting furiously with a handful of napkins. "Let's leave before we get thrown out," she said. "Can we see your car now?"

The cake that Uncle Seth custom-ordered for Sonny's birthday covered most of the surface of a card table. Baked in the shape of a huge number one, it was decorated to include a clumsy likeness of Dick Vitale, who had long been proclaiming that the Salukis were the best team in the nation regardless of what the polls said.

Aunt Jane took a Polaroid photograph of the cake before cutting a portion of it into generous squares. With his beer in hand, Uncle Seth asked, "How does chocolate cake go with the king?"

"You mean the king of beers?" asked Hufnagel.

"That's the one."

"Not too good, as I recall."

"Then you better eat your cake before you get too much brew in you," Uncle Seth cautioned him.

"It's a little late to be telling me now." He laughed out loud and so did Uncle Seth.

The TV was turned up loud. It was halftime in the Georgetown game, and the ESPN anchormen were reporting scores and highlights from around the country. It was unlikely that Georgetown, ranked number one in the nation, would blow its 12-point lead. Paepke was a real estate developer from Mount Vernon. His view was, "If we were in the Big Ten or the Big East, we would've been number one a long time ago."

It was the prevailing opinion. "You got that right," said Seth.

"It wouldn't even be close in the polls."

"It's enough to make you puke, isn't it?" said Hufnagel.

"It's too bad we aren't in one of those holiday classics," lamented Paepke.

Sonny reminded them, "We were in the NIT and the Memphis Invitational."

"That's not the same. It's these Christmas holiday tournaments where you get the most exposure."

"Yeah," said Oscar. "Look at Georgetown."

When the second half started, Sonny took the rest of the cake up to the kitchen, where Aunt Jane was mixing a large bowl of trail mix to supplement the potato chips. "I don't think you're enjoying the party much," his aunt said to him.

Sonny shrugged. "It's okay. It's lots of grins for the good old boy network."

"It gives them a chance to let off steam."

But where does the steam come from? he wondered. *What does it mean?* "Right," he said.

"Take these downstairs for me?"

"Sure." He took the bowls down to the den, where a Rutgers comeback was stirring some excitement. Sonny took an empty chair and munched on potato chips. He was familiar with Georgetown, having watched them on TV several times before.

Rutgers cut the lead to six points before Georgetown's six-foot-eight all-American, LeRoy Jackson, took over the game with a couple of leaners in the paint that he converted into three-point plays, three blocked shots, and a breakaway dunk. The lead was back to 14 points. With less than six minutes remaining, the game's outcome was not in doubt.

"They're not that good," Paepke said of Georgetown. "Jackson's not that good either."

Sonny couldn't believe it. "Are you serious? He's a first-team all-American. He's only a sophomore, but he could probably come out after this season."

"He's not ready to come out," Paepke insisted. "What makes him think he's ready for the NBA?"

"That's what I say," Oscar agreed. "You can't believe everything the Eastern press wants to tell you, Sonny."

"I don't care what sportswriters say. I've seen him play enough with my own eyes. Workman says he'll be a lottery pick."

"Could you guard him, Sonny?" asked Uncle Seth.

"He's six eight," Sonny reminded him. "I might be able to check him out on the floor, but not posted up." At times he got impatient with their remote expectations. Where was reality?

"Luther Cobb could guard him," said Oscar. "Luther would shut him down."

"Georgetown's not on our schedule," Sonny pointed out.

"We're talking about *the* tournament," said Hufnagel to Sonny. "The Hoyas'll be on our schedule in the NCAA tournament."

"If they're lucky enough to get that far!" exclaimed Uncle Seth. Then the two of them laughed out loud and clinked their beer mugs together.

After the game, when all the guests were gone, Uncle Seth was sound asleep in the easy chair. A monster truck rerun was showing, but Sonny didn't touch the set. He went up to his room. He found a paper clip to fasten together the five loose pages of his library report. Then he went to bed.

The two dreams, which were on the lip of consciousness, merged at times to seem like parts of the same dream: LeRoy Jackson soaring like a hawk to pin his finger roll against the backboard, and Sissy swallowing his finger wet and wild. He awoke with a sweat and a start; the nightstand clock told him it was only three A.M.

On the night of the 30th, it was dark as pitch, but the rain had slowed to a drizzle as Sonny guided the Mazda along the ruts and slush in Sissy's lane. He was relieved to see lights on in the house.

She was wearing her bathrobe. She only opened the door partway, but at least she left the porch light off. "This is a surprise, Cousin. Tell me what's up."

"I came to wish you a happy birthday."

"Liar. How did you even find out?"

"Aunt Jane told me."

"Still a liar. What's on your mind?"

His hesitation was caused by the foolishness he felt. "I don't know. I guess I just wanted to visit."

"Life in the fast lane must be slowing down; you came all the way up here for the sole purpose of visiting *moi*?"

"I guess."

She reached to open the screen door so he could come inside. Lamplit from behind, like a silhouette, she seemed large. But it was probably only because she was on the step up. Before Sonny could get inside, it started to pour again. The rain pounded the porch roof like falling marbles. "Oh, the plaster!" Sissy exclaimed.

"What plaster?"

"I put four bags of plaster by the barn; I couldn't get them any farther. The rain will ruin them."

"I'll put them away."

She smiled. "We can pretend you came for my birthday and you want to give me a present."

"What present?"

"Not goods, services. Putting the plaster away."

She turned on the porch light while Sonny jogged through the downpour. The barn door padlock was troublesome because it was partly iced; he was soaked to the skin getting the bags inside.

When he stood on the throw rug inside her door, he was dripping like a wet tree. Sissy brought him a huge towel, so he took off his sweater and shirt to begin rubbing dry. Sissy held the wet garments, so drenched they were heavy. "You're soaked, Sonny. Let me put your clothes through the dryer."

His hair was plastered to his face. His teeth were

chattering even though he stood near the heat from the fireplace. "I'll probably be okay."

"Don't be absurd. This isn't the locker room, you don't have to be tough here."

He started to answer, but his teeth were chattering too much from the wet and cold.

"I have a house rule," Sissy went on. "No superstar leaves the premises with pneumonia."

Sonny had to laugh. He found himself in her large bathroom, under the bright ceiling light fixture. He took off the rest of his soggy clothes and handed them out to her around the small door opening. "Run yourself a hot shower," she instructed. "These are so wet I'm going to put them through the spin cycle of the washer first."

He called after her, "There's a report folded up in my back pocket. Take it out first, okay?"

Her distant voice was playful: "Have no fear, I never deal in laundered reports." She sure seemed in a good mood.

For nearly five minutes he simply stood still under the hot water with the steam rising. When his skin began turning pink, he started soaping himself. It was only rote shower behavior, though, because he wasn't even dirty. Because of his height, Sonny could see over the top of the shower curtain. He watched the bathroom door swing open, and he could see the top of Sissy's head as she entered the bathroom.

When he heard the toilet lid clunk down, he realized that she had chosen a place to sit. "I brought you some wine," she said in a voice loud enough to clear the shower.

Wine? Sonny stopped in mid-soap. He was taking this shower, while she was sitting on the toilet lid for conversation. It wasn't possible to see her through the accumulated condensation on the shower curtain. He began soaping his genitals, which increased his self-consciousness.

"I said, I brought you some wine."

"What for?"

"Birthdays, Cousin. We're celebrating the anniversaries of our passage from the womb."

"How old are you, Sissy?"

"When you get past forty, you stop counting. Besides, you're not supposed to ask impertinent questions when you're using another person's shower." She pulled back enough shower curtain to pass him a large coffee mug. He extended his arm to take it. "Don't worry, you get to keep your privacy. Cheers."

The black coffee mug had a printed message in red letters: *Pardon me, you've probably mistaken me for someone who gives a shit.* He had to turn sideways to the showerhead, in order to keep the water out of the wine. He took a sip and enjoyed the warm slide down. The curtain was returned, so he assumed she was sitting down again. He wondered how many glasses of wine she'd had already.

Sonny wasn't sure what came next, but he guessed it ought to be conversation. He asked her, "Did you do anything on your birthday?"

"Mother came up. We had dinner together."

"What about Uncle Seth?"

"He did us both a favor by staying away. He did send a gift."

"What was it?"

Without hesitation she said, "Money, of course. What else?"

Sonny took two small swallows, then a much bigger one. It was hard soaping your ankles with just one hand. "Is this your first glass of wine?" he asked.

"It might not be, what makes you ask?"

"Just wondering." *Just wondering what's going on here,* would be more like it. But the wine and shower were both effective; he felt a warming of the soul and skin. "How's the project coming?"

"Still as far behind as ever. We don't have any six-eight all-Americans to reach the high places."

"Six feet five," he corrected her. "And it was *high school* all-American; that's the past."

"Leave some of that modesty behind, *Liebchen.* It will only slow your development."

He didn't understand what she meant, of course, but he was learning not to be overwhelmed. He followed his own thread when he said, "I'd like to help some more with the fresco."

"You've done more than your share, Sonny. You've gone the second mile and then some."

"But I like it."

"Are we getting hooked on art, Cousin?"

"I don't know about that, I just like working on the panels and the cartons. I guess I'm getting attached."

His mug was empty by the time he shut off the water. She handed him the towel around the curtain. Sonny felt like the wine was running wheels in his brain. He began drying off.

"I like being with you," he said. He couldn't remember saying such a thing to an adult in his whole life. "I like working with you."

"What a kind thing to say. People don't like me much as a rule; I'm usually too aggressive and blunt."

Sonny wondered if it was really true that people didn't like her. Maybe, like he'd said to Aunt Jane, it was a matter of getting to know her. "You could give me another hour of independent study, only for second semester."

"You're serious about this, aren't you?"

"Yeah." Sonny was thoroughly dry. Before he stepped out of the shower, he secured the towel around his waist. Standing on the bathmat, he had to stoop down considerably to look in her mirror, which was fogged anyway. Sissy had changed into a twill shirt and blue jeans. She was seated on the toilet lid with her mug in one hand and a cigarette in the other. She was using the sink for an ashtray. "Why don't you just sign up for art history? There's plenty of time left to add a course."

"I couldn't handle it, not with basketball. I can carry thirteen hours, but not fifteen."

"Mmmm."

"Besides, when I work on the fresco project, I can fit it around the rest of my schedule."

She was looking at his chest. "You do have a beautiful body, don't you?"

It was one of her abrupt subject changes, partly lost on him while he tried to rub the mirror clear. "I wouldn't put it that way. What do you mean?"

"Is there any fat on you at all? I guess I shouldn't be surprised, though; how much bodybuilding does the jock ranch put you people through?"

"We have to lift three days a week," Sonny replied. "But it isn't bodybuilding, it's weight training."

"An important distinction, I'm sure. I'd like to do a sculpture. How'd you like to model, Cousin?"

He looked at her. "Model? Why?"

"Because you have superb muscular definition. You have what we call striated planes."

"You mean just stand there? I don't want to go to the studio, I'll get soaked again."

"Not the studio," Sissy explained. "I'd just like to do

some sketches. Preliminary ones that I might be able to work from later on. It's warm as toast in the living room, what do you say, Cuz?"

Sonny looked at her again. "You mean like this? With just a towel on?"

She stood up and poured some more wine in his cup. Ran some water over her smoldering cigarette to drown it. She bumped against him. "No, no, no, Wingman, I mean without the towel. I mean life drawings."

He could feel the blood rushing in his neck and face. When he looked at her, she was staring straight into his eyes. "Are you serious?" he asked.

"Of course. Do you forget that I'm an artist?"

"No, it's just . . ."

"You wouldn't have the guts, would you?" She was laughing, but it wasn't scorn, it was warm and playful.

"You can't say I don't have the guts."

Her eyes were twinkling. "I already said it. Here, let me say it again: You don't have the guts." She handed him the refilled cup.

"You can't say that." His face was full-flushed, but not exclusively from embarrassment.

Sissy hooked an index finger over the towel fold, just below his navel. She tugged. "Let's see if you do. Come on."

"Are you drunk, Sissy?"

"What do you think? Come on."

He followed her clumsily, surprised and speechless, trying to hold a level cup. If he resisted, he would lose the towel for sure. Sissy had her back turned, like she was pulling a wagon. "I want to see if you can get naked," she told him.

"I've probably had more sex experience than you have," he protested.

"Who's talking about sex? Sex is easy. I'm talking about getting naked."

This typically cryptic remark didn't reduce his bewilderment. Sonny found himself standing next to the popping fireplace, watching Sissy turning on lamps and shoving furniture around. His face flushed and the fire hot, he stood up straight. "Okay, so tell me what you want me to do."

"Drink some of the wine, take the towel off, and breathe deep."

"If you don't think I have the guts, it's just another case of you underestimating me."

"If that's true, it's a positive sign. In my opinion."

I'll show you. Sonny took two large swallows from his mug, then he removed the towel. Draped it over the poker handle. He turned a defiant glare on his cousin, but it was wasted; her back was still turned. She was rummaging in her cabinet for materials. Sonny felt so naked, he felt helpless. This wasn't anything like undressing a sex partner so as to go flesh to flesh, this made him light-headed. Instead of looking at her, he stared through the rain-splattered window clear to the haloed effect of the dim but visible pole light next to the barn.

He heard the sound of pages tearing, but he didn't look to face her. Still staring through the window to the light beyond, he waited a few moments before he broke the silence: "So when do we start?"

"This is the third sketch," she replied.

He looked at her then, seated cross-legged on the easy chair. Most of her face was concealed by her long hair and the shadows in the corner. Making long and bold strokes on the sketch pad, then tearing off the page to begin another. She glanced up at him, then back down at her page, "Are you embarrassed?"

"What do you think?"

"The embarrassment won't last long, Sonny, believe me. Eventually, you'll just feel bored. What are you embarrassed about?"

"I'm naked, for God's sake." Then he felt defiant again. "I'm afraid I'll get a hard-on."

"If you do, I'll sketch it. Please turn a little to the left, just far enough so you're facing the door."

He turned a little to the left. "Okay, I'm afraid I *won't* get one."

"In that case, I won't be able to sketch it."

"Why are you being such a shit? It wouldn't hurt you to give me a little consideration."

"I'm not being a shit. At least I don't *mean* to be. I'm just trying to help you feel natural. Try thinking of yourself as a two-by-four, as if there's simply no *you*."

"I want a drink of the wine," Sonny said.

"Go for it. You don't have to stand perfectly still for these quickies."

After he drank two more generous swallows, he began to feel an inner glow like a small flame.

"Do that again," Sissy requested.

"Do what again?"

"Hold the position you were in when you set the cup on the mantel. Please. Just let your left arm hang free."

He did as she asked, but he said, "I can't do this for very long. The fire's too hot."

"Okay, that was long enough." She tore off another page. Sonny moved away from the fire and locked his fingers together at the back of his neck.

"You never talk about your father, do you, Sonny?"

"No."

"Ever think about him?"

"No."

"Do you have memories of him?"

"A few, but I'd rather spend my time thinking about happy memories. My mother used to wonder about him, where he might be or what he might be doing. I never got into that. All I know is, he fucked us over."

"He's a part of you though, Dear One. Your father's still inside of you. Please leave your arms up there a little longer if it's not too uncomfortable."

"It's comfortable enough. I told you I have a few memories of him."

"It isn't just memories I'm talking about, Sonny. I mean the whole population center that lives deep down inside of you. All the folks who want to know you. One of them is the father you never knew. Know what I mean?"

"Not hardly. Sometimes I don't even try to guess what you mean."

"What are you afraid of, Cousin?"

"Not that again." He turned once more to pick up his mug. This time he drained it. When he turned back, Sissy asked him if he would lock his hands behind his neck again.

"No problem."

"Turn to the side a little bit, please? I'd like to detail this one a little more. Do you think you could hold that for about three minutes?"

"No problem," he declared. Sonny assumed the position and even arched his back. He found himself in an unexpected comfort zone, warm and mellow. The lamps were haloes at the shades, and the warm fire tingled his skin. He had to remind himself that he wasn't wearing any clothes.

"What are you afraid of, Sonny?"

"You want to know?"

"That's why I'm asking."

"Okay, if you really want to know, I'm afraid of LeRoy Jackson."

Sissy stopped adjusting her sketch pad long enough to put her glasses back on. "So tell me. Who is LeRoy Jackson?"

"He plays for Georgetown. Sometimes I have bad dreams about him. He can jump out of the gym and he's strong as steel."

"And that makes him scary?"

"It isn't just him, it's what he *stands* for. No matter how good you are, there's always somebody better."

"I suppose that stands to reason."

"I mean, you can always keep turning the switch up higher, but there'll always be somebody better."

"We both know how little I understand about sports, but all the available information seems to say that you're one of the best college players in the country. Aren't you proud of that?"

Sonny's serenity carried him to the threshold of drowsiness. He yawned. "I guess so."

"Isn't it enough?" she asked gently.

"I always think it should be, but in a game situation it's not. When the ball goes up, nothing's enough. It's never enough." He yawned again. "So you like this body, huh?"

"You make a lovely model, *Liebchen*. If you ever grow weary of basketball, you might make an income at it."

"You can get paid for doing this?"

"Most definitely. If you can learn to get past the embarrassment. Speaking of which, how are we doing?"

"What embarrassment?" he giggled. "Are we almost done now?" *What was that smell?*

"I think we'd better be. Your towel's catching on fire."

6

Even though Coach Gentry was a composed and sophisticated man, the strain he felt was evident in his answers to reporters. He turned aside all questions about the impending NCAA investigation with a brusque "no comment." After two easy road wins at Tulsa and Wichita State, reporters asked him if the SIU schedule was holding the team back.

"We make no apologies for the Missouri Valley Conference," Gentry replied. "We think the teams in our league are quality opponents, and we expect we'll have to work extremely hard to beat them."

Sonny, squirmy in his seat at the press conference table, wasn't surprised at this line of questioning. It was becoming routine. Besides, it was standard grist for the discussion mill among Uncle Seth and his cronies.

But the reporter persisted, "Apparently, the national polls are suspicious of your schedule, or you would be rated number one by now."

"We don't spend our time worrying about the polls," Gentry said. "Polls are fun for the fans."

"Do you think you'd be undefeated playing a Big Ten schedule?" asked another reporter. Sonny recognized him as one of the Chicago writers. The question was obviously loaded.

Gentry had a smile on his face, but not in his voice. "I've already stated how much respect we have for our opponents. Our hands are full taking care of business in the Missouri Valley. The teams in the Big Ten and the Big Eight will have to take care of their own business. What happens in other conferences is not something we can control. Neither is what goes on in the polls."

Then another man asked Sonny what he thought when people impugned the quality of Saluki opponents. Sonny's heart beat a little faster, the way it always did when he was asked to give public answers. *Why couldn't it be Luther's turn, or Hooker's?* He licked his lips, then said, "Well, we beat Michigan and we beat Arkansas. We won the Big Apple NIT and the Memphis Invitational."

Sonny assumed it must have been a very good answer, because Gentry was smiling ear to ear. "Out of the mouths of babes," he said, and the reporters had a good laugh. The rest of the questions were for the coach, so Sonny tipped back comfortably in his chair.

On a free Saturday in the middle part of January, Sonny helped Sissy crate two large and awkward fresco panels in the Pyramid lodge. They transported them in the Bronco to Willie Joe's spacious workroom. From his wheelchair Willie Joe instructed, "Just push that shit out of the way. Take all the space you need." Sonny and Sissy got the crates into the flat position on one of the worktables.

"Are they airtight?" Willie Joe wanted to know.

"It's touching of you to ask," said Sissy, "but rest assured that the packing meets the highest professional standards. Our point guard sees to that."

Sonny had no comment; he'd given up correcting her basketball terminology. But Willie Joe asked him why he was free on a Saturday.

"We've got the Virginia game tomorrow," said Sonny. "They changed the date so the game could be on CBS."

"Oh, man, kick their ass on national TV."

"We'll do our best," said Sonny. "They're good, though."

"Would I ever like to see that game."

Sissy said, "He just told you the game's on television."

"No," said Sonny. "He means in person. Willie Joe, if you wanta go, I've got two comp tickets left."

"You serious?"

"Yeah. Uncle Seth usually uses them but he's in Florida this week. You can have them if you want them."

"You better believe," said Willie Joe.

Then Sissy said, "I'd like to come too, Cousin."

"You want to come to the game?"

"Don't sound so surprised. I need to find out first-hand what this madness is all about."

"I just didn't think you'd want to."

"That's because you always underestimate me," she said. Sonny looked to see if she was teasing him, but her back was turned.

By this time, Willie Joe was utterly psyched up: "Hey Sonny, you wanta take five and shoot a few?"

"What d'you mean?"

"You've seen our court; it's called Makanda Square Garden. Let's put a few up."

"Right now? It's cold, Willie Joe."

"It ain't that cold, and there's no wind."

"Aw, it's cold. Anyway, what about a ball?"

"In the corner there, behind the scrap box." Willie Joe pointed and Sonny looked. It was a bright orange playground ball with a rubbery, pebbled surface. Sonny walked over and palmed it up like a cantaloupe. "So who's gonna play?" he asked.

"You, me, and the man-eater. We go three-on-three."

Sissy stuck her tongue out at him, but Sonny doubted if Willie Joe saw it, as he was pulling on a heavy blue sweatshirt. Sonny felt like pointing out it would take six people to go three-on-three, but a bigger mystery was how a legless man expected to play at all.

It was amazing to watch, though, the way Willie Joe slalomed his way on his crutches across the intersection and the railroad tracks. He went clear to the court without breaking a sweat, so obvious by then was the powerful muscular strength in his arms and back. It was cold, but cloudless, and Willie Joe was right about the wind: There wasn't any.

Sissy held the ball against her bulky leather flight jacket, which she wore over her sweatshirt. "Is it necessary to say an invocation, or is it acceptable to just go ahead and take a shot?" Without waiting for an answer, she took a two-handed push shot with no arc; it banged hard off the rim and caromed clear into the street.

Astonishingly, Willie Joe could somehow balance himself on one crutch only, while shooting push shots next to his right ear. Then he would snatch the other crutch quickly to balance himself. The evidence of his playing days was in the rotation of the ball as it released along his fingertips. If the shot made or missed, Sonny retrieved the ball to hand it back to him. Sissy was bouncing up and down in a guarding posture, but asking for the ball all the same.

Willie Joe missed a ten-footer, but Sonny tipped it in gently. "Shit," said Willie Joe. "Go ahead and tell me this is cold."

Sonny grinned at him. "Okay, it's not cold."

"Tell me this is cold. How many times you been on a playground in weather ten times worse?"

"Hundreds," laughed Sonny. "Okay, a thousand."

"You get to be a superstar, and you want carpet in the dressing room. Am I right?"

"Okay you're right." Sonny passed the ball to his cousin, who tried another of her flat push shots. It made contact with the chain net, but not the rim. Sonny watched his breath hang in the still air. Oddly enough, there was something about this moment that he found liberating and exhilarating.

"You shoot like a girl," Willie Joe said to Sissy, and then he laughed.

She was retrieving the ball. "I do lots of things like a girl," she responded. "But thank you for noticing."

Sonny kept tipping in Willie Joe's missed shots, but then the black man said, "How 'bout a dunk?"

Sonny jumped up slightly to snap the ball down politely. The chain net made a soft *chunking* sound. None of it satisfied Willie Joe: "I don't mean that pussy shit, I mean a *slam*. I mean a *gorilla* slam."

"Come on, Willie Joe." This was embarrassing.

"*You* come on."

"Go ahead, Sonny Youngblood," said Sissy. "We want a gorilla slam."

"Do you even know what a dunk is?" Sonny asked her.

"Of course I do. It means forcing the ball down through the ring instead of allowing it to drop through by means of gravity."

Sonny had to pause a moment. "You think that's it?" he asked Willie Joe.

"Who gives a shit how you describe it? You know a slam when you see one."

Okay, Sonny was convinced. He pivoted quickly to lob the ball underhand, so that when it made contact with the backboard, it caromed upward at a 45-degree angle. The moment it reached its highest point, when it would have begun its fall, his hands were there to seize it and drive it down through. The basket vibrated while Willie Joe howled his approval.

Sissy shook her head. "Is there an adolescent fantasy anywhere that doesn't torment you?"

But Willie Joe was hollering much too loud to hear her. When Sissy tried another push shot, Sonny blocked it by snatching it clean with one hand. She tried to get the ball back, but Sonny teased her by holding it too high. Sissy doubled her fist and took a swing at him, but he ducked it. Her momentum lunged her off balance, and she fell in a heap on the concrete.

Willie Joe's uncontrolled laughter echoed down the silent main drag of town. There were tears in his eyes. From her prone position, Sissy kicked his crutches out from under him. Two bodies on the pavement now, and Sonny wondered who might be hurt, or at least pissed. But they were both laughing their heads off, from flat on their backs. *What a hoot*, Sonny thought.

He jumped up swiftly to drive down a two-handed tomahawk so vicious it left the backboard swaying like a willow in the wind. He sat down on the pavement and pulled his knees up under his chin. Willie Joe's blue jeans, where they stopped, were folded and safety pinned. In the sunlight, Sissy's hair showed traces of red that Sonny had never noticed before.

In the cold but peaceful moment, Sonny had no desire to be anyplace else.

Gentry's game plan for Virginia was unusual. "Coach wants you to post up every chance you get," Workman explained to Sonny. "We want to run every baseline pick we can. Down low, posting up. Okay?"

Sonny knew it was because the Virginia guards were so short. Coach wanted to capitalize on the height advantage he would enjoy. "What if they zone?" Sonny asked.

"If they zone, you'll go back to the wing. But they won't. They've only played eight minutes of zone in twelve games. They would have to be in extreme foul trouble before they would go to a zone."

The huge and noisy crowd filled the arena thirty minutes before tip-off, partly in anticipation of CBS personalities and game-of-the-week preparations. It seemed so odd to Sonny, jogging through the pregame drills, to look at the comp seats where Uncle Seth and company were usually in place, and see instead Sissy and Willie Joe. Right next to them, Julio and Andrea. The two other seats were occupied by businessmen from Marion with familiar faces, but Sonny didn't remember their names.

Even before the ball went up for the tip-off, as the players pushed and shoved for circle advantage, the refs made it plain that they meant to keep the game under control. The oldest one paused before tossing the ball to say to both teams, "Let's get it together right now. Keep your hands off. We're here for basketball, not football. Are we okay?" This well-intentioned speech was essentially a waste of breath. The Salukis concentrated on pounding the ball down low to Sonny on the blocks, but the Cavaliers weren't surprised. They doubled down at every opportunity and thrashed him.

At the first TV time-out, Sonny had five points, but it felt like twice as many bruises, especially on his wrists and forearms. The restless, angry crowd made it hard for him to concentrate on Coach Gentry, who was saying, "Just keep your composure. They've got fouls to give, so that's what they're going to do. All of this is predictable."

Sonny nodded, while taking deep breaths. He wiped his dripping sweat and tasted the blood from the cut inside his mouth. The coach continued, "From now on, when they foul you, they're going to put you on the line. Just stay cool and make your free throws."

Gentry was right, but Sonny had to wonder if it was worth it. By halftime he had 20 points, 13 of which had come from the free throw line. But it felt like his nose was broken, and the ringing in his ears from an elbow shot wouldn't go away. The Virginia guards were short, but they were strong; they were powerfully built like fullbacks. They could dish out physical punishment and so could their backups, who were like clones coming off the bench.

Sonny even had to wonder about the strategy itself. Virginia couldn't stop him, but it took the Salukis out of their regular offense, and the game was too close for comfort at 45–36. For the first time in his life as a player, he had the urge to tell his coach to change the game plan. They didn't need this offensive gimmick to beat this team. Maybe not any team. Instead, he sat still and took deep breaths while the trainer painted his cuts with a styptic pencil and applied Vaseline.

The second half was more of the same. Sonny was so wired up late in the contest, it felt like high voltage galvanizing every pore of his body. He pounded home two monster dunks with the fullbacks hanging on him; each time, the bellowing crowd seemed to rend the air. The third time he tried it, though, he was undercut off the end of the court. He bounced up with his fists clenched and went chest-to-chest with Greene, one of the Virginia hatchet men.

"Go ahead, you pale motherfucker," Greene hissed at him.

"Fuck you, nigger."

"Ooooooeeeee!" exclaimed Luther Cobb, with a grin on his face. Luther was bending over and grabbing at his shorts, exhausted; if there was going to be a fight, it seemed as if he would use it as an opportunity to get a breather.

The refs stepped in quickly to separate Sonny from his stocky tormentor. On their feet, the 11,000 spectators were deafening, yet the referee's words were somehow audible: "Both of you come with me."

This referee stepped between them while the other two kept the rest of the players apart. Two Virginia players restrained Greene, while Hooker, with a firm grip on Sonny's arm, followed along to the scorer's table, where both head coaches were waiting.

"I want these two on the bench for a while to cool off," the ref informed them. But it was hard to hear him above the din.

"That's five on Greene anyway," someone from the scorer's table shouted. "He's out of the game."

Taking him by the other arm, Coach Workman helped Hooker lead Sonny toward the bench. "Just be cool, man."

"Is that fuck out of the game?"

"Just be cool."

Sonny felt the shakes. The trainer stuffed a gauze cylinder up his left nostril to stop the bleeding. "Leave me in. If Greene's gone, just leave me in."

"I can't leave you in with this blood, you know that."

He pushed the trainer away. "Just leave me in."

"Just be cool, Sonny," Workman told him.

The ref wouldn't hear it anyway. Coach Gentry told

Sonny, "Just have a seat and cool off. I haven't got a choice here."

By the time Gentry finished his statement, it didn't matter anymore; Sonny's shakes turned to weightlessness again. He was floating, his feet weren't making contact with the floor. He was cut loose, out of himself, precarious. He got to the bench somehow and sat down while the game resumed.

He felt his skin burning. The team manager draped a fluffy towel across his shoulders and gave him a cup of water. He was still floating and shaky, though. Sonny swallowed all the water in two gulps, then blew some bloody snot into the empty cup. Some of the Vaseline was smeared into the corner of his right eye; it filmed his vision.

Sonny didn't re-enter the game. The final score was 83–68. Georgetown was still number one in the nation, but the Saluki hold on number two was solid as a rock.

After the game he had recovered enough to do a post-game interview with Jack Sikma, who did the color for CBS. Sikma asked him if he liked playing low post in a game this physical.

"Not hardly, but it's what Coach wanted." At least his nose wasn't bleeding anymore.

Sikma said, "By consensus, you're the number one freshman player in the nation. How does that make you feel, Sonny Youngblood?"

"It's fine, I guess," answered Sonny, feeling bored. "I just have to play. We have to keep winnin'."

"You made twenty-eight free throws today. Did you know you set a school record?"

"What else could I do? They were poundin' ass on me in there."

After they went to commercial, Jack Sikma told him,

"You can't say *pounding ass* on the air. But nice game, man. We'll be seeing you down the road, I'm sure."

Sonny shook his hand, then jogged to the locker room. There was some reassurance: He was surefooted again.

"I never knew," was what Sissy said. And then she added, "I never understood." These were her words of introduction as she slid beneath the covers to lie beside him.

"You didn't understand what?" He was now wide-awake. *Had he heard the floorboards creak beneath her feet?*

"The report you wrote on the Isis legend was the first thing."

In the dark. "You read it?"

"Right away. Just as soon as I realized what it was. Oh Sonny, there's no written work required for independent credit."

"I know that. I wanted to write it anyway, maybe even *because* it wasn't required. What did you think of it?"

No hesitation. "I thought it was deliciously childlike, like a junior high report taken from an encyclopedia."

Sonny lifted his head to protest, but Sissy pushed it back down onto the pillow. On his arm, he felt her skin brushing. *Was she naked?*

"Hold still," she insisted. "It was so touchingly naive and literal I almost cried when I read it."

He wondered why she was using words of admiration to describe a report she found so juvenile. "I just didn't think it could ever really happen," he said. "A woman goes around the world collecting her husband's body parts, or her brother's, or whatever, and then putting them back together until he's healed.

Are there people who actually believe that happened?"

"Probably. Regrettably."

"Regrettably?"

"If they believe that resurrections literally happen, they can never understand them."

"Why not?"

"Because they can't see through to the meaning that may be there. Do you understand?"

"Not hardly." He also didn't understand why she was in his bed, although there seemed to be a remote corner of his deep-down self that *did* know. Not in a way that went into words, of course. By this time Sonny's eyes were accustomed to the dark so he could see, but her abundant hair concealed most of her face.

He tried to lift his head again, but with the same result. "Hold still," she told him. "The report was only the first thing. I haven't told you the second yet."

"You might as well, since I don't understand the first one."

"You understand more than you know, Sonny Youngblood, which is the whole point. The second thing was your game — the one I came to watch."

"What about it?" Even though the Virginia game was three days ago, the emotional drama of the second half was still vivid to him.

"It was the intensity, *Liebchen*. That's what I didn't understand."

"You have to play hard. When you come out of high school you think you know how to play hard, but you really don't. I can always turn it up another notch, that's maybe more important than talent."

"I'm sure that's how your coaches motivate you, but I'm talking about the expectations of thousands and thousands of people. The unspeakable pressure to succeed and never fail, and then to have your success or failure so public and so immediate."

Sonny fumbled for words. "We do have good crowds."

"Not to mention the millions of dollars hanging in the balance," she said. She turned on her side. "The rest of us can't comprehend that kind of pressure. Even those of us who are given major responsibility, so-called, don't have to *perform*. We are expected to succeed, but it's all so conditional." Sissy's voice was now scarcely more than a whisper. "We don't have to be *heroic*."

"I don't like being called a hero," Sonny answered right away.

"Unfortunately, you aren't given a choice. It's called the hero's burden."

He could feel the warm flesh of her thigh. "Are you naked, Sissy?"

"No, I'm wearing my nightgown. Are you naked?"

"No."

At this point, Sissy sat up to take a sidesaddle position on the edge of the bed. "I had to be at your game to truly understand the dimensions of the burden. To expect all of this from willing young men and then to pretend, somehow, that they can function as college students."

"I got a two-point-five, don't forget." He was still smarting a bit from her condescending description of his report.

"I'm not forgetting." Playfully, she reached over to scratch his head like a dog. "The hero's burden is that he's expected to compensate for those thousands if not millions of empty lives. People who are hibernating, as Anaïs Nin liked to put it, in monotony, boredom, and death. You are the children asked to fulfill the fantasies of the childish."

Then she stood up.

"Children?" protested Sonny. "Only three of us are freshmen. You saw Luther Cobb. Did he look like a *child* to you?"

Sissy didn't answer right away. She was looking out the window, apparently lost in thought. Most of her face was concealed by her hair and shadows, but the strong moonlight that framed her torso turned her nightgown semitransparent. Sonny had a clear view of her full breasts and generous hips. His moment of arousal was embarrassing and would have to be perverse, he thought.

Sissy finally said, "The very same boy who wrote the report has to be the hero for the legions who have gone to sleep in the snow and never awakened. You will make them feel significant for a brief, shining moment but no one will count the cost. Do you understand?"

Sonny had no interest in understanding, but instead in suppressing the surge of testosterone that was claiming him. And shaming him. *What did she expect of him? What did he expect of himself?*

She turned her face in his direction. "You're looking at me."

"I suppose I am."

"If I'm old and fat, let the darkness hide it."

"You're not old and fat."

"I'll see you tomorrow, Cousin. Sorry I woke you. Sweet dreams." And then she was gone.

It was a long time getting back to sleep. Disconcerted by the welter of emotions stimulated by this encounter, he tossed and turned. Eventually, remembering how the moonlight silhouetted the contours of her torso, he relieved himself the tried and true way, with swift and careless strokes. His good fortune was the box of tissues on the nightstand.

Before he fell asleep, though, he took offense once again at her description of his report.

7

Of the two men, Yates and Brosky, the latter was the older. It also seemed to Sonny that Brosky was the one short on patience. Especially when Sonny said he couldn't remember details. Yates was asking him about a conversation he'd had with Gentry at Abydos High when he was still a junior. "You say you don't remember what was said, but do you remember where the conversation took place?"

"I think so."

"You think so?"

"Yeah, I remember it. I talked to Coach Gentry in the hall outside the coach's office in the gym."

"What did you talk about?"

Sonny stared out through the conference room window at McAndrew Stadium across the way. He wondered why Coach Gentry wasn't here, but not really; they wanted to find out if his story would be different from that of the coach.

"Did you hear the question?" Brosky asked. "Mr. Yates asked what the two of you discussed."

Sonny looked back. He didn't like the way Brosky's eyes were hidden by the reflection from his glasses. "I heard the question. I can't remember, but we probably talked about basketball."

"You think this is funny, Mr. Youngblood?"

"Okay, we probably talked about SIU basketball."

Yates asked him, "Do you remember how long the conversation lasted?"

"Are you serious?"

"Very serious. What we're trying to determine, if we can, is whether the contact was simply a case of the two of you exchanging pleasantries in passing, or if it was an actual recruiting visit."

Sonny couldn't remember. "I can't remember," he said. He looked at the slow-moving wheels of the tape cassette. Whenever there were long silences, Brosky tended to shut the recorder off.

"Then let me ask you this. You had recruiting visits from Gentry that spring in your home. Is that correct?"

Sonny shook his head. "I have no idea. Probably. What is it you want from me?"

"Some straight answers, for one thing," Brosky declared.

Gardner interrupted: "Do you really expect a high school all-American to be able to recall this much detail about his recruitment during high school? Don't you realize we're talking about hundreds, maybe even thousands, of phone calls and visits?"

Brosky sniffed again. "What we expect, Mr. Gardner, is to be stonewalled. It seems to be the nature of our business."

"Nobody's stonewalling you. Please turn the recorder back on."

Yates said, "We always ask. Sometimes it's amazing the way people can recall details when they really try. Sonny, we understand your uncle was very active in your recruiting experience."

"That's true." The difference between this investigation and the *Checkpoint* procedure was the focus. This time, all the questions were aimed at learning information exclusively about the SIU basketball program. Mr. Ernst, the university attorney, was present but he didn't speak; occasionally, he made notes.

"Your uncle Seth spent a lot of time associating with businessmen from other cities while you were in high school. Is that correct?"

"Yeah, I s'pose he did. Still does."

"Did you ever wonder about that?"

"No, why? They're all men in the booster club."

Reading from his index cards, Brosky said, "An insurance man from Mount Vernon, another one from Belleville, a Buick dealer from Carbondale, the list goes on and on. You never wondered about your uncle's far-flung network of friendships?"

"Why should I?" Sonny found himself getting annoyed. "Booster club members are from all over; they don't all live in the same town."

Gardner had a smile on his face. Sonny assumed he appreciated the answer.

"Did your uncle screen your phone calls?"

"In my junior and senior years he did."

"How?"

"He set up an answering machine to take calls from recruiters. For his own calls, for him and Aunt Jane, he got an unlisted number."

"Didn't you think that was a little odd?" Brosky wanted to know.

"Not really," answered Sonny. "The calls were coming night and day. I think it was really my aunt Jane's idea to have the unlisted number, just so she could get a little relief. Besides, I've heard of other players doing the same thing in their families, just to deal with recruiters."

"So have these gentlemen," said Gardner wearily. "Don't you think we've plowed this furrow long enough?"

Brosky turned on him: "I'll tell you what, since Mr. Yates and I are in charge of this investigation, we'll be in charge of deciding what information we need. I'm not particularly fond of your tone of voice, either."

"I'm not particularly fond of your investigation," was Gardner's crisp response. "Is it just a coincidence that this inquiry comes within two weeks of our number one ranking? All those weeks that Georgetown was number one, did you have them under investigation?"

The attorney, Ernst, removed his glasses and began squeezing the bridge of his nose. Sonny wanted to think Gardner was on his side, but what kind of an ally would he be if all he did was get the investigators pissed off? Yates asked Sonny, "Do you understand NCAA policy governing complimentary tickets?"

Gardner interrupted again. "All our people are thoroughly briefed about matters of NCAA compliance. It's my job to keep players and coaches updated."

Ignoring the interruption, Yates repeated the question. Sonny squirmed a bit before he answered. "Some of the rules get pretty technical. The way they nitpick, I get confused at times, to tell you the truth."

"I'm asking you about complimentary tickets. Are you clear about the rules?"

Sonny shook his head. "Not exactly. Sort of. I think a certain number are for relatives, and a certain number can be used by other people."

"You know this stuff, Youngblood," Gardner declared. *Great. Now Gardner's against me too.* "I've been told all of it," Sonny admitted. "It gets confusing after a while. Who can give you a ride, or buy you a Coke, who you can talk to, who gets the tickets, et cetera."

"Don't play dumb, Sonny. You're not stupid."

"Mr. Gardner, please do us all a favor. Let Sonny provide his own answers to the questions."

Gardner sighed, took off his glasses, and slumped in his chair. Yates asked Sonny, "For example, can you remember who used your comp tickets for the Virginia game on January tenth?"

"Are you kidding?" asked Brosky sarcastically. "Do you expect him to remember something from three weeks ago?"

"I do remember," said Sonny.

"Hallelujah!" exclaimed Brosky.

Sonny was beyond irritation; he felt humiliated. "Why don't you kiss my ass?" he snapped at Brosky.

"What did you say to me?"

Sonny could feel his own flush. "You heard me, kiss my ass."

Yates was holding his two hands up like a third-base coach stopping a runner. "Equilibrium please," he begged.

"Right."

"May I ask why you remember?"

It seemed like an odd question. "Because my uncle Seth didn't use them. He and my aunt Jane were in Florida."

"Does your uncle ordinarily use your tickets?"

"Yeah, I usually give him all six. He distributes them how he wants."

"Okay," said Brosky. "Let's go back to the tenth. And I apologize for being so sarcastic." He sniffed.

"It's okay," said Sonny. "Sorry I lost my temper." He told the two of them that for the Virginia game, his tickets were used by Sissy, Willie Joe, Julio, and Andrea. The remaining two by his uncle's booster friends.

Yates asked, "How many of those people are members of your immediate family, Sonny?"

With a knot forming in the pit of his stomach: "Well, Sissy's my cousin."

"We don't consider cousins immediate family."

"But she's my first cousin. Uncle Seth is her father. The others were friends from high school or just . . . just friends."

"Do you understand you're not in compliance with NCAA rules when you distribute tickets in that manner?"

Sonny was looking down. He made a sidelong glance at Ernst and Gardner, but they were looking at their hands. Before he answered, Sonny drank some of his water. "Yeah, I knew. I just gave the tickets to Uncle Seth all the time so I wouldn't have to think about who would use them."

"I appreciate the honesty of that answer," said Yates, who seemed, in spite of the circumstances, to be a fair-minded guy. At least to Sonny.

Yates continued, "Is it fair to say that your uncle has always been glad to have your tickets?"

Sonny shrugged. "Yeah, I'd say so. He almost never misses a game and there are plenty of people who always want to come." Then Sonny had a start. "Are you going to be talking to my uncle Seth?"

Yates smiled. "Who knows? We never know for sure where an investigation will lead."

It was a remark which gave Sonny a burning sensation in his chest like angry bile. *Do they know things that I don't know?* "I'm telling you the truth here."

"I believe you are, Sonny," Yates admitted. "We'd like to ask you just a couple of questions about Erika Neil, and then we should be finished."

"Sissy? You're not going to talk to her, are you?"

"Like I said, we can never predict exactly where the trail will lead, but it isn't likely. Okay if I ask you one or two things?"

"Yeah, sure, go ahead."

"First of all, you earned one hour of independent study credit from Ms. Neil in art history. Is that correct?"

Gardner broke his long silence to interrupt again. Sarcastically. "You've seen his transcript, why the charade?"

"Excuse me," said Yates. "Am I correct, Sonny?"

"Yeah, that's right."

Brosky added, "An hour of A, and she made it retroactive."

"Teachers do it all the time. It's not unusual."

"Tell me if this is accurate," said Brosky. "You got an hour of art history credit retroactively, from your own cousin. And she gave you an A. Is that an accurate statement?"

Sonny squirmed and fumed. "If you put it that way, it sounds totally lame."

"You said it, not me. Is it also true that this particular hour of credit kept you eligible for basketball?"

"I worked my ass off for that credit. Sissy told me I did enough work to earn two or three credits. Look it up somewhere, teachers make that arrangement all the time. You're pissing me off, so get off my case."

Yates took a pause long enough to drink some coffee. For his part, Brosky worked his right nostril with the nasal mist. Then he asked Sonny, "You don't live with your cousin, do you?"

"No, I don't live with her. I live in the dorm."

"It's true though, isn't it," asked Yates, "that you spend a great deal of time at her house?"

"That would depend on what you mean by a great deal of time."

"You don't live with her, then. Do you ever spend the night at her house?"

Before he answered, Sonny wondered where this was headed. "Sometimes, if it's any of your business. Is that a violation too?"

"I wouldn't know," answered Brosky. "What does your uncle think about it?"

"I'm not sure what he thinks, if he even knows about it." But even as he was giving this answer, it made him uneasy the way their questions seemed so rooted in information. "Let me ask you a question: Why are you wasting your time asking me about Sissy? I thought you wanted to know about basketball and recruiting."

"Is that what we're doing? Wasting our time?"

"If you think my cousin Sissy gives a shit about basketball, or who plays for who, you're wasting your time for sure."

"Why don't you tell us about that aspect of it, then?" asked Brosky.

"That's what I'm trying to do. My cousin hates basketball almost as much as she hates football. If she had her way, the only college teams would be debate teams or scholastic bowl."

"This is too funny," said Gardner, who was trying not to laugh. "Too, too funny." He asked Yates and Brosky, "Do you honestly think Erika Neil had something to do with recruiting a basketball player for the SIU program?" But Gardner couldn't go on; he was laughing too hard.

*　　*　　*

The Bradley game was when it first happened. Round one of the Missouri Valley Conference tournament in the St. Louis Arena, a game in which the Salukis coasted by the Braves by 30 points. At the ten-minute mark of the first half, Sonny was floating again. A cold, clammy sweat in his palms was followed by shortness of breath. His legs went wobbly like he just missed a head-on collision on the highway. He went to the locker room, light in the head and with a towel draped over his shoulders. Daley, the team trainer, walked beside him.

Before the rest of the team came in at the half, there was time for Dr. Kelso to take his temperature and use the small flashlight to look in his eyes, ears, nose, and throat. No apparent abnormalities, so the doctor told him to rest up and get ready for the second half. Sonny lay flat on his back, listening to the distant, muffled roars of the crowd above. He thought to himself, *This is all in my head*. The most mysterious part seemed to be found in having knowledge of something so unfamiliar.

He felt strong enough at the start of the second half to swish a pair of quick three-pointers, but with 16 minutes showing, his legs were suddenly full of sand again. He was drained of color and drenched in sweat. For precautionary reasons, Gentry took him out of the game; it was a blowout in any case.

Sonny slumped on the bench with towels draped and his head in his hands. Workman took the seat next to him and said, "What's the matter, Sonny?"

This is all in my head, Sonny thought again. But instead of answering, he simply shook his head.

"You're not out of shape, are you?"

"Are you serious? You see me in practice every day, how could I be out of shape?"

"Okay, okay, I take it back."

The next night Sonny sucked it up as best he could. Tulsa played a 1-2-2 zone, so there were open shots on the wing, especially off Otis's quick penetrations. Sonny's jump shots were true as crosshairs, but they were only the stationary type; against a man-to-man, he wouldn't have had the strength to *get* a shot.

His defense was enervated. During time-outs and free throws, he clutched at his shorts and fought for breath. Mopped his sweat while trying to conceal his low-level case of the shakes. Sonny had 20 points, but only because the Tulsa defense was tailor-made for a series of undemanding jump shots. He breathed relief when the lead reached 30 points and Gentry began clearing the bench. After the game, Sonny threw up in one of the stalls, but nobody saw him.

Getting two days of rest seemed to help. By Monday night, when the Salukis played Creighton in the conference championship game, Sonny felt stronger. It seemed providential to be renewed in front of the 12,000 noisy fans and a national television audience.

He was quick to the basket against Creighton's overplay man defense, although he did pick up two charging fouls. They ran the double stack for a while, which freed him up for 15-footers near the free throw line. By halftime, when the lead was ten, Sonny had 21 points. He felt like he was all the way back.

But then came the second half, when the inexplicable weariness invaded his limbs. It was as if all his bodily fluids were much too heavy. He was about to get the shakes again, and he had some minor vertigo. His slow-motion defense led to two more fouls, which forced Gentry to sit him on the bench.

The lead was safe, although Creighton made a couple of runs late in the game. Sonny sat in his impotent cell of frustration and bewilderment, broken in a cold sweat. His legs shaky as pudding, a towel across his lap, and another around his shoulders. Grateful, as his teammates put the game away at the free throw line, that Gentry wouldn't send him back into the game.

During the post-game celebration, while his teammates cut down the nets, Sonny held the ladder. Or it held him. There would be no postgame interviews, in compliance with Gentry's current policy that made the players off-limits to reporters.

In their locker room, the players watched Gentry's press conference on closed-circuit TV. It didn't take long for the reporters to raise the issue of the NCAA investigation, but Gentry turned it aside with a crisp, firm disclaimer. "I don't intend to answer questions about that subject. Even if I wanted to talk about it, I'm not allowed to. I'll be happy to answer questions about the game, or about our team."

After that, it didn't take the press very long to resurrect the strength-of-schedule agenda. A reporter wanted to know if SIU's "soft" schedule would hurt the team's chances in the NCAA tournament.

His struggle for patience clearly visible, Gentry answered in monotones. "Okay, let's do this one more time. 'Soft' is your word. We won the Big Apple NIT, the Memphis Invitational, and the regular-season Missouri Valley championship. Now we've won the MVC tournament. We're the only undefeated major in the country and we've been number one in all the polls for nearly three weeks. Now you people tell me: Who votes in the polls? You do. If you don't think we're that good, then I suggest you exercise your ballot-box rights and vote us lower."

"Tell 'em, Coach," said Robert Lee, who was seated next to Sonny. "These fucking writers. What the hell did they ever play except maybe a few games of pocket pool?"

Sonny didn't say a word. He watched the monitor as one of the reporters asked the coach, "Can you tell us anything about Youngblood's condition?"

"He may have a touch of the flu. Our team physician is working with him. He'll have a few days of rest now, to get ready for the first round of the tournament."

"If he were unable to play, how would that affect your team's chances in the tournament?"

Gentry smiled for the first time. "How much would it help any team to lose a key player? But we don't expect anything like that. A little rest and Sonny should be just fine."

A writer wanted to know if Gentry thought it was important to be seeded number one by the NCAA selection committee.

"Only because our fans would benefit. It would mean they'd put us in the Indianapolis regional," the coach replied. "It's close to home, so our fans would be able to watch us play."

Robert Lee was wearing an uneven necklace of nylon net. When the press conference was over he asked Sonny, "Are you okay, man?"

Sonny didn't feel the shakes anymore, and there was no floating. But he was still cold and clammy. "I'll be fine," he said. Most of the players, having lost interest in the press conference, were in the showers. The steam crept like fog to permeate the locker-room area, but Sonny felt like the real fog was wrapped around his brain.

"Come on," said Robert Lee. "Let's hit the showers."

"Go ahead. I'll be there in a minute."

"He knows, Sonny."

Sonny switched off the radio and lifted his turn signal lever before he made an answer. "You mean Uncle Seth."

He used his side mirror to merge while Aunt Jane said, "Yes."

Before he said anything, Sonny got the car into the left lane flow of traffic. "He was bound to find out. Nobody's been trying to hide anything." At the edge of the highway, some dirty residual slush clung to its position, but the pavement itself was merely wet. The wipers were on intermittent.

"I didn't tell him, Sonny. He found out on his own."

"Like I said, nobody tried to hide anything. Is he pissed?"

Aunt Jane popped a Life Saver before offering him one. "Of course he's upset. Of all times for you to be spending time with Sissy, the worst would be right in the middle of all this SIU basketball glory. At least that's how it would seem to him."

"You'd think it might make him happy. Me and his own daughter getting to know one another." Not that he believed his own words for a minute.

"It makes me very happy," Aunt Jane said, "but it will only make Seth angry."

"Why does he hate her so much?"

"It isn't hate, Sonny. It's rejection."

"Okay then, why does he reject her so much?"

"Once upon a time there was a condition known as the generation gap."

"I've heard of it. You're talking about that Vietnam-era protest stuff from the sixties."

"You've heard of it, but you never lived through it. He just can't forgive her for rejecting his way of life."

Sonny turned the heater fan up to the next number. "That's a lot of grudge for a long time just over a different view of life."

"You can say that again."

When they got back, the part of the driveway nearest the road, where the lindens were clustered, was a partly frozen, treacherous surface, covered by an inch of water. Further back, by the house and shed, the gravel was simply wet. It was starting to rain again.

The blue Olds was parked beside the back porch. "He's back home," his aunt observed. "Are you coming inside?"

"Hell, yes. I'm not gonna start hiding from my uncle just because he might be pissed."

They were only at the kitchen table long enough for Aunt Jane to get the pot boiling when his uncle lumbered in. He slumped in one of the kitchen chairs, only half recovered from his nap on the den couch. Seth fished a cigarette from his shirt pocket before he said, "Just tell me why, Sonny. Tell me why."

"Why what?"

"You know what. I mean, why Sissy?" Seth was rubbing his sleepy eyes with his fists. Trying to flatten down his scattered, thinning hair.

"I like Sissy, Uncle Seth."

"Oh, God. You have no idea."

"No idea of what?"

"No idea the trouble you're askin' for. You know what a ball-buster is, Sonny?"

Aunt Jane at the stove had tears in her eyes. "That's enough of that kind of talk."

"You're talking about your own daughter, Uncle Seth."

"I know goddamn good and well who I'm talking about!" He lifted his eyes for the first time to look Sonny in the face. "The thing is, Sonny, she just doesn't have regular values."

"Let's say she has different values. Isn't that a right people have?"

"What are you, *living* with her?"

"No, I'm not living with her. I spend time at her house, but I'm not living with her."

"Don't you know what we're talking about here? My God, you guys are on target for a national championship! You can't let people like Sissy distract you from something this big!"

Sonny was losing patience with this. It felt like another NCAA grilling. "When we lose a game, we can worry about it. You better think about this, Uncle Seth: If it wasn't for Sissy, I probably wouldn't even be eligible."

This reminder gave Uncle Seth reason to pause. He got a beer from the fridge before he said, "Are you going to tell me that Sissy cares about SIU basketball all of a sudden? She's been an anti-sports fanatic for twenty years."

"No," answered Sonny evenly. "I'm telling you that Sissy cares about me."

"Aaaaach!" his uncle exclaimed. Stood up abruptly to put both hands on top of his head and begin pacing. "I have to take a piss. Don't go away."

"Why should I go away?" While Seth was gone, Aunt

Jane brushed her eyes once or twice, then poured two cups of steaming cocoa. It looked like Seth would be drinking beer. Sonny warmed his fingers by wrapping them around the ceramic blue mug, but he didn't say anything.

When Seth returned, the first thing Sonny said to him was, "Do you want to hear about my mom?"

"What's that supposed to mean?"

"We just got back from visiting her in the hospital. Don't you want to hear how it went?"

"Is there somethin' to tell? I'm trying to help you out of a situation that could be a lot worse than you realize."

"I'd say it's my mom who's got a situation. She's in the loony bin."

Uncle Seth looked embarrassed. He lit up another cigarette and played with his lighter by adjusting the flame up and down. "So what's to tell?"

"She's taken up smoking."

"What are you saying to me?" So tortured was his body language that his to-and-fro shifting nearly thrashed his chair. On his face was an infinitely pained expression. "How can she smoke? Does she have enough wits about her to light a cigarette and smoke it?"

Aunt Jane said, "Not really. You remember the blue cashmere sweater we got her for Christmas?"

"Let's say I do. What about it?"

"She's burned some holes in it. Apparently, when the cigarette burns her fingers, she lets it drop on her clothing."

Seth was holding his head again. "Are we going nuts here? Why would they let her have cigarettes in the hospital, or something to light them with?"

"That's what we said," Sonny answered. "It was like they didn't even know she had them or where she got them. Someone probably smuggled them in. They promised it wouldn't happen again."

"Okay, then it's taken care of."

Finished with his cocoa, Sonny stood up to leave.

"Where are you going?"

"Back to Carbondale," Sonny replied.

"Just like that? I thought this was your spring break."

"It is, but I'm going to spend it on campus. We've got practice, don't forget."

"Are you gonna be with Sissy? Is that the part you're not telling me?"

"That, too," Sonny admitted. He was zipping his coat. "We've only got two more fresco panels to bring up from Makanda, and then we should be done."

"Fresco panels," said Uncle Seth. "Great."

When Sonny got the car started, he looked up to see Uncle Seth stumbling toward the passenger door, in the rain. *Now what?* He put the window down. Seth said, "I forgot to tell you something. Brother Rice died last night."

"Rice is dead?"

"He died in the nursing home."

Sonny was surprised, but he felt neutral about the information. For several moments he didn't speak. Seth just stood in the rain, breathing hard, but with no other apparent discomfort. He finally said, "End of a legend, huh, Sonny?"

"End of a douche bag would be more like it."

"How could you say a thing like that?"

"If I can't, who can?"

Seth was shaking his dripping head. "I just don't see how you could say that."

"You should go inside now, Uncle Seth. You're getting soaked."

Sonny spun gravel on his fishtail path out of the driveway. He got the car up to speed and turned the wipers on medium. If Rice was dead, he asked himself, why should it be a surprise? Carrying around that extra 150 pounds, smoking his three packs a day, sitting around on his fat ass instead of getting any exercise. Why would his death ever be unexpected? The only surprise would have to be that his death didn't come years earlier.

Maybe Uncle Seth was right: Maybe Rice was a legend. People die, but legends don't. *Was that it?* Maybe he and Seth were both right: Brother Rice was a legend *and* a douche bag.

Whatever, this new information was a distraction. Sonny meant to concentrate on the road, but he kept seeing the interior of the old gym. The day Brother lost it in practice. *Was that a good day or a bad day?*

He listened to the wipers whining his windshield. He watched the broken white line at the center of the wet pavement. He didn't see them though. He saw only that afternoon in practice, four years earlier. The fat man on the bleachers who was pissed because they were screwing up the fast break.

"Goddamnit! When I say fill the lanes, I mean fill the lanes! You stand around with your thumb up your ass, how d'you expect to get it done? Do it again, and this time, move!" Thursday practices were always the worst because they usually came just before game day. Rice was working them on the fast break following a missed free throw. Butch Cross was the shooter.

Hands on hips, Sonny took the third spot along the

lane; Mickey Stanley and Dick Lynch had the lane positions under the basket.

Butch made six free throws in a row, but Rice seemed patient. "It's okay," he said to Butch. "Just keep shooting. Don't miss on purpose."

The next time he missed, Mickey Stanley grabbed the rebound. He turned to make the outlet pass, but only after a moment's hesitation did the players start to break for the other end of the court.

Brother Rice blew his whistle with a special fury. "*Goddamn!* How many times do you people have to be told?!" He walked heavily over to the free throw line. He took off his glasses, then used his shapeless handkerchief to wipe the sweat from his eyebrows and the bridge of his nose.

"Listen to me and get this straight. When we have to practice the same things repeatedly, we waste time. Wasting time means we're inefficient, and inefficiency makes losers. Am I making myself clear to you?" He paused, for breathing and for sinking in. He put the glasses back on.

At the top of the circle, and outside Rice's range of vision, Julio arched his back to stick out his scrawny belly as far as he could. As soon as Sonny saw the mockery, he felt a frightening impulse to start giggling. He turned his head away so he could stare at the bleachers and bite down on the insides of his mouth.

"If you people can't learn this by five o'clock, then we'll stay till six. If you can't learn it by six, then we'll practice till seven. Whatever it takes. Do it again and this time fill the lanes. You see where Julio is? By the time the ball is rebounded, you should have the lanes filled this far out. Now goddamnit, get it right or I'm going to start kicking some ass!"

Sonny watched him walk to the side of the court where two players not involved in the drill were standing.

Butch Cross missed the next free throw, and Lynch grabbed the rebound. This time, the other players bolted instantly. Lynch snapped the outlet pass to Julio on the left wing; he took two quick dribbles and fired a long pass to Sonny, who was in the middle. The pass had perfect lead time. When Sonny gathered the ball in, he was closing on the free throw line at the other end.

Rice blew the whistle. "Fair. C-minus. Do it again."

They did it again, and again, and again. It was obvious to Sonny by this time that Butch was missing free throws on purpose, but if the coach noticed, he didn't seem to care.

Then another break that was too slow to develop. Rice blew the whistle in rage, but Julio dribbled on anyway, with weary body language, to the other end. He shoveled a feeble layup off the glass. Coach blew the whistle again. "Goddamnit, *Chico*, give me the ball!"

In his flushed face, Julio's frustration was evident. When he threw Rice the ball, he threw it too hard, from too close. The ball smacked onto the fat man's belly before he could react with his hands. He went red in the face and doubled over, fighting for breath.

It was 30 seconds, but it felt like 30 days to Sonny, watching the disabled coach sink to his knees. All the players stood so motionless and silent it was as if mannequins had replaced them. Sonny felt his own pulse pounding in his head. He couldn't imagine what the consequences would be for Julio.

When Rice finally recovered, he was flushed and

sweating. Slowly, he pulled his huge carcass erect. His eyes like two pinpoints of metallic light, he approached Julio deliberately, without a word. The closer he got, the more Sonny sucked in his breath, certain he wasn't the only one. When Rice stood in front of him, Julio, five feet six inches and 120 pounds, stood like a condemned criminal with head hanging and hands on hips.

There was one more moment of terrible silence before the coach drew back his right arm and delivered a powerful slap upside the head, right on the top of Julio's left ear. *Crack!*

Julio fell to the floor like a doll. When he landed, he thumped. He stood up slowly with his eyes brimming and the left side of his face bright red.

In a ringing voice, Rice made an announcement: "I should be kicking this little spic sonofabitch off the team, but instead, I'm going to do him a favor. I'm going to teach him a lesson he'll never forget."

Almost as soon as the words were out of his mouth, he hit Julio again, in the same spot, maybe even harder. Again, he was knocked off his feet.

"Get up, *Chico!*" commanded the coach. "Get on your feet."

When he stood up the second time, Rice didn't hit him, but instead gave him an order: "Take off your shoes and socks."

The wiry point guard stood with slumped shoulders and a look of bewilderment. He had the guts to meet Rice's eyes, even while wiping tears with the back of his hand, even with the rose-colored swelling that was already smoothing out the left side of his face.

"You heard me. I said take off the shoes and socks."

Standing and watching, Sonny felt his stomach tighten by the moment. Moving slowly, as if in a trance, Julio removed the shoes and socks. He stood barefoot in the center circle.

Coach Rice turned to speak to the other players. "We're going to have a scrimmage. Full scrimmage, red against gold! During the scrimmage, you're going to step on his feet. You hear me? Step on his feet!"

Sonny heard, but he didn't understand. Whatever it meant, since he was wearing a gold jersey, the same as Julio, it probably didn't apply to him.

But as if he could read minds, Rice declared, "I don't care if you're on his team or not! Step on his feet! Every chance you get, step on his feet! You're not hurting him, you're doing him a favor! He's not worth a shit now, and he never will be without humility!" With no further guidelines, the furious coach blew his whistle and ordered them to start the scrimmage.

Sonny's dilemma was no less than anyone else's. It was an acute one, to somehow participate in the scrimmage while looking for opportunities to stomp on the unfortunate teammate's bare feet.

"Step on his feet!" screamed the coach.

Julio moved aimlessly about the court, his left eye purpling into a slit, the right one liquid with tears. Some players made a halfhearted attempt to step on his feet, but faked it like pro wrestlers, anything to avoid the coach's wrath. Sonny decided if he ran the fast break like they practiced, it would keep him away from Julio, but at the same time send Coach Rice a signal of his dedication.

"I told you to step on his feet!" the frantic coach screamed again.

The one thing you couldn't do, though, was disobey Brother Rice. Sonny wasn't sure when his confusion turned to rage, or how, or why. He only knew that inside he felt like a simmering volcano. Each time down the floor he was more desperate to target his anger and frustration. *This is the switch*, he thought to himself, in an unexpected and incongruous moment of reflection. *This is turning it up a notch and maybe even more. This is the switch.*

"Goddamnit, step on his feet!"

It was Dick Lynch who stole the ball and headed for the other basket. Gliding on the dribble, he might try one of his semidunks, or he might just lay it in soft, but there would be no reason to expect any interference. Sonny felt electrified; he bolted down the lane with the quickest acceleration he'd ever known. His attempt to block the shot would be too late, but it would be extra effort, and it would let off steam. He left his feet from ten feet out.

The ball traveled gently from Lynch's fingertips to kiss the glass eight inches above the rim. Sonny flew from behind like a blur, barely brushing the back of Lynch's head. With his left hand, he spanked the ball savagely against the glass. It ricocheted all the way to the free throw line. Sonny's left-handed blow left the backboard vibrating.

"Jesus Christ!" said One Gram.

The stunned Dick Lynch yelled, "Goal tending! Coach, that's goal tending, you saw it!"

Brother Rice only threw back his head and laughed savagely. "Way to go, Youngblood!"

Most of the players were standing around in the aftermath, trying to absorb what they'd seen, but it was more humiliation than Lynch could endure. He turned to Sonny, "You dumb fuck, you ever do that to me again, I'll beat the shit out of you."

Sonny felt out of control. He just laughed and said, "Piss off."

"Are you crazy? You say that to *me*?"

They were faced off, but Rice's whistle re-established his agenda. "I told you girls to scrimmage full-out. Now get moving." He blew the whistle to restart the scrimmage, but the stress of it was reduced now that Julio was no longer the exclusive focus. He was still barefoot, but there were no further orders from the coach to step on his feet.

When the practice was finally over, Rice sat them down on the first row of bleachers. "You have just had a demonstration of what happens to a player on this team if he is insubordinate. The only way to win is with total discipline, and total discipline is what we will have. Is that perfectly clear?"

No one spoke.

"Maybe you didn't hear me. I said, is that perfectly clear?"

"Yes," the players mumbled.

Then Rice laughed, but it was still the savage laugh, the one without humor. "I presume," he said, "that our little *Chico* will want to wear his shoes and socks the next time we practice."

It was supposed to be funny but no one laughed.

"We're going to take all twelve of you to Dongola tomorrow. The bus will leave at five-thirty sharp. I expect a big lead at halftime because I want to get some more playing time for the reserves. Are there any questions?"

When no questions were forthcoming, Rice dismissed them.

It was a very subdued locker room. Butch Cross spoke softly, but in the quiet moment his voice was clearly audible: "I'm quittin'."

"You're quittin', Butch? Come on."

"Buc-buc," said Lynch.

"Kiss off."

Could you just quit? It was a shocking idea to Sonny, who was slowly peeling off. Did Butch really mean it? Could you just quit and that would be that? Why not, though, maybe it was that simple.

"Come on, Butch, you can't quit," said Mickey Stanley.

Butch looked up at him. "Who's going to stop me? Not even Brother Rice can force you to stay on the team. It's my decision, right?"

Sonny wondered again if he really meant it, then turned to look at Julio, sitting in his jockstrap. Head bowed down, elbows resting on the thin but sinewy legs. Even with his face lowered, the swelling around his left eye was still visible.

Sonny asked him quietly, "You're not quittin', are you Julio?"

Julio answered without looking up. "Are you kidding? The fucker's not scaring me off the team."

Uneasy, Sonny pulled his car off the road. He left the engine running and the wipers wiping. *Are you kidding? The fucker's not scaring me off the team.*

If he was going to sit in his car and think, he decided he should turn his hazard lights on *Was that what Brother wanted all along? Was that what made him a genius?*

It was a curiosity to him how his flashbacks assumed a pattern. They weren't random phenomena, they had focus. Rice might be dead, but this latest memory conformed to the pattern. Almost exclusively, it seemed, the events of his past that came a-calling were ribbed into a spine of events that occurred during March of his ninth-grade year.

That meant Brother Rice and Barb, basketball, and his mother's slow but sure slide into final madness. The vividness of this cluster of memories convinced Sonny they must be important. *Was Sissy like Barb?* He had to wonder if his current malaise of floats and shakes and disorientation was somehow the flip side of wiring it up over and over, turning the switch ever one notch higher and then higher still? But if he felt disposed to look for parallels, where would he find one between Brother Rice and Coach Gentry?

When the rain stopped, Sonny turned the wipers off. It was his plan to drive clear to Carbondale, but the Makanda turnoff was just ahead. It would be more convenient to spend the night at Sissy's.

8

In March of the ninth grade, by which time Sonny was the established star of the Abydos freshman team, by which time his mother had been in and out of the hospital twice, and by which time Seth was in the habit of introducing him to coaches and businessmen, he took Barb to the Ides of March dance at the YMCA. It was sponsored by the English classes to coincide with the *Julius Caesar* portion of the curriculum.

Sonny had little interest in Shakespeare, but he would use any opportunity to be with Barb. On the walk to her house, his fingers nearly froze from holding the flower, a long-stemmed rose still in the paper sleeve from the florist shop. A message in scripted letters embossed the wrapping: *A single rose means I love you.*

He felt clumsy with the flower when he gave it to her on the front porch, but she didn't notice: "Oh, Sonny, thank you."

"My mother picked it out," he said. "She's good at stuff like that."

"I'm going to put this in water right away." While she and her mother looked for a vase in kitchen cupboards, Sonny talked to her dad in the living room.

"You played a hell of a game against Anna-Jonesboro. I haven't had a chance to tell you yet."

Sonny felt a mild embarrassment, but basketball players were held in such high esteem in Abydos that after a while you more or less got used to the attention. "Thanks a lot," he said.

When Barb was ready to go, Sonny helped her on with her coat. She thrust her chest to access the coat sleeves, and tossed her hair to clear the collar. They walked along the sidewalk, holding hands. It was cold, but clear and still; a canopy of stars glittered the moonless sky. She asked him how his mother was.

"She's okay, I guess." He could have added that she was drinking again and missing work, but he didn't. Instead, he stopped her under a corner streetlight and kissed her, a long, wet kiss with teeth and tongues.

As soon as they started walking again, she said, "I heard about Julio."

"What did you hear?"

"I heard how Brother Rice beat him up in practice."

"That's not what happened, it's not like he beat him up. How did you find out about it anyway?"

"Silly, you can't keep a thing like that secret. It was Andrea who told me about it and I'm like, no way."

Sonny didn't understand the trace of impatience he felt. "I was there. It's not like he beat him up. It's old news anyway."

"Did he hit him?"

"Well, yeah, he did hit him a couple of times."

"Don't you think something should be done about that?"

"Done? Like what?"

"He can't just get *away* with it, he's a *teacher*." Then she added, "I think Julio should turn Brother Rice in or quit the team. Maybe both. I just can't believe he can get away with it."

Quit the team? Butch Cross did it, but it wasn't something you even thought about. "Turn Rice in?" Sonny asked. "Why?"

She looked at him before she answered. "Because it's the right thing to do."

"For you, maybe, but it's up to Julio, right?" He was thinking that if your dad was out of work and your mom went for handouts, it might give everything a different slant. He didn't want to go into that, though. He suggested, "Maybe he wants to be somebody."

"Julio?"

"Yeah, Julio. Maybe he wants to be somebody."

"That's not how you get to be somebody, silly, not by being a big star so you can impress lots of other people. It's what you are on the *inside* that makes you somebody."

Sonny was sure she believed it. He had a point to make, but how would he get it across? He could see the YMCA in the next block; they wouldn't have to talk about it anymore. The last thing he wanted was to have an argument with her; he was hoping this was the night she would let him handle her breasts.

Like most other old buildings in downtown Abydos, the YMCA was advanced in its deterioration. The crooked sign attached to its second-story brick-and-concrete facade was torn loose from two of its bolts. There were some guys hanging out in front of the corner entrance. Up the street, several hoods were clustered around a Camaro with lots of chrome.

It cost two dollars each to get in. It was with pride that Sonny paid the four dollars to cover both admissions. Mrs. Fowler, one of the chaperones, stamped the back of their hands with a purple ring and told them where refreshments were located.

The dance floor of the dark community room was already crowded when they went in. When people spoke, it wasn't just to *her* anymore, it was to *them*. A Michael Bolton tape blasted through the stereo speakers. Barb liked the fast songs, but Sonny liked the slow ones, even though slow dancing always brought with it the ongoing dilemma of holding her body close without sprouting the public hard-on.

Julio Bates was there without a date, and without a trace of damage to his face, that you could see. He was mimicking Brother Rice by sticking out his stomach as far as he could and getting lots of laughs. When Sonny took a bathroom break, One Gram was using the next urinal. It didn't take Warren long to repeat his speech about the need to be aggressive if you wanted to score.

"Girls want the same thing we want," he assured Sonny. "Only they're supposed to act like they don't."

Sonny thought about Warren's date, Joan Mason, who had an easy reputation. Then he thought of Barb and her plum sweater. He said, "I'm hoping for the best."

"Not good enough," declared One Gram. He was shaking off the last drops while making a face. "You don't get anywhere by hoping, you have to make it happen."

It usually felt safe to be honest with Warren. Sonny said, "I guess I just don't have enough confidence."

"You didn't have basketball confidence before this year, but did that slow you down?"

Sonny looked into his eyes. It was One Gram who had lost his position when Sonny made the starting five. But there was no malice in the eyes, he was still a good friend. "Basketball is different," Sonny observed.

"It's not different." They both washed their hands,

checking their hair in the mirror. Sonny was taller now. "A girl wants the same thing you want, so if you're aggressive, you give her the excuse she needs. It's like she can tell herself she's just givin' in to pressure. You see what I'm sayin'?"

"Yeah, I get the point." He wasn't sure he believed it, though, at least not enough to act on it.

After ten, they went downstairs for a Pepsi. Since Barb was talking to Andrea, Sonny decided to step outside for some air. Dick Lynch was there, laughing loudly with several guys including Skoog Weems, a hood who was smoking a cigarette.

"Hey, look, guys, it's Tampax!" exclaimed Lynch. Everyone laughed.

"Why don't you shut up?" said Sonny.

"Oooooo, you're a superstar now, ain't you, Tampax?"

Sonny didn't answer. He didn't want anything to do with this. But when he turned to go back inside, Lynch reached out from behind and grabbed his neck chain, the one with Barb's ring. He jerked it hard. Sonny was so unprepared, he lost his balance and stumbled backward, the thin chain cutting into his throat like piano wire.

"What's the big hurry, Tampax, you afraid Barby Boobs might get horny when you're not around?"

Lynch tightened his grip so the chain cut even tighter into Sonny's flesh. He couldn't breathe. He tried desperately to dig his fingers in under the chain, but he couldn't. As much as he tried to force his chin down he couldn't do that, either. Then there must have been someone else behind him, because he felt himself being tripped over backwards. He fell so hard the curb rose up to smash him beneath the shoulder blades.

Pain, and shock, and no breath. Sonny heard Lynch say, "I forgot, he doesn't like to be called Tampax." That got the biggest laugh of all.

On his side and doubled up, Sonny groped around his collar but the chain was gone. It must be broken, the chain and the ring were both gone. His fingers searched momentarily in the cold concrete of the gutter, but his rage was suddenly so total he was oblivious to the pain and shock. He twisted himself violently to get on his feet.

Inflamed as he was, and out of control, he didn't wonder when two of the guys helped him to his feet. It turned out they were framing him up so Lynch could deliver any blow he wanted. The punch to the stomach doubled Sonny over like a rag doll; then Lynch said, "This is for blockin' my shot in practice, motherfucker." Lights exploded in Sonny's head the moment the fist drove into his face.

On the sidewalk, he was so groggy his contact with reality was purely elliptical; he faded in and out. The lights kept flashing. Eventually, he was able to roll onto his side and prop himself with his right elbow. Out of eyes that didn't focus, he watched the blood dribble from his mouth to spot the sidewalk.

There was no way to gauge the passing time, but there was a crowd of hushed people looking on. Sonny felt ridiculous. He could hear Mrs. Fowler saying something, but that was just before he passed out.

When he came to, they were helping him stumble into the conference room. In addition to Mrs. Fowler, Mr. Tuttle, the YMCA director, was propping him up. Thank God the door was closed; the humiliation seemed even worse than the pain.

"We've been trying to call your mother, Sonny," explained Mrs. Fowler. "But we keep getting a recording."

His headache sliced in his brain like a cleaver. If he told them their phone was cut off, what good would that do? His mother couldn't handle this anyway. "What about the ring?" he asked.

Mr. Tuttle looked dumbly at Mrs. Fowler, but she said, "Barbara found the ring; you don't need to worry about that."

"Where's Barb?" he asked thickly. His mouth didn't want to work.

"She called her dad; he's coming to get her. He'll be glad to take you home, too, or to the doctor." She was dabbing gently at his mouth with the corner of a wet towel, while Mr. Tuttle had gone to find some ice.

"I don't want to see her. No doctor, either." It hurt to talk, but he didn't want to see anybody. Or *be* seen. His tongue tested two upper teeth; a bicuspid and an eyetooth were loose. He swallowed down the blood that ran in his mouth.

Mr. Tuttle was there with a freezepack, wrapped in a soft cloth. As soon as he delivered it to Mrs. Fowler, he left. Through the closing door, Sonny had a glimpse of Barb standing by the water fountain.

Still inspecting his face, Mrs. Fowler said, "Sonny, I'm going to call a doctor. Who's your family doctor?"

"No, don't need to."

"No matter how tough you think you are, I'm going to have to overrule you. These aren't just bumps and bruises, these are injuries. I want you to hold this cold pack in place while I use the phone in Mr. Tuttle's office. Keep your head tilted back and hold still."

She left. The cold pack ached his throbbing face while he swallowed more blood. He saw the other door, which he knew led out the back way and into the alley. He could go down the alley to the *Daily Leader* building, turn left, and no one would see him.

The main thing was, he had to be alone. He stood up slowly, gripping the cold pack to hold it tight against his cheekbone. The throbbing intensified and he felt dizzy, but he steadied himself against the table. He was miserable, but he was pretty sure he could make it. He ducked out the door quickly without looking back. Since he didn't have his coat, he tried to jog but he was too dizzy; he walked fast. He knew his mother would be in bed, so he wouldn't have to face her. By the time he turned the corner at the newspaper building, his fingers were freezing. He dropped the ice pack in a trash barrel.

The unexpected part was how resourceful his mother proved to be during the days subsequent to the beating. Late afternoon before the Carbondale game, he counted 22 bowls of pudding forming rows on the bottom two shelves of the refrigerator. In the mirror made by the chrome lid on the dairy compartment, he got a distorted glimpse of his swollen, disfigured face.

His mother was at the stove mincing hard-boiled eggs and adding butter in a saucepan. "There is protein in pudding and protein in eggs," she said simply.

"Mom, I can chew." But if she heard him, she made no sign. It wouldn't surprise him if she was up all night making the pudding; it was for sure she didn't go to work. Some of her hair was out of place and her wrinkled clothes looked like she'd slept in them.

"What will become of the thug who hurt you?"

"Lynch is kicked off the team. There's a rumor he's suspended from school, but I don't know if it's true. He wasn't there today."

Then she had the far-off look. Staring out the window while she stirred the pan mechanically. "None of these problems would have happened," she began. "When your father left us he passed a sentence. He condemned us."

Who could tell if she meant the fight with Lynch or some other problem? Sonny fingered the wide tape that tightened down on the smooth terrain of his swollen, broken nose. She was going to talk about his father, but his mind was on the Carbondale game.

"We'll never know why he abandoned us." Setting a bowl of the mashed eggs in front of him, she added salt and pepper vigorously.

"Mom, I can chew."

She didn't hear, or didn't acknowledge. "You have no idea how often I've prayed about it. The Lord wants us to find room in our hearts for forgiveness, but I don't know if I ever can."

She was close enough that he could smell the booze on her breath. Sonny wanted to leave. *Carbondale is eighteen and four,* he thought to himself. Using a tablespoon, he began devouring the buttered egg bits.

Back at the stove, she said, "Please tell me about your coach, Norman. See if you can give me some reassurance. I've heard such awful stories."

She's heard the stories about Rice. "I'd say the stories are mostly exaggerated. The guys call him Brother."

"They call him Brother? But that's such a term of endearment. Surely he's not a monk. Do the members of the team have affection for him?"

Sonny had to think a minute. "I wouldn't say that. To be honest, I'd say they hate him, but they also have respect for him."

She was speaking into her small circle of pan. "But

how can it be that you hate someone and respect him at the same time? It seems confusing."

"I didn't say I hate him."

"I'm so happy for your success, but it would cause me such grief to think of you as a member of a team with a cruel coach."

"I don't know about cruel. He's real strict a lot of the time."

"I'm so glad you're playing basketball and not football. Basketball seems like an elegant game of finesse and grace. Still, there's a proliferation of cruelty in the world beyond our comprehension. Practically everywhere you look. Sometimes I pray to the Lord that he might put a mark on you so that the world's cruelty might always pass you by, just as the chosen were marked to be spared in the original Passover." His mother wasn't looking at him as she spoke. Instead, she was staring across the room at nothing in particular, as far as Sonny could tell. A semitransparent film seemed to glaze her eyes.

It was hopeless to try and talk to her when she got into one of these grooves. He was done with the eggs so he said, "I have to go now."

"Don't you want some pudding?"

"I'll have it later." He was putting on his jacket.

"But you won't be playing basketball in your condition?" She reached for him with tears in her eyes.

"No," he lied. When her fingers brushed the side of his face he said, "I'm just gonna watch."

When he got to the basketball office it was still so early the guys weren't even dressed yet. He said to Coach Rice, "I've got to play."

"Are you kidding? Here, Youngblood, take a look." Rice closed the medicine chest door above the sink so

Sonny could look at himself in the mirror. The left side of his mouth was swollen twice its normal size, particularly the upper lip, which had a long, vertical crack. The black-and-blue swelling across the bridge of his nose seemed to remove the definition from his features; it was hard to believe the face was really *his*.

"I know what I look like," said Sonny.

"Do you really? Do you have a doctor's permission to play?"

"No, but I don't have a doctor's order not to play, either."

The crooked smile. Rice leaned back in the swivel chair before he lit up. "You've got balls, Youngblood, I'll say that for you. Why are you so unglued about this game? We start the tournament on Friday, and you should be ready to play by then."

"I have to play," he said. But that sounded like a demand, which you could never do with Rice. So he added, "I'm afraid we'll lose. With me and Lynch both missing, I'm afraid we'll lose."

Brother Rice was already shaking his head. "No, no, that's not it, Youngblood. I decide what it takes to win. We don't have two players, we have twelve; the system is bigger than the individuals who make it up. You understand?"

Sonny didn't understand, but he didn't care. He only knew he had to play. He thought his chances would be best if he didn't say anymore, so he just sat still to watch Rice smoke his cigarette down.

The coach finally said, "I admire your guts, though. What about your loose teeth?"

Using his index finger, Sonny carefully lifted the damaged lip. "I've got this retainer; it holds them real tight."

Rice stubbed out the cigarette. "There's a protective face mask in the supply room. See if Jake can get it adjusted to fit you. You won't start and I'm not sure you'll get to play at all. If you pester me on the bench, it's for damn sure you won't play. We understand each other?"

Sonny was elated. "Thanks a lot, Coach."

The pliable face mask was white. It was made of a plastic material used for soft casts. Sonny was the last one in uniform because of the time it took to get the mask adjusted. Jake fussed with the straps while Sonny shifted his weight from one foot to the other.

When the mask was fastened in place it hurt, but not too bad. He looked weird in the mirror, like a voodoo creature or like Jason in one of the *Friday the 13th* movies. The bad part was, the pressure of the mask made his nose bleed. Jake didn't see it though, so Sonny stuffed cotton wads up both nostrils. They hurt too, but the bleeding stopped.

He left the mask on the bench when he joined the team for warm-ups, already in progress.

"How come you're not wearin' the mask?" asked One Gram.

"I don't need it for warm-ups," Sonny answered.

The large crowd filled two thirds of the gym. Sonny went through the warm-up drills breathing through his mouth. He could see Lynch leaning against the wall by the drinking fountain partway down the hall by the ref's dressing room. When the horn sounded, Sonny gave him the finger, down by his waist, so Lynch would see it but not other people.

For the first time all season, Abydos was behind after the first quarter. Carbondale was very good. A tall, black player named Collins, who was a quick leaper, was tough to handle under the basket. Then there was

Wheeler, a stocky point guard with terrific ball-handling skills. He was beating the Abydos press and laying the ball off for easy baskets. Sonny squirmed on the bench, but he knew he didn't dare pester the coach to put him in.

Abydos made a spurt in the second quarter to take the lead, but then One Gram got into foul trouble trying to guard Collins, who was taller and quicker. Rice stomped the sidelines pouring verbal abuse on the refs as well as the players. But playing without One Gram, Lynch, and Sonny, Abydos was overmatched; they fell behind by five points at halftime.

Brother Rice was so furious at halftime he chewed butt the whole time. "Goddamnit, *Chico!*" he hollered at Julio. "This is your game now, you have to be the man! You remember anything at all about defense?"

When they went back on the floor for the second half, Coach took Sonny by the elbow. "Put on the mask. You're going in."

Sonny was pleased, of course, but not surprised. With Rice there was winning and nothing but winning. When they lined up to inbound the ball, Sonny felt like everyone was staring at his weird appearance. His own teammates as well as the Carbondale players. Just before the ball was handed to the Carbondale player by the ref, he remembered the cotton wads inside his nostrils. He pulled them out and stuck them down inside his socks. He hoped too many people didn't notice.

Sonny was at home on the right wing of the diamond press, so it surprised him when a couple of ordinary passes got by him. He felt a little shaky, which caused him to wonder if he was more injured than he realized.

But the first time down on the offensive end he made a three-pointer, and then another. The second one cut the lead to three points and brought the crowd roaring to its feet. Carbondale had the press on, so Julio's next pass gave Sonny a lane to the basket. He could see Collins flying at him from the corner of his eye, but he decided to take it right to the hole. If there was a collision, it wouldn't be charging.

It was something in Collins's face. In his eyes. Just as Sonny soared up to lay his finger roll over the front of the rim, Collins brushed him on the way by and took a useless swipe at the ball. Sonny saw the fear in those eyes, if only for an instant; it was fear of Sonny's face, or his mask, or maybe even fear of hurting him. Either way, Sonny understood how it was an advantage.

With the score tied and three minutes left in the quarter, Rice called a time-out. He wanted them to go to man-to-man full-court pressure, and he put Mickey Stanley in the game. The coach was giving in-detail directions, but Sonny's nose was bleeding again. He crouched down, pretending to tie his shoes, got the stale cotton wads from inside his socks instead, and pushed them back up inside his nostrils.

After that, he was in a zone where nothing could intrude. To the spectators, astonished by the ballistic intensity of his movements, he might have seemed out of control. But he was very much in control. The zone was a visionary location, impervious to any would-be distraction. There was no pain in his face, no crowd noise, not even any Brother Rice. Most important, there were no obstacles. He saw passes before, during, and after. Intercepted them lightning-quick, then took them in for layups.

Sonny poured in automatic three-pointers, with the ball out of time, frozen in amber, in the orbitlike path of its rainbow arc, swishing the net it seemed even before it left his fingertips. Layup after layup off defensive turnovers, trey upon trey on the offensive end, electrified and galvanized but never out of control. Until, with less than four minutes remaining in the game and Abydos's lead swollen to 66–50, Sonny saw One Gram sitting beneath the scorers' bench. He knew that Coach Rice was taking him out.

The next pass went to a Carbondale player named Gleeson, who raised the ball above his head to make a downcourt pass, but Sonny ripped it away from behind. Three quick dribbles and he was behind even Collins, the inbounds man. The path to the basket was clear, and Sonny knew he was coming out. He soared at the rim, looked it right in the face, and cocked the ball behind his head with both hands. It was a tomahawk dunk. As soon as he slammed it through, the backboard shimmered the aftermath.

When he left the game to take his seat on the bench, he must have high-fived his way down the row of teammates. He was remotely aware of the earsplitting, standing ovation that the crowd bestowed, but he had no knowledge at all of his 31 points in less than one half.

He did know he was having trouble breathing. He grabbed a towel and ran to the locker room. As soon as he took off the mask, he could feel a line of pain behind his eyes; he started running cold water full out in one of the sinks.

Sonny blew his nose on the towel to get out the cotton wads, but lots of snot and blood came with them.

When Jake poked his head in, Sonny asked for some aspirin. He had a slight case of the shakes, so he lay on his back on one of the benches between the lockers. His pulse was too fast and the headache was worse. His head down flat, Sonny piled the cold, wet towel on top of his face and didn't move.

It was about a week after that, in the bandshell gazebo, when she asked him for her ring back. It was cold if you didn't keep moving; with his large hands stuffed in his pockets, Sonny prowled the perimeter, counting all eight sides. He was still restless when he came full circle.

"Why?" he asked her.

She had her hands in the pockets of the navy blue coat. Around her neck was the angora scarf. She looked at him and said, "Sometimes I feel like I don't know you anymore."

"I don't know what that's supposed to mean."

"I don't know either, Sonny. The way you played against Carbondale was truly awesome, but I only felt sorry for you."

"Yeah, right. *Sorry* for me."

"I don't mean to hurt your feelings, but it just didn't seem like *you* playing."

Sonny took another uneasy trip around the sectioned circumference, kicking at the dirty slush preserved along the southern baseboard. He tongued the uncomfortable retainer, which anchored the two damaged teeth that were still sore, but firming up. "I'll tell you why you didn't recognize me, it's the same reason nobody else did. How often have you seen a guy score thirty points in one half? Even *less* than a half."

"I said I don't want to hurt your feelings. I know how well you played."

"Barb, that was better than playing *good*. Rice said it was the best half ever by one of his players."

Barb turned away. "Don't bring him up. You know how I feel about Coach Rice. Sonny, let's don't talk about this now; the bus leaves for Cairo in an hour."

"It's not my idea to talk about this stuff, but you asked for your ring back. What d'you expect me to do?"

"I know, I'm sorry."

"I'll tell you something about Brother Rice. He may be a jerk, but he knows what it takes to win. That's why he's such a great coach. Why do you think we're undefeated?"

She went clear to the other side of the gazebo to look in the direction of Goldie's Cafe. "How can you say that? He beat your friend up in practice and you still stand up for him. Even Julio just took it and went right on playing. I don't understand."

"You have to be on the team to understand," said Sonny.

"He put you in the game with your face the way it was. You could have been injured for life. D'you think he cares?"

"We were behind. He knows what it takes to win. Besides, he took me out as soon as the lead was safe." A knot of frustration was forming in his chest. He wouldn't know the words to make her understand what a turning point that game was, that face, that pain, that zone.

"You know what the truth really is, Sonny? Coach Rice should be fired for the things he does. Butch is the only one on your team with enough courage to quit."

Now he was pissed. *What does she know about courage?* It

was the way she was putting *him* down when she put the coach down. "What makes you so perfect? You're a cheerleader, what about that?"

"That's different."

"What makes it different? Cheerleaders are like a part of the team, right?"

"We cheer for every team. Every sport. That's why it's not the same."

If it wasn't a satisfactory answer, he didn't know how to dispute it. They were sitting side-by-side on the gazebo's east-side bench. The low sun reflected in the bank's plate glass windows was so glaring it hurt his eyes. He moved to sit on her other side.

She said to him, "Sonny, I know we've talked about this before, but you think you'll be somebody if you're a basketball star. That's not what makes a person important, it's what they are on the inside."

Her tone was sincere, but he hated the way she didn't understand. "Before basketball, what was I? Who cared about me then?"

"*I* cared about you then."

"Why?"

"Because of who you are; who you were."

She didn't get it. He got up to pace some more. "I don't know how you *could* understand. Your father's rich and your mother's the PTO president. You've been somebody your whole life." They were his honest thoughts, but he was surprised by the bluntness of his words. He unhooked the chain from behind his neck.

He was standing in front of her with the chain and ring hanging from his index finger. "There's no way you can understand this," he said.

When she reached for the ring, she had tears in her

eyes. "Like I said, Sonny, sometimes I feel like I don't know you anymore."

The ring and chain nestled into the hollow of her open palm. He would go home now, make himself a peanut butter sandwich, and eat a couple of bowls of stale butterscotch pudding. He would get to school ten minutes early for the tournament bus.

He might have two black eyes, but the tender swelling across the bridge of his nose was reduced. He might even play without the face mask. With or without it, though, it wouldn't matter; he knew all of the teams in the tournament and all of their personnel. No one could stop him. No one from Cairo, or Egyptian High, or Mounds Meridian, or Anna-Jonesboro. No one could stop him.

The national pollsters might have been slow to recognize the achievements of the Salukis, but not so the NCAA selection committee when tournament pairings were announced. Their number one seed in the Midwest guaranteed them a spot in the Indianapolis Hoosierdome if they won their two subregional games in Louisville. Since Louisville and Indianapolis were both relatively close to Carbondale, SIU fans could participate in large numbers.

For nearly a week, the campus was a media blitz. The hysteria that gripped the region seemed to intensify with the arrival of each new contingent, whether from *USA Today*, ESPN, or CBS. In the midst of all this glory, though, Sonny felt alienated. His heart was not in it, could not get in it. Instead, he found himself lost in the peculiar and mystifying malaise that he labeled "the float," the ongoing condition of distracted ennui.

His heart was not in the photo sequence arranged by *Sports Illustrated* and neither was his head. The sequence, which *SI* editors intended to call "Jam Session," required Sonny and Luther to wear tuxedos and hold trumpets or saxophones while dunking basketballs. He had no focus in the press conferences, each one of which opened with Coach Gentry's disclaimer that he would not answer questions about the NCAA investigation into the Saluki program, nor would he answer any more questions about SIU's so-called "soft" schedule.

At Wednesday's press conference, the day before their first tournament game, Warner the sportswriter rescued him by taking him for a walk around McAndrew Stadium.

According to Warner, the SIU basketball program was in line for some severe NCAA penalties. His candor in saying so in his columns made him *persona non grata* with Coach Gentry; Warner was no longer allowed to travel with the team.

"You really pissed him off, I guess," said Sonny.

Warner just shrugged. "It's not my job to make Gentry happy. Athletics has a sports information office to take care of the propaganda. What's the story on your slump?"

"I'm in a slump," Sonny agreed.

"You haven't had one all season, so I guess you're entitled."

"I guess," Sonny mumbled.

Warner was walking with his hands wrapped around his Styrofoam coffee cup. No notebook and no ballpoint. "You know what it looks like?"

"No, I don't." Sonny replied. "You're not writing any of this down."

"This is just between you and me. I'm only curious about what's going on with your game."

"Okay, what does it look like?"

"Like you're sleepwalking. Like you're not motivated. It looks like you're gliding, just on talent."

How much does he know? Sonny wondered. "Some games you get pumped more than others, Warner."

"Bullshit. Not you, Youngblood. I've been watching you play for four years. You never put it on idle. Never."

Sonny tried to brush him off. "If you say so."

"Are you losing your nerve?"

"What's that supposed to mean? Are you a psychiatrist or something?"

Warner laughed before he said, "No, just a Wal-Mart psychologist. Are you going to answer the question?"

But before he could even try to answer, unexpectedly and abruptly, Sonny was whisked in memory to eighth-grade football. In a game hopelessly lost, Coach Risby had assigned him to kick-off return. When the ball tumbled fearfully out of the sky, Sonny's main concern, other than fumbling, was keeping his loose-fitting pants from falling down. With his head down, he hoped to more or less fall to the ground, so someone could drop on him. But there was no contact.

"I guess there must've been some pretty good blocks," he said to Warner. "By the time I got my head up again, I was in the clear. I was all the way to the forty, and the only thing in front of me was sixty yards of green grass."

"I can't picture you playing football, Youngblood."

"Not after the eighth grade, not after I discovered hoops."

"So what happened? Did you take it all the way?"

"Not hardly. It was too scary, because it was too un-expected. By the time I got across the fifty, I could feel my legs start to shake. I knew there was a guy chasing me from behind, and I didn't want to get tackled by someone I couldn't even see. I started stumbling at about the forty, but it took at least ten yards before I went down completely. I was flat on my face, and no-body touched me."

"You didn't fumble, though?"

"No. I probably would have, but I landed right on top of the ball." Sonny listened to his own words res-onating remote, like an unfamiliar echo.

"That's losing your nerve," said Warner. "I think it's called the fear of success."

"Okay, Mr. Psych."

"What does your cousin tell you?" Warner asked.

Sonny looked him in the eye. "Do you know my cousin Erika?"

"I know *of* her."

"Then you don't know her," Sonny declared. "Let me ask you a question, Warner. In your articles, you keep saying that the NCAA has got the goods."

"Is that the question?"

"The question is, how do you know?"

"I know from gathering information. From talking to lots and lots of people, then putting two and two to-gether."

"You know more than you're saying, then. Right?"

Warner smiled and answered, "Doesn't everybody? Sonny, when they interviewed you, did it seem like they were on a fishing expedition?"

Sonny thought of Yates and Brosky and their inten-tional questions. "No. It seemed like they already knew a lot of stuff, which made me feel like I was gettin' jerked around."

"Exactly. They *do* have a lot of stuff; they may have more stuff than they need."

"They asked me so many questions about my uncle Seth."

Warner's head was bobbing. "What they're doing at this point in time is gathering additional information to corroborate the charges they're planning to bring against the program. You could say they're strengthening their case. Just one man's opinion, of course, and I could be wrong."

Sonny doubted if Warner was wrong. "Are you saying they're going to put us on probation? Are you saying it's already decided?"

This time Warner shook his head. "Nobody knows what penalties the committee on infractions will impose, but there will be some. No doubt the NCAA has a prepared list of allegations; in my opinion, they have the goods to make the allegations stick."

"And what if they don't?"

"I don't think it matters. It's their game, and their rules. If they want to stick you, there's nothing to stop them."

"Terrific." Sonny glanced around to see if there was anyone within hearing distance before he said quietly, "Robert Lee says they're going to get Luther for using steroids."

"Is that what Robert Lee says?"

"Yeah. He also says that Luther's transcript from junior college was doctored." Sonny watched Warner's face to see if there was any reaction, but the sportswriter was simply using his tie to clean his glasses. "You know all of this, don't you?"

"I know a few things, and I've heard a lot more things. You can't really know about a transcript unless you've seen it."

More impatient, Sonny said, "Okay, what *can* you tell me?"

"What can I tell you for sure? I can tell you this, Sonny: Get yourself a good attorney."

His heart sank. "We have Ernst."

"I don't mean the university attorneys. I mean your own personal attorney. The last thing I want to do is alarm you right before a tournament game, but you asked what I can tell you. Get yourself a good lawyer."

The first-round game, against Texas A&M, was a blowout after eight minutes. Weak as Sonny felt, he scored comfortably from the perimeter against a sagging 1-2-2 zone. His three-pointers were effortless smart bombs. It was junior high P.E. Under no duress, he scored 19 points, then spent most of the second half on the bench with the other starters.

But the second-round game was scary, and not just to Sonny. Matched against the intelligent efficiency of Princeton, the Salukis were missing shots and losing composure. They lost composure on the defensive end mostly, where Princeton's methodical passing game ran as much clock as possible. A crew-cut guard named Applegate was swishing threes, and Sonny was too shaky to stay with him. The Tigers had a six-eight grunt player as well, who used his body skillfully to get Luther into foul trouble.

The lead at halftime was only three points, and to make matters worse, Luther would have to sit out much of the second half. "At least you don't have any fouls," Workman said to Sonny.

Sonny might have told him, *I'm too weak to foul anybody*, but he didn't. When Workman asked him if he was feeling okay, Sonny replied, "I'll be fine." With a stomach that felt like it housed a shotput.

His shakes got so bad in the second half that Sonny started faking it and grabbing onto his shorts. For only the second time all season, SIU was behind in the second half. Most of the neutral fans cheered even louder for the underdog Princeton Tigers, while the lethargy of the large SIU contingent testified to a condition of shock.

Sonny's frustration brought tears to his eyes. The body that refused to do what he commanded. When C.J. Moore shook the ball loose in a corner trap, Sonny snatched it and drove straight to the hole. He cocked the ball behind his head, preparing to slam it, but the takeoff in his knees was weak as pudding. It devastated him in his airborne impotence to realize that he was going to come up short.

When a Princeton forward collided with him from the side to knock him from the end of the court, he almost felt relieved. He hit the floor with a thud that hushed the crowd, then lay still on his back. Even though his collision with the floor was a shock, Sonny knew at once he wasn't injured. Neither did he feel the urge to get up. Inexplicably at peace, he stared into the huge circle of ceiling lights and watched them coalesce like distant traffic. But surely he must have heard the shower of boos pouring forth from the SIU section to remind the Princeton culprit of his sin.

"Are you hurt, Sonny?" It was either Workman or the trainer; they were both crouched over him.

"I'm not hurt."

"Don't get up in a hurry, just lay still."

Sonny wasn't in a hurry at all, just the opposite. He felt numb but relieved, like someone just pulled the plug. A burning line of sweat entered the corner of his eye from the bridge of his nose. With the back of his hand, he wiped it clean.

"I'm not hurt," he repeated.

It was a long time before they finally got him to his feet to lead him to the bench. When they did, the roaring crowd's approval was distant and muffled. He slumped on the bench as the game resumed. The trainer looked into his eyes, then Dr. Kelso did the same thing, except with the small flashlight. Gentry checked Sonny briefly before asking Kelso, "Can we put him back in the game?"

"We need to hold him out. I'm going to have to examine him tomorrow. Couple of X rays probably, just to play it safe."

Without a word, Gentry returned to his seat. He sent Luther back in to play with four fouls.

Dr. Kelso asked Sonny if he felt well enough to stay on the bench or if he needed to go to the locker room. Without looking up: "I'm fine right here." He used the towel to sop some of the sweat from his face.

"I know how disappointed you are, Youngblood."

Sonny nodded but didn't speak; disappointment was the farthest thing from his mind. The only feeling he still had was the relief. Luther and C.J. led a comeback that won the game, 81–74, in overtime.

Naturally, whenever the ball bounded off the court and into the ditch, the job of retrieving it was Sonny's. Under clear skies, the temperature reached into the fifties; it was only in the low-lying ditch with the northern exposure where traces of slush clung stubbornly. Sonny palmed up the ball, then used his sweatshirt to wipe the dirty ice crystals from its pebbled surface.

Even while in the prone position, Willie Joe could make chest shots from out near the free throw line. Sonny could do it, too, but with the added advantage of leg whip for extra leverage.

"I could play, you know," said Willie Joe. "Once upon a time."

"I know."

"How do you know?"

"I've seen the rotation on your shot," Sonny answered.

Willie Joe made another ten-footer. The pinned overalls twitched ever so slightly when he released the ball. Sonny returned it to him by means of a soft bounce pass. Willie Joe said, "I played with Charlie Vaughn. Can you top that?"

Sonny laughed. "I play with Luther Cobb."

"We'll see about Luther. Charlie played eight years in the NBA; give Luther a little time, then we'll see. I didn't actually play *with* Charlie, I played against him. But we were friends."

"Charlie Vaughn scored thirty-six hundred points in high school," said Sonny absently.

"How you know that?"

"I just know," Sonny replied. He could have added, *Because he's the only player in the state who ever scored more points than me.* But he didn't. He remembered a conversation he once had with Brother Rice, when the coach underscored for him the supreme importance of Charlie Vaughn's place in the cosmos.

Before he took his next shot, Willie Joe said,

"They're gonna retire your number, huh, Sonny?"

"Yeah, I guess so."

"Jesus Christ, think of that."

"Come on, Willie Joe, stop it." This was embarrassing.

"They gonna retire your number and y'all ain't even black. Jesus."

It gave Sonny a chance to laugh, which reduced the embarrassment. Willie Joe returned to the Charlie Vaughn agenda: "Charlie could play, no doubt about that."

Sonny sat down beside him. "You could play, too, before you lost your legs. You must have regrets, big time."

"Sure," said Willie Joe with a shrug. He had out a tin of Kodiak smokeless tobacco, evergreen scent. The offer he made to Sonny was only out of politeness. Sonny shook his head. "Sure I have regrets."

"You can tell me if I'm being too personal."

"No problem. It was one of those things. You try all kind of bodacious things when you're young, even goin' up against a train."

"You wouldn't do it again though, right?"

"Hell no. But losing out on basketball ain't the end of the world. I've got a good life mostly. Millions of people a lot worse off than me."

"You find other things."

"You do find other things. Ain't no use cryin' over the piss that misses the pot."

"You find other things," Sonny repeated, this time while staring down the railroad tracks to watch them disappear in the heavy timber of Giant City State Park.

Sissy was wearing a skirt. "You want to put one up, Sissy Sue?" Willie Joe asked her.

"Put one up what? Is this a code?"

"I'm asking you if you want a shot."

"What if I told you that shooting your basketball was very low on my list of priorities?"

Willie Joe laughed loud and long. Sissy thanked him for the use of his workshop. "You've been uncommonly generous with your space. Now we'll be out of your hair."

"You ever heard me complain?"

"No, but I have breeding and manners, so I thank you." Then she said, "You should see how toasty our studio is, now that the wingman keeps the woodbox full. He splits logs like Abe Lincoln."

They lingered in the clinic coffee shop while Sissy drank her coffee. She said to him, "The first time we bumped into each other was here."

"Mhmm."

"Did they make you piss in a bottle, Sonny?"

"That, too. What they didn't do would be more like it."

Elbows on the table, Sissy gripped her coffee cup with both hands. She wore her hair pulled back in a ponytail, which made the gray more evident. "Could they give you any results?"

"Not yet. Kelso is supposed to tell me all about it in a couple of days."

"It seems such a shame, poor *Liebchen*. Poked and probed while your teammates bask in the limelight of nationwide media attention."

Sonny made a face. "Maybe that would be a bigger pain in the ass. There's nothing wrong with me, not physically, anyway."

"Maybe there's nothing wrong with you at all."

He was impatient. "Can we go now?"

"What about my coffee, Dear One?"

"You want a cigarette worse. Besides, it's not every day they retire your number."

"Fair enough, but you have to drive."

A light rain was starting, so Sonny turned on the wipers. Just enough moisture to make them squeak. She lit up while he thought to himself, *I feel great. There is nothing wrong with me.* It was dusk, so he turned on the headlights. They were a mile out of town when he asked her, "Did you ever have an EKG?"

"A couple of times. Most recently at the end of last summer, when I had my surgery."

"You never told me what the surgery was."

"And you never asked."

"Maybe I thought it might be nosy."

"Maybe you did. I had other people in my life for that kind of sharing. You and I were just getting acquainted." She rolled down the window far enough to toss out her cigarette butt. "Do you want me to tell you about it?"

"I guess I do."

"Okay then, I had a complete hysterectomy. They took out every reproductive organ in my body."

Her tone of voice provoked Sonny to glance in her direction, to see her expression. But it was too dark. All he could see clearly was her profile. She went on, "They weren't going to take my ovaries but the surgeon decided it would be risky not to."

This information subdued him. He wondered why he'd never asked. "It makes you sad," he said.

"After the operation I was depressed. I suppose it was the full realization that I would never be a mother. It was grieving over loss."

He knew she was looking at him now, but he kept his

eyes on the road. "I never knew you wanted to be a mother, it seems out of character."

"It was never a conscious goal of mine to be a mother, but when the door is closed, when the possibility is utterly excluded . . ." Sissy stopped talking long enough to take a Kleenex from her bag and blow her nose. "I wasn't prepared for my own reaction."

"Are you okay?" Sonny asked her.

"I'm fine."

"We don't have to talk about this."

"Talking about feelings is good, Sonny. You should try it yourself."

"What would I try it on?"

"How about your current condition, the thing you call the float?"

"What could I say about it?"

"Tell me what it's like."

Impatiently: "I think you already know what it's like. When I play in a game, I'm losin' it. I get this like sickness. I don't know what the hell's goin' on, but I either have to fake it or take myself out of the game. Never in practice though, so maybe Warner's right."

"Who is Warner?"

"He's a sportswriter. You should see the NCAA investigation. They treat you like a criminal. All I wanta do is play."

"I know."

"I don't know shit about doctored transcripts or drugs or money changing hands. All I want to do is play, but now whenever we have a game I end up gettin' sick. You tell me."

"No, Sonny, you tell me. What do you think is wrong?"

The only answer he could think of, he hated to say

out loud. When he did speak, he didn't look in her direction. "I think it's in my head."

"In your head?"

"Yes," he growled. They were approaching the city limits of Anna. "I think it's psychological."

"Let me ask you something, Cousin."

"Go ahead. Ask me something."

"When was the last time basketball was fun?"

"Fun?" It really did sound preposterous.

"That's the question."

"Basketball fun? When was the last time it was fun?" Then he thought to add, "When was it ever fun?"

In the parking lot at the Clyde L. Choate Mental Health and Developmental Center, Sonny left the engine idling. The flower beds were bare, but he had seen them red and white with bloom many times. Even in the dark, even with naked sycamore limbs and wet pavement, he knew how attractive and serene the spread-out grounds of the hospital seemed.

"Are we waiting for something?" Sissy inquired.

"I was just thinking. It looks like such a beautiful place but all the lives inside are so fucked-up."

"I think that's called appearance versus reality. There seems to be a lot of it going around."

"Things aren't always what they seem to be."

"Let's go inside, Sonny."

Clad in pale green hospital garb and accompanied by a nurse, his mother landed in her usual chair by the picture window of the sitting room. Stared like stone into the dark great beyond on the other side of the glass. When it was plain that neither Sonny nor Sissy had medical questions, the nurse left.

If it was possible, his mother looked thinner. But then, didn't he always think that? The skin on her hands and wrists, where the prominent veins snaked in high relief, was white as china. Glazed like pottery baked in a kiln. *If you squeezed her fingers, would they break like china?*

Sissy took a brush and comb from her carpetbag. Standing behind his mother, she began brushing out her long hair, which reached to the middle of her back. It seemed like his mother's reddish hair was gone completely to gray and pale yellow. Sonny might have felt the urgency to get to the Abydos gym for the ceremony, but Sissy's brushing, slow and measured, tripped his memory to a time four or five years earlier.

It brought to mind a November evening when he sat on the balcony of their apartment listening to the distant ringing of One Gram's basketball as it spanked on the concrete of the alleyway. Sonny thought to himself, if he knocked on his mother's bedroom door she would be tired. *I don't have any plans for supper,* she would say. *I seem to be so tired all the time,* she would say.

But it was after six o'clock, so he knocked on her door anyway. When he went in, she was seated on the edge of the bed, wearing her bathrobe. She was staring out the window in the direction of the dim streetlight. Her hair was down and loose; in her lap, her hands held the heirloom hairbrush.

Sonny switched on the dresser lamp so they wouldn't be in the dark. She turned to look at him. "I'm afraid I don't have anything planned for supper, Sonny. It's nice to have a job, but it makes me so tired."

Sonny sighed. He said to his mother, "It doesn't matter, we've got stuff for sandwiches. We've still got some of the sliced ham."

"You're so resourceful, Sonny. Sometimes you make me so proud."

What was that supposed to mean? he wondered.

She lifted the hairbrush almost like it was supposed to be a visual aide. "I've been doing some thinking. Sometimes it seems so cruel the way moral dilemmas are visited upon us, unexpected and gratuitous even. Through no fault of our own, just . . . circumstances you might say."

Sonny had no idea where this was headed, but it was clearly a prelude to something, and it gave him the funny feeling.

"There was this special on *Discovery* last night about elephant poaching. It was set in Africa, but I don't remember which country. After these men kill the elephants, they cut off their heads with chain saws. That's so they can get tusks and everything out in a hurry, in trucks; by taking the whole head, they make certain they don't lose even one inch of the tusk." Now there were tears running down her cheeks, but she still sat erect. "They had pictures of these poor headless beasts humped up on the ground and covered with buzzard droppings. I just can't tell you how unthinkable it all was, and how desperate."

It *was* sad, hearing her describe it, but what could he do? Maybe he should just ask her if she'd like a sandwich now.

His mother took some Kleenex to wipe her eyes and blow her nose. So when she spoke, it sounded like she had a cold: "My hairbrush is made of ivory. This very one handed down to me from my own grandmother." She stopped long enough to blow her nose again, while her fingers traveled the long, sculpted handle.

"That means some poor innocent beast had to suffer and die, maybe even die horribly, simply to make a hairbrush. A hairbrush is a thing of vanity, Norman, any old brush would do as well, even one made of wood or plastic."

She turned to look at him. He felt uncomfortable and impatient. "The fact remains though, that my brush is a treasure. It has a history of generations in my family, so I can only see it as a precious possession. Do you see what I mean by unwanted dilemmas? It seems so unfair." She began to cry again.

Sonny felt helpless. He finally told her, "Whatever tusk was used to make your hairbrush, it came from an elephant that was killed a long time ago."

She sniffled some more before admitting, "I keep telling myself the same thing, Norman. It's *true*, isn't it?"

"You can't feel guilty about an elephant that was killed before you were even born." His own voice sounded cold. He stood up, impatient. "I'm going to get the ham out."

That was then. Now, watching Sissy lift with her left hand and stroke with her right, Sonny knew there would be no conversation involving his mother. No discussions of dilemmas or anything else. Sissy lifted and then she brushed, slowly and then slower still, as if she could go on forever. When the large body of hair was shiny and full and symmetrical, she began to braid it. Her strong but gentle hands were expert as they sectioned and tucked.

Sonny found himself captivated by the tranquillity. It was his cousin who finally reminded him, "Hadn't you better be going?"

"Probably."

"It isn't every day you get your number retired," she said with a smile.

It was funny enough to make him laugh. With the absence of urgency still prevailing, he took his mother's small, cold, dry hands in both of his. He tried to warm them without squeezing. "I'm going to the gym in Abydos, Mother; they're going to retire my number."

Without turning in his direction, his mother blinked. Sonny couldn't be sure, but it looked as if her eyes moistened and her crow's-feet softened.

Sonny said to Sissy, "Are you sure you don't want to come with me?"

"Thank you, but I'm sure I've had all the basketball excitement I can stand for one year."

"I better be goin'. I'll pick you up afterwards."

"I'll be here."

When Sonny got to the house, Uncle Seth was keen to discuss his malaise and the team's apparent decline, but Aunt Jane told him to hush. "This is Sonny's special night. If you want to talk about problems, that can wait."

Uncle Seth drove. When they got to the parking lot outside the gym, the crowd surged close to the car. Sonny got his back slapped so many times by well-wishers he got separated from Seth and Jane, but it was okay since he wouldn't be sitting with them anyway.

He took his place on the temporary stage beneath the south basket, which was winched up out of the way. By the time the festivities began, the bleachers were filled, along with 500 folding chairs arranged in rows on the gym floor.

The costumed cheerleaders led the crowd through an earsplitting chorus of the standard Abydos cheer:

Rah! Rah! Go, fight Ras!
Go, fight, win,
Go, fight, win,
Rah! Rah! Go, fight Ras!

After the roar subsided, the first order of business was to honor the Abydos High team on its recent third-place finish in the state tournament at Assembly Hall in Champaign. All 12 players came on stage, wearing their tournament medals, as their names were called. The last one up was Bobby Reed, the captain. A wiry forward who'd been Sonny's backup one year ago, Reed was a 17-point scorer and honorable mention all-state. With the help of Collins, the new coach, Reed hoisted the massive trophy on high. The standing ovation, which was deafening, lasted more than two minutes. Sonny wondered how the roof stayed in place. Finally, when the players and coaches left the stage, the cheerleaders twirled their way through two more rounds of cheers.

Mr. Doyle, the principal, approached the microphone and waved for quiet. Eventually, the crowd honored his request. "I don't have to tell all of you how proud we are at Abydos of our rich basketball history."

The principal was interrupted by loud applause, so he paused long enough to take a drink of water. "Even by our standards, however, Sonny Youngblood's chapter in that history will stand out in boldface."

Again, he was interrupted by enthusiastic applause, as many in the crowd came to their feet. Sonny squirmed in his chair. He looked down at his feet and wished there was some way he could become invisible. As soon as the quiet was restored, Doyle went on: "The thirty-five hundred points he scored in his career at Abydos places him second on the all-time IHSA scoring list, just behind the legendary Charlie Vaughn. To put this achievement in some kind of perspective, let me just point out that further down the scoring list, looking up at Sonny, are such names as Cazzie Russell, Quinn Buckner, Isiah Thomas, and Mark Aguirre."

Listening only with part of his focus, Sonny was searching the crowd for familiar faces. There were many, of course, but the person he was surprised to locate was Barbara Bonds. Seated with her parents, she was high up in the balcony at the far end. Sonny wished their eyes could meet, but it was difficult to make out her face, which seemed partly occluded by one of the hanging banners. Or maybe it was simply looking over too much time and space. The twist of regret he felt had no chance to develop, though, since Doyle was asking him to come forward.

Sonny got to his feet. The loud and long ovation gave him time to lick his dry lips and swallow several times. Doyle presented him with his high school jersey, the shiny gold with the maroon number 14, and a large plaque of glossy wood with a brass plate affixed. The plate listed Sonny's most singular scoring records.

"You can take the plaque home, Sonny, but we'll keep the jersey here, safe in our lobby trophy case. From this time forth, no player at Abydos will wear the number fourteen; it is officially retired to its place of honor."

Doyle sat down while Sonny stepped to the mike in the eye of an ovation that seemed to shake the building. It went on and on. It was good in a way, because it gave him time to try and establish some emotional composure. He draped the jersey over his shoulder and when the noise died down enough that he might be heard, he adjusted the mike upward. It squealed with feedback on the way up, which set his teeth on edge, but also turned down the volume of the crowd.

When there was enough quiet that he might be heard, he said, "I want to thank you all for this honor." But his mouth was so dry he had to swallow again before continuing. "I guess you all know we're in the NCAA tournament."

The huge applause that interrupted him gave him a chance to drink from the glass of water at the podium. "I don't know how far we'll get, but we're ranked number one in the country and we've made it to the round of sixteen. That ain't too bad."

Another raucous ovation gave him a chance to drink more water. He looked up to the far corner of the balcony but he still couldn't make out her face, at least not distinctly. He felt a sudden urge to say something *meaningful*; was it her presence that precipitated the impulse?

When the noise subsided to only a few lingering hoots and whistles, he found himself saying, "I think I've learned a little something this year."

Now the crowd was quiet. Sonny felt his heart pumping up but he went ahead: "We're all crazy about basketball. Sometimes it's almost like if there was a nuclear war, everything would still be cool just as long as the gym wasn't blown up. We eat basketball, and we drink it, and we sleep it; but the truth is, there's more to life." He had to stop for more water. His knees were suddenly shaky. The crowd was gone now from quiet to silent, but it wasn't the whoop-it-up kind, the kind that simply anticipates the next opportunity to explode. It was now the uneasy, curious kind. *Why am I doing this?*

"What I'm trying to say is, your whole life can't be just one thing. A person's life can't be just one thing because there's more to every person than just one thing." More dry mouth now, because it all seemed so absurd; this huge throng was programmed to go crazy, not listen to a jock with a 20 on his ACT reflect on the meaning of life. Sonny turned to look briefly at Mr. Doyle, who had a knit in his brow.

He turned back to the five thousand faces, now gone a little bit blurry. They were silent as a Sunday morning congregation about to begin the pastoral prayer. Was it simply the fact that he would probably never again in his life hold the undivided attention of thousands of people? Was it Sissy's influence? Was it an unexpected opportunity to get it right with the girl (now a woman) seated in the far end of the balcony? These were some of the questions, but what were the answers?

And what would he say to the people about the *other things*, the *important* things? Would he tell them about his cousin Sissy who hated big-time college sports but was nevertheless important in his life somehow? Would he tell them about the legless black man with oceans of humor and generosity of spirit whose success in life was rooted in his refusal to be a victim? Or maybe the meaning of murals rescued tediously with skill and courage but without recognition or public spotlight?

Or maybe something else altogether? But by this time the silence, extended past two minutes, was thoroughly embarrassing. He felt woozy. From behind, he could hear Doyle's voice: "Are you okay, Sonny?"

"I'll be okay," he murmured.

"Are you sure?"

"I'll be okay." Still woozy, Sonny looked up again at

the blurry crowd. There was a way out of this. He wouldn't say the important things, but he knew the way out. He breathed deep before he spoke into the mike again: "Most of you know me," he said. "You know I'm no good with words. What I know how to do is play, so let's leave it at this: See you at the Hoosierdome. Who knows, maybe we'll kick some ass."

Quickly, although not immediately, the crowd's recognition of Sonny's return from the brief sojourn into pensiveness generated a long, firm swell of applause that was somehow still polite. He shook hands all around the stage, then was almost grateful for Uncle Seth's scheduled bash back at the house, since it gave him the opportunity to whisk away in the car.

As soon as he hung up his coat, Uncle Seth went right on past the kitchen refrigerator to the one in the pantry, where the open door revealed how the cases of beer were double-stacked.

"You want a cold one?"

Sonny shook his head.

Seth took a seat at the table and snapped back the pop-top on his gold can of Miller's. "Maybe you can tell me what's goin' on with you."

Sonny stretched his legs. "Maybe I could. If I knew, maybe I could."

"That's exactly what I'm talkin' about, remarks like that. What the hell were you trying to do in the gym? I couldn't believe it was you up there."

"Me neither."

The interruption was Aunt Jane's voice from the bottom of the stairs. She wanted to know how many people he expected.

"Maybe a couple dozen," Seth hollered.

"How soon?"

"It'll be a few minutes anyway."

So she asked him to take the pizza rolls out of the freezer. While he was getting them, Sonny said, "I've got a question of my own, Uncle Seth."

His uncle thunked the frozen cartons on the counter, then sat down again. "You changing the subject on me?"

"I guess so." The question wouldn't come easily, though; he had to clear his throat before he asked, "My question would be, how much?"

"How much what?" Seth was fishing a cigarette from his shirt pocket.

"How much money, Uncle Seth? When I signed my letter of intent at SIU, how much did you get from the boosters?"

"What, are you serious?"

Sonny thought for a moment. "I must be."

"What is this shit?" Uncle Seth flattened his thin hair at the crown and lit the cigarette before looking up again. "Sonny, what is this shit?"

As nervous as he was, Sonny said anyway, "I'm askin' you a simple question. How much money?"

"Why are you talkin' to me like this?"

"Because I have to know. They're putting us through a meat grinder; it's called an NCAA investigation. The other question would be, what about the comp tickets? How much do you broker them for?"

"Where are you gettin' ideas like this?"

"A little at a time. I'm not as stupid as some people think."

"I don't know anybody that thinks you're stupid." Seth downed the rest of his beer aggressively, then broke open another. "Sonny, you don't really believe all the rumors the NCAA investigators are stirring up?"

"Are you gonna answer the question? Fifty thou is the figure I hear the most."

"*Fifty thou.* Jesus Christ, listen to it. I don't know where you get stuff like this." Uncle Seth looked so pissed his eyes were filmed over, but he also looked frightened.

"I've heard it even higher than that," Sonny declared. "I've heard it all the way up to a hundred thou. I don't know what to believe, so you tell me. How much?"

Without a word, Seth stood up to go to the counter. With his back turned, he started breaking frozen pizza rolls apart by rapping them on the Formica. "Sonny, you got something to complain about? You got a complaint about the team you're on?"

"That's got nothing to do with it. Why would I complain about being on the number one team in the country?"

"Exactly. That's the bottom line, isn't it? Wasn't I with you every step of the way when it came to recruiting? Did I ever leave you hangin' out in the breeze?"

"You're not gonna answer me, are you?"

"You're a superstar on an undefeated team ranked number one in the country. You're on ESPN more often than Dick Vitale. You're drivin' a new car. I swear, it's getting so I don't even know you anymore."

"Uncle Seth, you're not going to lay a guilt trip on me." This hiding from the question seemed to Sonny the same as admitting the truth. "I'm just going to have to believe the most common rumor: thirty thousand for the booster club payoff, and twenty for the tickets."

Uncle Seth let go of the pizza roll boxes and spread his hands on the counter, but he didn't turn around. "What do you want from me, Sonny?"

"Just the truth, is all." Sonny answered. None of this was easy, but he didn't feel nervous any longer. The several moments of silence caused him to notice his own even breathing. Then he said, "You brokered me, didn't you, Uncle Seth?"

"Don't say that."

"That's what you did, though. When I didn't have any parents left, you took me in and I'll always be grateful. So maybe you had the right. Who knows? But the fact is, you brokered me."

"Don't say this, Sonny. Not tonight." His uncle sat down in the chair again and slumped. He kept running the thick fingers through the thin hair. His western string tie was caught in the cuff of his shirt.

"For fifty thousand bucks," said Sonny. He stood up and arched his back to get the stiffness out. "That, and the chance to feel like a big deal, like you're somebody real important. Are you gonna get fifty thou for my sophomore year, or does the price go up?"

"You're just not gonna get off of it, are you, Sonny?" Then he asked, "Why are you getting up?"

"I'm getting ready to leave. I'm picking Sissy up at the hospital, then we're going back to Makanda."

"Jesus Christ. You can't leave now, what about the party?"

"Leaving is what I'm doing." He took his coat from the doorknob on the back porch door and began putting it on. "It'll be a better party without me, because like you said, you don't know me anymore."

"You can't leave like this, Sonny, the party's for you."

"No, it's not." Zipping the coat, he turned around to face his uncle straight on. "It's not for me, Seth, the party's for the brokers. It always is."

"You're not really leaving."

"Please tell Aunt Jane good-bye for me. I'll call her later." Sonny went outside, closing the door firmly behind him. As soon as he started the car, he scanned for K-SHE, the funkiest nighttime rock 'n' roll he could find. He spun gravel on the way out the drive. It was a climactic moment; he didn't know how, exactly, but he knew that's what it was.

9

It wasn't thinking, but somehow it was still knowing all the same. The rim had to be turned on its side.

After he brushed his teeth, Sonny got dressed and went downstairs. He tiptoed past Sissy's room so as not to wake her. In the kitchen, he drank several swallows of orange juice rapidly from the carton. The open refrigerator emitted enough light to illuminate briefly the burnished plaque, which was still propped there on the kitchen chair. He knew the plaque said 3500 points, but he paid it no attention.

The light at dawn was so faint and, around the barn, where the huge sycamores and oaks stood, it was nearly eclipsed. He could tell the haymow door was swung open on its hinges because it made a rectangle darker than the siding. But he had to get closer to make out the rim and the net, fastened lower down.

He needed the toolbox from the Bronco and the stepladder from the studio. More light would have made it easier, but because of his height and his long arms, he could reach from the second step. Even though it was cold, it was calm; he could finish the job long before his fingers began to go stiff.

Lag bolts held the rim in place. As soon as Sonny began to loosen them with the socket wrench, the startled barn swallows set up a shrill racket. They flurried in and out, even swooping at times near his head. They were a surprise, but not a distraction; as soon as the bolt on the right side of the base was removed completely, he was able to pivot the rim upward. He used a vertical seam in the barn siding to line it up. There would have to be a pilot hole to reset the bolt, so he reamed one with his strong hands and a gutter spike.

When he drove the bolt, its large threads chewed out small slivers of the weathered siding, but it was a quiet process. The only noise came from the swallows, who lost interest shortly after Sonny stepped down from the ladder.

Looking up, he tried to comprehend the results of this project: the rim anchored firm in the vertical position, the net hanging limp like butterfly netting from top to bottom. A ball could only pass through it from one side to the other. Instead of a backboard, there were now *sideboards*, one on the right and one on the left. And where would you measure the ten feet? To the bottom, or the top? To the middle maybe?

But even sideways, a basket on a barn and memories were awash down the channels of Sonny Young-blood's inscape. The ineffable surge within when the undersides of your forearms pounded the rim, driving home a two-handed dunk so pure that the ball exploded straight down a line absolutely vertical, hitting the floor almost before there was time to pull your hands back. The countless days and nights on the playground courts, even Uncle Seth's barn, on metal backboards and wooden ones, nets of steel chain, nets of cotton like string mops, nylon nets and no nets at all, straight rims and bent ones. Still shooting baskets after your friends were gone, and the streetlights were on, and your freezing hands were numb way past the point of pain, but your fingers still worked. Somehow.

The puddles in the low spots were fringed with ice. Sonny put his cold hands in his jacket pockets; he looked again at the incongruous, perpendicular goal, and straight on through to the east at the brightening sky behind the silhouette of bluff and timber. Incongruous and urgent at the same time, *But don't ask me why*, he said to himself. "It just needs to be this way," he said aloud but quietly. "It belongs to *me* this way," he said, wondering all the same what he meant.

When he put the ladder away in the studio, he didn't pay attention to the new section of fresco Sissy was working on, but he did notice the thermometer at only 55 degrees and how low the woodbox was. He put the three remaining logs inside the Franklin stove and dampered it up to a full blaze. On the way to the woodpile, he thought briefly of Uncle Seth's treachery. *So what does it matter really if they retire your number?*

Sonny called it the hax because it was about three-quarters, too long to be a hatchet, but too short to qualify as an ax. Its blade was lodged so firm in the chopping block he had to use both hands to work it loose. The first dozen logs, mostly pine and sycamore, were easy to split. The sharp blade halved them in only two or three of his long strokes, the cold steel clunking the chopping block like a stone, making its hollow echo in the still morning air.

The brightening sky along the timber ridge meant there would be sun; cold as it was, it was still March. It would be warm by noon. Using the hax with his right hand only, he split another dozen of the small pine logs until his shoulder ached and his cold fingers were going numb.

He could switch to his left hand, though; he wasn't ambidextrous for nothing. The next log was seasoned oak. Its irregular shape made it awkward to balance, so Sonny clamped it with his right hand to stabilize it. Somewhat clumsy, though, with the semistiff fingers. If he could hold the log steady to frame it up for a strong blow with the left hand, just to get the blade in two or three inches, then he could hoist it back up with both hands and bring it down to bust it.

Cutting his fingers off wasn't part of the plan.

When the bad-aim blade came flashing down, it only grazed the log. It cut off his thumb and index finger complete, along with the middle finger at the second knuckle and the ring finger at the first knuckle.

The only damage to his pinky finger would turn out to be a bruised nail.

Since the impact was more like a blow than a cut, he felt immediate disbelief when he looked at his own cleaved digits resting on the chopping block like butcher shop offal. The hax was there, too, on its side. Sonny sucked in his breath; this was nothing at all like slamming your fingers in the car door.

At the first surge of nausea, he sat down light-headed in his dumb shock. He was in two places at once; it was him with his butt on the pea gravel, but that was him on the chopping block as well. The pain came fast and furious, but it fascinated him how some part of his brain maintained an informational function: It was for sure he wouldn't be playing in the UCLA game; this wasn't like a broken nose where you could put on a protective mask and just go for it.

Sonny's elbows were clenched in tight against his stomach. The sun was high enough to peek above the treetops, causing him to squint. The conundrum of rim on its side, backlit suddenly like a production number, had its own hypnotic effect; he stared at it and right on through it for several moments. Even took long enough to track the vertical column of smoke from Winslow's cabin beyond the ravine. Rim on its side and fingers on the chopping block, *Those aren't me anymore*, he thought to himself. *Those fingers aren't mine now.*

The elements of hypnotic disbelief that threatened to paralyze him gave way to fiercer pain and an increased flow of blood. For the first time, he felt panic. He had to find Sissy for help, because he knew all of a sudden that he could die here. He could bleed to death in the lassitude of his state of shock.

He shoved the savaged hand down inside his jacket pocket to stem the flow of blood, but when he tried to get to his feet, he was too dizzy. He fell on his back without losing consciousness. A three-legged crawl for about 20 yards with the shakes and the chills and a swimming head.

Ferocious as the pain was, the fear of passing out was greater because if he did, he would bleed to death before Sissy could know he was at risk. He couldn't die alone. He recovered sufficiently to make it to his feet, and stumbling hunched over with his left arm holding down on the right elbow, he made it clear to the house. Even to her bedroom. He must have made noise, because she was awake and sitting on the edge of the bed in her white flannel nightgown. Her sleepy face was quickened by startled confusion. Sonny sat heavily on the bed beside her, slumped over, gasping for breath while the raging pulse pounded in his head. Her arm was around his shoulders. "My God, Sonny, what's the matter?"

With slow, clumsy movements, he used his left hand to lift the right one out of the jacket pocket. He couldn't look when he laid the bloody hand softly in her lap.

"Oh, God no," she whispered, but didn't look away.

Doubled down, Sonny was resting his face on his knees. *My mother will never really know about this*, he thought to himself, *because she won't be able to know*.

"How did this happen?" Sissy was pleading. "Tell me what happened to you."

He just shook his head back and forth. He didn't feel the strength to talk and, anyway, she would know her own answer. His chills and cold sweats were accelerating, which served to increase the nausea.

Sissy got to her feet suddenly and pulled the nightgown off, up over her head. When she sat down, she carefully wrapped it around the wasted hand several times. The clump of flesh and flannel now rested in her lap. From the corner of his eye, Sonny could see her large, brown nipples.

Unexpectedly, she took his head firmly in both her hands, and twisted his neck to drive his face into her sternum. She locked her chin down on top of his head till it seemed like her flesh was engulfing him. Her voice quivered: "Not your fingers, Sonny, not those fingers."

Helpless as a baby, what could he say? It was an accident.

"No, Sonny, not your fingers." Sissy locked down all the tighter with her chin, while Sonny tried to breathe inside the breast flesh swallowing his face. Then he could smell her sweat; she had tremors of her own. As if to quell them, she began to squeeze him even tighter. He couldn't trust his own sense of time, disoriented as he was on the threshold of unconsciousness, nevertheless he couldn't help asking himself, *Shouldn't we be driving to the hospital?*

It was almost like she was trying to give him the release of a quick euthanasia. It might be okay to die like this in her arms, she would know what to do. Anyway, would it be worth living if you couldn't play basketball?

He couldn't be sure how long she held him that way, sweating and shaking; it could have been no more than a few seconds. But it seemed like a long time. Desperately, he pulled himself free.

The sweat was gathered on Sissy's forehead and temples, but her eyes were clear. She told him, "I'm going to put something on now and get the keys to the Bronco." He stared dumbly at the blood in her loins, but then he realized it was his blood, not hers. It was soaking clear on through the saturated nightgown.

It only took her a minute to slip into a T-shirt and a pair of overalls; she emerged from the kitchen, clinking keys. When Sonny started to get up she put her hand on his shoulder. "Sit still, Sonny, I'm going to back all the way down here to the porch."

He stayed put on his butt. He was trying not to lose consciousness, but then he wondered why. If he went unconscious, the pain would be gone.

Since the hospital had a large menu of codes vis-à-vis public access to patients, Sonny had a good deal of control. He took no phone calls, and the only visitors on his approved list were Aunt Jane and Sissy. It usually worked out that his aunt came to visit in the afternoons, and Sissy in the evenings. Sometimes Aunt Jane reported a list of people who wanted to visit him, everyone from Rick Telander of *Sports Illustrated* to Pastor Roberts of the Abydos Baptist Church. But Sonny declined them all.

By the third day, he cut off floral deliveries, which threatened to avalanche him; his room was so banked with sprays it smelled like a greenhouse. One of the nurses told him the flowers could go to other patients who didn't get any, and it sounded fine to Sonny.

But it wasn't until the third day that he had any clear recognition of this data relative to hospital procedures. So much of the time he traveled in and out of consciousness. The drips of morphine that entered his veins by means of his IV line, the frequent shots of Demerol, those things that mitigated his pain also sedated him so thoroughly that reality was as elliptical as his suffering.

The steady flow of cards and letters. A lot of them were from young kids he didn't know, well-wishers who were avid Saluki fans. If he was in a lucid head, he read the letters or listened as they were read to him. They were touching but painful. He didn't answer them, but asked Sissy to save them. How could he write letters as a left-handed person?

So many flower smells. The great, huge dressing that swallowed his hand like a snow-white oven mitt was in traction much of the time. Was it attached to him or was it some kind of grotesque mobile suspended above his bed? There were hallucinations to transfigure his welter of dreams and memories: Once Sissy propped beside him on his pillows. She lifted her shirt to free up her right mamma, the swollen surface laced with tracer veins, the rigid brown nipple framed between her first two fingers. "You turned the rim vertical," her voice declared. "We can pitch the ball through it when you get back home. If I beat you, though, it's off with your head."

Pitch the ball. He turned on his side to correct her terminology, only she wasn't in his bed anymore, she was in the chair by the window. "You don't pitch the basketball, you shoot it," he reminded her.

Only it wasn't Sissy at all, it was his aunt Jane. "What's that, dear?"

Without answering, he turned over and went back to sleep.

On Saturday, with Aunt Jane and Sissy both in his room, Sonny watched the UCLA game on television. The Salukis lost, 92–83. They were eliminated from the tournament. Although he dozed intermittently, Sonny could track the game well enough to know that his teammates ran out of gas in the second half. Luther Cobb had to sit out long portions of the final 20 minutes in foul trouble. It was the first loss of a sensational season, but it was the end of the road.

His aunt sought to console him: "Don't feel bad, Sonny; it was still a wonderful season."

"I know."

"You can't win them all."

Sonny appreciated Aunt Jane's good intentions. He might have been consumed by grief or regret, but his drugged condition had a neutralizing effect. "Life goes on," he said glibly.

At the postgame press conference, Luther announced that he was coming out.

"Is he gay, is that what he means?" asked Sissy.

"Very funny," Sonny replied.

"But he said he's coming out. That must mean out of the closet."

"No, it means he's leaving school a year early to play in the NBA."

"He'll finish his junior year, then?"

Sonny adjusted his traction mechanism in order to turn in her direction before he answered. "To be honest, now that the season is over, I doubt if Luther will go to another class."

"That's wonderful," said Sissy scornfully. "And to think I've been so cynical about the student-athlete concept."

It was Aunt Jane's turn: "Please don't be quarrelsome now, Sissy. Sonny needs to get well."

"Okay, but as soon as he's recovered, I'll be as quarrelsome as I need to be."

The fresh surgical dressing on Sonny's right hand was encased in a plastic soft cast that reached nearly to the middle of his forearm; the arm itself was housed in a stitched canvas sling secured around his torso by nylon straps. People stared at him. In the library, or on his way to classes, or even locating his car in a parking lot, he could feel the uncomfortable, curious eyes. He was used to being gawked at, but not in this fashion; he didn't like it.

The solitude at Sissy's place was comforting. He didn't have to answer questions or take phone calls, not from reporters, not from anybody. He didn't have to feel the eyes. There were many nuts-and-bolts frustrations associated with learning how to be a one-handed, left-handed person. Everything from driving a car to brushing his teeth was an annoying adjustment taking extra time. Still, he could learn alone; he didn't have to be embarrassed because his adjustments could be private.

One afternoon he went to the dorm to move his stuff out. He was hoping he could accomplish the exodus alone, without encountering Robert Lee. There was the frustration of trying to operate exclusively with the left hand. By the time he had most of his clothes out of the closet and his books and notebooks packed in the computer paper boxes, he was uncommonly fatigued. He sat dispirited on the edge of the bed with shortness of breath and a case of the shakes. He felt weak. *How could he be so far out of shape so fast?*

Then Robert Lee came in, sweaty in T-shirt and gym shorts. Wearing a headband. "Sonny. Jesus Christ, how are you?"

"Wore-out I guess. Look at me."

"Jesus Christ, how are you? Are you okay?"

"I'll be okay when I get my strength back. You been shootin'?"

"Nah, just some team Frisbee. You're packin' your stuff. You're leavin', aren't you?"

"I'm not leavin' school," Sonny assured him. "I'm just movin' in with my cousin for a while."

"Oh man, are you sure?"

"Yeah. It's what I have to do."

"I'm gonna miss you for sure."

"I told you I'll still be in school."

"In a way I don't blame you though. The phone never

stops ringin'." Robert Lee asked him about the cast and the sling.

"I don't wear the sling a lot of the time. The cast'll be on for at least another week, maybe longer."

"Does it hurt?"

"Not as bad as it used to. I have pain pills anyway."

"Did you cut off your whole hand, Sonny?"

"Just about. I still have my little finger and part of my ring finger."

"Jesus Christ, what are you going to do? What about your scholarship?"

Robert Lee had his shirt off and was toweling his sweat. Sonny didn't have an answer for the question. "I don't know, *amigo*, I don't know. I guess I have a lot to think about."

"I probably shouldn't even ask you that," said Robert Lee, looking uncomfortable and embarrassed. From the top shelf of his cubby, he brought out a gold medallion at the end of a slim chain. "I saved this for you from the ceremony they had for us at the arena. Everybody got one."

Robert Lee let the medallion drop in Sonny's open palm. It was shiny gold with a Saluki in relief on one side and the words NCAA TOURNAMENT on the other. The delicate chain sifted through his long fingers like sand. Sonny looked at it, but didn't know what to feel; maybe it would have more meaning than the plaque that said 3500.

"The place was jammed. Charlie Vaughn was there. I wish you could have been there, my friend."

"I heard all about it from my aunt. I wish I could have been there, too."

"Anyhow, I wanted to make sure you got the medallion."

"I appreciate it."

Robert Lee sat down across from him before he said, "You know what, Sonny? We almost did it."

Sonny knew what he meant. "Yeah, we almost did, didn't we?"

"We almost won the fucking national championship. We almost did that."

Sonny didn't want to talk about it, though. He said, "Yeah, that's what we almost did."

"I probably shouldn't even say that though; you probably feel bad enough without that."

"Don't worry about it, Robert Lee, just say what you say. Just be yourself."

"Yeah, I guess. Can I help you out with anything?"

"There's one thing. Would you mind helping me take this stuff downstairs? Sissy's coming by in the Bronco."

"When am I going to be seeing you?"

"I'll be around."

"No, you won't. We aren't going to be seeing you."

"I told you I'll be around. Are you going to help me with this stuff or what?"

Sonny spent more time at his studies. More time in the library. More time on walks in the woods, every now and then with Aunt Jane, when she came to visit.

Sissy wasn't pleased. "Life doesn't stop," she told him.

"This is just a period of adjustment. Don't you remember what my doctor said?"

"I'm glad you're here, Sonny, but I don't want you living with me to escape from reality."

"Reality? I'm just being contemplative; I thought you'd like it."

"You're just being a hermit. You don't have to withdraw from the world to be contemplative."

"I need more time," he said again.

On the day he went to the hospital to have his stitches removed, he sat with his eyes closed. There was no pain, but when the doctor pulled on the sutures, it tickled. Sonny could feel the fingers that weren't there anymore. The new dressing was small. Held in place by an Ace bandage, it left his little finger and the stub of his ring finger free.

In the hospital parking lot, his right hand resting in his lap while the left reached across to move the car into reverse, he felt tears running down his face. He had wondered when, if ever, they would come. He pushed the gear back into park. The smaller, freer bandage was supposed to signify liberation and a new beginning. Instead, it delivered the harshest confrontation with reality with the force of a two-by-four between the eyes: He was now a one-handed man without a future as a basketball player. There would have to be life after basketball and he would have to discover what kind of life that would be.

Was he resourceful enough to do that? Could he ever? Sonny shut the engine off while the tears ran down his face. He had wondered when, if ever, they would come.

It was the first of May when he was using her tape measure to find dimensions on the old haymow door. He watched Sissy's Bronco as it bounced its way up the gravel lane before lurching to a stop. When she got out, Sonny could see she was holding a basketball.

"What's with the basketball?" he asked.

"What's with the tape measure?" she countered.

"I asked first."

"I asked better." She was wearing the Donald Duck T-shirt and her overalls. She was picking hairpins out of her hair to let it loose.

"I'm measuring the haymow door," he told her. "It's almost four feet by six. If I could frame it up, we could put a window in it. It wouldn't be a skylight, exactly, but it would let in lots of light."

"*Bueno, Chico.* You can do it all left-handed?"

"I won't have a choice, will I? So what's with the ball? You know I don't want to shoot."

"*I* want to shoot."

"You do?"

"Yes. I do. Are you going to make me play alone?"

They shot baskets through the rim on its side. The mechanics of it were about what Sonny expected, except you had to drive the ball hard against the siding to expedite its horizontal path through the rim. It took a while to get the hang of it; Sissy seemed better at it in a way, because her two-handed push shot tended to gather altitude after it contacted the siding.

After thirty minutes they were sweaty and tired. For May, it was hot. They drank the ice water while leaning against the car. "Look what I found," she said to him.

He recognized the small gold pin she handed him as his fraternity pledge pin. "Where the hell did you find this?"

"In the kitchen, next to the coffee canister. I thought you quit your fraternity, Sonny."

"I did."

"So, what's with the pin?"

"I just never got around to takin' it back. I didn't even know where it was."

"So what do you think of basketball turned on its side?" she asked him.

"Is there any other kind?"

"We're not going to be negative now, that's one of the rules."

"Rules for what?"

"Rules for sideways basketball."

"Okay, I think basketball on its side is terrific."

She changed the subject. "Your sportswriter friend called this morning. The one called Warner."

"I know; he called back. I ended up talkin' to him."

"That's good, Sonny."

"Oh yeah, what makes it good?"

"Anything that makes you less of a hermit is good for you. In my opinion, that is."

"We've talked about this before, Sissy."

"What are you afraid of, *Liebchen*?"

"We've talked about this before, too."

"So what did Warner want?" she asked.

Before he answered, he took a drink of the water and put the small pin away in his pocket. "He has a theory. Warner's theory is that I cut off my fingers on purpose."

"Oh, my."

"Not in my conscious mind, not that I *knew* I was doing it on purpose. It was only on purpose in my subconscious mind."

"Oh, my," Sissy repeated. "And does this theory include any motivation for such a drastic form of behavior?"

"You mean the why of it?"

"That's what I mean."

Sonny looked at the way the net hung flat against the rim's opening. A rim on its side didn't really have a top or bottom, what would be the need for a net, anyway? There was nothing to prevent him from modifying further; he could take away the net if he felt like it. He said, "Warner thinks I did it because I could never stand to be second-best. He calls it losing your nerve. There's always the next level; no matter how good you are, there's always a higher level."

"The only level higher than college would be the NBA, isn't that so, Sonny?"

"Yes, but there's always somebody better. Even in the NBA there are stars and superstars, and they're all above the role players. No matter how good you are, there's always somebody at a higher level."

Sissy said, "And the rest of the theory would be, you're off the hook now, because you're a handicapped person. If you're ambivalent about winning and losing, it makes no difference if you can't be expected to take responsibility."

Sonny was amazed. He turned to look in her eyes. "I don't know how you can do that. How can you do that?"

"You mean I'm right?"

"Almost word for word." Sonny repeated himself: "I don't know how you can do that. You're too smart for your own good."

"I'm not the only one, though. It's possible your friend Warner is in over his head."

"How do you mean?"

"I mean, if we follow his argument to the end of the line, pretty soon we'll be asking ourselves if there are any such things as accidents at all."

"Can you stop now? Isn't it deep enough as it is?"

Sissy laughed. She grabbed him by the short hairs at the nape of the neck. "Come and sit down, Cuz; I'm tired of standing."

They sat on the chopping block, the scene of the crime itself. Its diameter was nearly three feet, so it provided enough room if Sonny sat between her legs. There were no longer any dressings or bandages on his mangled hand. Only bumps and stubs and molded, folded flesh, tender but hardening. He resisted the self-conscious urge to secure his right hand in the left armpit. He said, "I need some more water."

She passed him the pitcher. "Are you drinking out of the same side?"

"Who knows? Who cares?" Slaked, he passed the pitcher back. "No matter what you say, I keep thinking about Warner's theory. I can't help it."

From behind, Sissy put her arms around his midriff; the side of her head rested against the back of his neck. "And what about it?"

"I cut off my own hand unconsciously on purpose because I've never resolved winning and losing."

"Do you believe that?"

"It's what *he* believes. I don't know what *I* think."

"What if he's right?" Sissy asked. "Is that so scary?"

"It has to be sick. Perverse, to use one of your words." He could feel her breath on the back of his neck. He was staring at the huge, old sycamore by the barn. He knew sycamores were always last to recover in spring.

"I'm not sure I've ever resolved winning and losing," she said to him. "Is that something we're supposed to do?"

"You're doing it again, aren't you?" he said wearily.

"Doing what? In sports there has to be a loser for every winner. Does that have anything to do with reality? Maybe that's what's perverse."

"You *are* doing it again."

She pulled the hair on the back of his neck. It hurt. "I'm just asking some pertinent questions. You want to be contemplative, so I'm getting on board. We rescued the fresco from the brink of destruction, and who was the loser?"

"That's different," he said.

"Exactly. It's different because there can be winners without losers. Maybe the resolution to winning and losing is to think of succeeding."

"We can succeed, but no one has to fail. That's what you're saying."

"Yes."

"You say winners without losers. You can have one without the other." He could see her point but couldn't think of a response. "What do you think of my idea?"

"Which idea?"

"Turning the haymow door into a window. We'd have to take out some of the upper floor."

"It sounds terrific. Let me know what materials you need." She pulled his hair again.

"Ow! Would you knock it off?"

She stopped pulling, but she asked him another question. "Guess what I did?"

"I'm afraid to guess; tell me what you did."

"I made you another appointment."

Sonny was shaking his head. "No more sportswriters. It was different with Warner, because he's more like an old friend."

"This is not a sportswriter, this is different."

"When did you decide to start making appointments for me?"

"About the time I got tired of being your press secretary."

Turning to look into her eyes, he saw how serious she was. "Okay, who is it this time?"

"It's Barbara Bonds, your old flame. She wants to visit you."

"Barby Boobs," said Sonny hypnotically. "My old flame."

By using his little finger and the heel of his hand in a kind of pincer movement, Sonny was making his right hand functional and stronger. For example, he could easily pick up a cup or glass, or he could use the hand to steady lumber in a building project. It was also true, though, that his left-handed capabilities improved every day; when he needed to rely exclusively on that hand, he discovered ever more possibilities.

He could shift easily through the gears, as he was doing now, without clumsiness, so it posed no logistical problem when she took his right hand and placed it in her lap. Her fingers caressed the fresh but toughening stumps. She seemed in no hurry; her fingers traveled slowly like a blind person reading in Braille, trying to come to terms with a particularly difficult passage.

"Willie Joe thinks I could still be a basketball star," Sonny said. "Even this way, with one good hand."

"What do you think?" asked Barbara.

"I think maybe I could be a lot of things," he answered. "But the only basketball I plan to play will be for fun, at Makanda Square Garden. That's what we call that court we passed back by the railroad tracks."

They were sailing down the highway. "Sonny, how are you?"

It seemed like an odd question. Didn't she already ask him that back at Sissy's? Besides which, the way she cradled his truncated hand in both of her own, made him feel embarrassed and edgy. "Aren't you Teague's woman now?" he asked her.

She responded by lifting the back of his hand to press it against her cheek. "I told you I was dating Teague, I didn't say I was married to him."

Sonny wished he was at the point where he could be secure while someone was holding his ruined hand, but he wasn't. He needed to make conversation: "You left the gym that night they retired my number. You were there at first, but then your seat was empty."

"You saw that?"

"I saw. I was looking for you."

Barb was working her chin on the fold where an index finger had once been. "I had to leave or I was going to cry," she said. "I knew what you were trying to say."

"Lucky for you, you could leave when you felt like it. I felt like I was going to cry, and I didn't even know what I was trying to say."

"Yes, you did. Tell me how you are now."

"I'm better."

"I don't mean just your hand. I've thought about you so much."

"You've thought about me so much?"

"All the time. Whenever I watched you play on television or read the newspapers. I wondered if you were happy."

"I think I have to learn what it means to be happy,"

he replied. "It doesn't mean being a star; that has more to do with fear."

Barb made her eyes round. "Sonny, you're so deep now."

"Don't make me laugh. You know how *deep* I am. It's my cousin Sissy who's the intellectual. A lot of the time, she reminds me of you."

"How is that?"

"She wants to improve my mind."

"Oh, how awful."

Sonny ignored her sarcasm. He took back his hand to steady the wheel, while using his left hand to fetch the gold team medallion from his shirt pocket. He handed it to her. "Here," he said. "Hold this." He watched the way the tiny gold links of the chain spilled into her waiting palm like liquid drops.

"What is it, Sonny?"

"It's a team memento. All the players got one. I figure my mother needs it more than I do."

"You're giving it to her?"

"Might as well."

Barb turned the medallion over in her hand to inspect it. "It's very nice," she declared. Then she added, "Will they let her have this in the hospital?"

"No way, she can't have anything with a chain. She'll only be able to have it under supervision."

"Will she know what it is?"

Sonny shrugged. "Who knows?"

When they reached the street where his old fraternity sat, he downshifted to bring the Mazda to a stop next to the curb. They were sitting in front of the house with the Greek letters.

"Why are we stopping here?" she wanted to know.

"It's just for a minute. I have to drop something off." He got out of the car.

"Don't be long, Sonny."

"This is just for a minute," he repeated.

The tulip tree in the front yard was glorious, and there was a row of red-hot sally in bloom along the foundation, but Sonny was focused on the front door. *Just stay cool,* he cautioned himself.

He found Harris in the house basement, shuffling fraternity records in manila folders. It was clearly end-of-the year housekeeping, no doubt one of the thankless, low-profile duties of a fraternity president. Nothing colorful like leading a lineup, for sure. Pinky was there as well, sipping at a Bud Light.

Sonny handed the pledge pin to Harris while apologizing for not returning it sooner. "To tell you the truth, I didn't know I still had it."

"Think nothing of it," said Harris with a smile. "Better late than never." Sonny watched Harris and Pinky staring at his right hand. He fought the urge to hide it in the pocket of his jeans.

Both fraternity men expressed their regrets about his accident, and asked him how he was doing.

"I'm okay."

"I hope so," said Harris. "You know, Sonny, a fraternity is a support system; that's the kind of brotherhood it is."

Sonny knew he could leave now, if he wanted; he didn't have to listen to this. "Terrific. I hope you get all the brotherhood you can handle."

Pinky stared at his beer can. Harris paused before he went on. "What I'm trying to say is that brothers in a fraternity form a bond that helps them through the rough times."

"Wonderful. I'm just bringin' the pin back; I wouldn't want to interrupt your bonding." In spite of his good intentions, he found himself getting pissed. He doubted if Harris would ever understand what real bonding was all about, the kind of connection he knew with Sissy, where the freedom to be yourself was the spine of a relationship.

For whatever reason, maybe from a level of discomfort, Harris persisted by saying, "I'm just sorry you never *got* that part, the part we call house loyalty."

"You can go fuck your house loyalty," Sonny snapped. *Now what am I doing?* "I brought your pin back. You sound like one of the kiss-ass grad assistants who works for the coaching staff. I'll tell you what you don't get, Harris: You think this fraternity makes you important. You're no different than all those sorry-ass boosters who think a basketball team will make them important."

"What are you, a thinker now, Youngblood?"

It was the question Sonny might have asked himself. "Maybe; stranger things have happened. I'll tell you something else: I could turn this fraternity in. All that hazing shit, that lineup shit, that's all illegal."

He watched Harris and Pinky to see what sort of response there might be, but neither of them spoke; neither of them looked in his direction, either. He went on, "I could turn your ass in to the office of student life and they'd close this fucking fraternity down."

"You could try that, I suppose," said Harris quietly. "It'd be your word against ours. But if all you can see in hazing is abuse, then you still miss the meaning of humility and subordinating oneself to the group."

"I know more about humility than you'll ever know.

Whatever it is I don't get, the university must not get it either. They'd close you down, so then you could go lookin' for a new set of brothers. How would that be? Then what would you do to feel important?"

"It'd be a chickenshit thing to do, Youngblood," added Pinky. "Somehow I don't see you as a chickenshit."

"You don't get it either, Pinky," said Sonny with a laugh. Even though this kind of verbal confrontation was foreign to him, he somehow felt comfortable, being pissed but in control at the same time. *Will I be different now, and will this be part of the difference?* he asked himself before continuing, "As far as that goes, what *do* you get, other than drunked up every chance you get? It's got nothin' to do with chickenshit. If I don't turn your sorry ass in, it'll be because you're not worth it."

"Fuck you, Youngblood," said Pinky.

"Maybe you ought to go now, Sonny," said Harris.

"I am going." Sonny thought of Barb in the car and how any more time he wasted here would postpone the drive to the state hospital. Or some other potentially meaningful activity. His breathing was even. "You aren't worth it," he said again. "Your fraternity is about as important as a fucking booster club, and about that far away from anything real."

If there was any reply, Sonny didn't hear it. He was gone out the door. Approaching the car slowly, he told himself, *I just made a speech.*

Barb wanted to know why he was laughing.

"I just got something off my chest; it's a good feeling."

"I've always thought so. Okay, let's go to Anna; I want to see your mother."

"Let's go to Anna."

At the edge of Carbondale, he was driving too fast, with the rock 'n' roll too loud. He felt a touch of euphoria. Barb wanted his hand again; she took it into her lap at the same time she turned down the volume.